CLANDESTINE
Bound in Blood: Book 1

Nicole Rae

Published by Euphoric Publishing & Design
ISBN-13: 978-1475196719
ISBN-10: 1475196717

DEDICATION

This book is dedicated with much love for my two beautiful daughters Alexeea and Ellyana. Without you I would not be me. Thank you for being my inspiration and my life every minute of every single day. PS… GO CLEAN YOUR ROOMS!! Just kidding… well, kinda.

From this moment on, my first published novel will forever have the same birthday as my oldest daughter… Happy Birthday, sweetie.

Clandestine

CONTENTS

Clandestine

ACKNOWLEDGMENTS

I would like to thank everyone for all your support and assistance during the editing process. It takes a village to raise a baby and I'm grateful that you've all helped me with mine. I can't tell you how much I appreciate you being my eyes and my counselor when I wanted to pull my hair out. You guys rock! I love you all very much and I couldn't have done this without you.

I am a lucky author. I already have a number one fan, as well as a best friend. I love you Gram and thanks for all of your support and wisdom. Also, I expect good placement on your book shelf... just sayin'

I would also like to give special thanks to J.D. Stroube at Dreamscape Covers (www.dreamscapecovers.com) for putting together a gorgeous graphic art design for my cover and chapter headings. You went way above and beyond the call of duty. I've come to value the friendship we have made very much and consider you one of my besties.

Clandestine

1

The blinds on the huge store front windows were closed. Emily spread apart a section of the blinds and peered out into blackness. Crap, she knew it! She was hoping maybe teenagers were loitering around or something so she wouldn't feel so alone. It was silly but a wary feeling always crossed her mind when she had to be out at night, especially by herself.

Lakeview was an okay town, not a lot happened most of the time, but she couldn't help her apprehension. Especially here lately, at times, she had been getting a wrenching pain in her gut that nearly drops her to her knees. It was so bad sometimes that she thought for sure she would die. It always coincided with the hair on the back of her neck standing up. She let her fingers release the blinds obstructing her view from the outside world.

It took her way to long to close the book store. Her tyrant of a boss wanted the inventory done and the new books on the shelves before closing. Well that wasn't going to happen. The store had been closed for over two hours. Too bad he wasn't generous enough to pay overtime.

Main Street wasn't very appealing at night. There are no street lights, or at least not regular ones. Some idiot somewhere along the line thought it would be a brilliant idea to use lantern light instead. It's supposed to bring a romantic ambiance to the store fronts for the tourists that Lakeview never has. The solar lights turn on at dusk. However, the whole street is still covered in shadow. Because everything is closed, there isn't much traffic. The only visible signs of life after dark are usually from the tenants of the apartments above the shops.

Emily willed herself to relax. It wouldn't do her any good to sit and dwell on it. The only other option was to sleep here and the boss wouldn't like that very much. He was a very cranky old man. His frame was slight, but anyone who knew him knew not to be fooled. He had a boiling temper on the verge of spilling over at any moment, pretty much all of the time. Crossing him was futile. She just did her job and kept her nose to the ground. Every now and then though, there was a hint of a crack in his otherwise mean demeanor but she never let him know that she noticed. This job was necessary at least through the summer to earn money for when school started in the fall.

Lakeview was the home of a local community college. Emily was enrolled and attended there for now. There were only a few semesters left and then she would transfer to UCLA where she had received a scholarship. It wouldn't cover everything though. That's why a few semesters here were unavoidable. It allowed her to get prerequisites out of the way so the cost of the University would be cheaper.

The heavy class load didn't leave much time for a job, so she was working all she could this summer to make up for what financial aid didn't cover. Her family wasn't poor. Their money was just tied up into other things. Emily pushed the thoughts of college and her family's financial state out of her mind. It was either that, or she would sit there and sulk about it forever. She didn't have time or the energy to be bitter about it anymore. It is what it is and making herself miserable about it wouldn't do her or anyone else any good.

She hauled the last box of books to a shelf in the back. The rest of the books would have to wait for morning. Her boss George would just have to get over it. Blake's Books would not burst into flames if one box of books wasn't stocked. She had to hurry up, her dad would be home soon and he hated when dinner was late. She flipped off the remaining lights as she headed out the door locking up behind her. As she took the key from the lock and crammed it into her purse, shivers raced down her spine. It felt like someone was watching her. She quickly gave a scan to her right and left trying to look nonchalant about it.

Don't be crazy there's no one out here. Why would there be? Pushing her paranoia to the back of her mind as best she could, she headed off down the sidewalk holding her chin up and alert. She remembered someone telling her this would exude confidence and would make a bad guy less likely to attack. Even though it seemed absurd, she couldn't help carrying the position anyway just in case. What could it hurt?

It was just then that her stomach convulsed into another spasm that contracted so hard that almost brought her to her knees. Her hand came up to put pressure on the pain but it didn't really alleviate it. Emily clenched her teeth together so she couldn't cry out. Why was this happening again?

Her long medium brown hair whipped behind her in the wind as a big breeze seemed to blow right through her. She found herself fighting a violent shiver that made her teeth chatter. The sudden wind wasn't doing much for her creep out meter that was for sure. Buying a car really needed to jump up the list of priorities.

A noise from behind her made her jump and stop abruptly. For a second, she was afraid to turn around. Her curiosity trumped her fear, she had to know what that sound was. It sounded like a piece of paper or some garbage shuffling on the pavement. Yeah that's what it was, garbage, she told herself as she hurriedly started walking again trying not to give the noise a second thought. There it was again. This time it sounded like a shoe scuffing the concrete. She gave a quick glance behind her and to her relief saw nothing. It was probably just litter flying by in the wind, or maybe even a cat. There were apartments a block up from where she was after all.

The apartments above the businesses on Main Street are not very nice, well at least the few she had ever seen anyway. Emily once had a friend who lived in a studio there that was so small the kitchen was literally in a closet and the fridge was in the living room. She supposed that would be a bachelors dream. He could watch the game on Sunday comfy on the couch and reach over and pull out a beer, never having to get up. All it would need is a toilet on the other side she thought laughing to herself.

Her comfortable laughter was brought up short by more sounds coming from the opposite direction that she was headed. This time though it was evident what it was, someone was walking a ways back behind her. It's just a harmless person walking home to their apartment after work. Get a hold of yourself Emily. They're not running and they are not sneaking so clearly they are not after you. Right? Yeah that's it, just walking home. Well then why was there a knot in the pit of her stomach that seemed to clench with every second that passed. A voice screamed in her head to run. She couldn't do that. This person hadn't posed any threat to her. There were no signs of immediate danger, at least not yet. STOP IT! You're psyching yourself out, Emily instructed herself firmly. This was ridiculous just because there is a man walking on a deserted street in the dark, did not mean he was a serial killer. After all, she was walking alone in the dark and she wasn't dangerous.

Then, through the endless babble in her mind she heard the strangers foots steps quicken. She picked up her pace too, trying to make herself move faster than whoever was behind her. She could see the corner up ahead where the wonderful glow of a street light promised safety. There was no point in yelling, the noise from the cross street was too loud. Besides, maybe he was just in a hurry too. She sped up again anyway. Better safe than sorry. Emily risked a glance over her shoulder to see her possible pursuer. She couldn't tell who it was, just that it appeared to be male. The figure was broad shouldered like a linebacker. She couldn't make out a face but she could tell it was looking right back at her. Well, at least it seemed to be. Why did it have to be so dark? Never mind, she told herself. It's not important, just keep going.

Her breath was shallower as she tried to be as silent as possible. She listened for any possible sign that he was getting closer to her. Man, he looked really big. If she panicked, he could probably catch up to her in a millisecond. There was no point in running. The guy was really tall. One of his strides probably added up to several of Emily's. Besides, she couldn't take a chance she tripped or something. He would have her for sure then and all her efforts would be wasted. Oh God, her mind exploded. It sounded like he was speeding up again. He had to be following her. Why else would he speed up every time she does? She still couldn't help but hope and pray that he was just an innocent bystander like she was. Even though she knew in her gut it wasn't true, she had to hold onto something. She had to get out of there and fast.

As she started across the alley an overwhelming blow hit her back sending her sprawling. As she fell, she vaguely wondered how in the world he caught up so quickly. A voice screamed out in her head to stay awake. Despite the sound advice, her lids just got heavier and heavier. Everything seemed to be in slow motion, she didn't think she was ever going to hit the ground. She tried to position herself somehow to break the fall but she was helpless against it. All she managed was to stretch her arms out in front of her.

Emily must have passed out for a minute because she didn't recall hitting the ground. Her next awareness was of being flat on her face in the dark. There was a gritty dirt taste in her mouth from the gravel that lined the alley way, but she didn't dare spit it out. Her forearm stung where a jagged rock was biting into her tender skin. Maybe if she lay very still, it would all just disappear, at least that's what she prayed for.

She soon realized her prayers would go unanswered when she heard a slight sound of something slipping across the rocks near her feet. She could hear deep ragged breathing and felt eyes boring into her but she didn't dare move. She knew there was no point in trying to escape. Her speed was mediocre at best, no match for his. So what was the use? She asked herself. Plus, she felt intense pain from the fall and didn't think she could make her limbs cooperate anyway.

What was taking him so long? Why hadn't he done anything yet? From all the stories she had heard in the news growing up, this was definitely not their style. Was it? Don't killers usually just attack for the thrill? What was the thrill in letting her lay there and eat dirt? For all he knew, she wasn't even awake yet. As long as she couldn't drag herself up, she would let him think so. He must be anticipating what he wanted to do to her next.

"Turn over." His voice was forceful but quiet. The sound of it made Emily's body tense and her skin crawl.

Heart pounding, she did what she was told. As she moved she felt a sharp pain stretching across her back. It must have been from when he pushed her down. She carefully moved into a sitting position and looked up into her attackers menacing eyes. They were emerald green. What was even more startling was that they seemed to glow brightly in the darkness. The sight made Emily cringe away from him. Those were like no human eyes she had ever seen before. Even though he was average height his frame seemed towering compared to Emily's. His hair was short and she thought it might be dark but it was hard to tell. It looked like he was in a crouch ready to pounce at the first sign that his prey might run.

"Why aren't you running or screaming? Don't I scare you?" He almost seemed like he was genuinely curious. His voice held an eerie fascination that made Emily's skin prickle all over. "I've been observing you for a while," he continued. "You're different from the others, but I still smell the stench of *them* on you." The attacker's voice was thick with disgust. Just as quickly he switched it up and purred, "no matter, I've got you now and I won't be wasting this opportunity. After all, you don't even seem to realize your potential or abilities, so they must not have summoned you yet. Therefore, they probably won't even miss you or hold me accountable for your loss."

Through the curiosity though, she could tell he was growing angry. He took a slow purposeful step towards her, and she still didn't move. She didn't know if it was fear or pure stupidity that held her still. She sure as heck knew it wasn't courage, her inner voice was screaming at her like a little girl to run but as usual, she couldn't respond. Her fight or flight mechanism was apparently broken. She was frozen, totally and completely locked in place where she sat utterly defeated on the cold hard ground.

Somewhere in the back of her panicked brain there was another voice that didn't sound like her own. It sounded safe somehow and that made her feel a little bit better. It reminded Emily of the old rule that when approached by a bear, never run. Only this was no bear, it was a man, and he wanted to do more than just hurt her.

Then as if he were trying to be friendly, he squatted down in front of her and asked her if she was okay. His rough voice had a peculiar sense of concern.

Emily wasn't fooled. Something inside her knew he couldn't be trusted. It was important that she didn't show him her fear either. People like this creep thrived on the fear of others and she refused to give him the satisfaction. She drew from her own strength and forced her nerves to steady. Emily squared her shoulders and said simply, "I'm fine, I'm not really loving your social skills though. Don't you know this is no way to start a conversation?" Emily's mouth clamped shut at the expression on the monsters face.

His sneer was a mixture of sarcasm and anger. Was that a hint of red she saw in his eyes? It couldn't be. That's just not possible. Her fear was just making her delusional.

"That's funny. You would think after being followed and shoved into a dark alley by a stranger, you would be at least a little shaken. Don't tell me, you are a black belt just waiting for the perfect moment to strike." He laughed soundlessly. "I mean your words do sound brave but your eyes and the fact that you're trembling like a scared little kitten say something else entirely." Even though the alley was submerged in darkness and shadows, it was obvious there was a devilish grin stretched across his face.

This sickened Emily to the very pit of her stomach. Even though he was just mocking her, she still wished it were true. If it were, she could kick his worthless butt. She didn't answer him. He was clearly just baiting her and she didn't want to give him the satisfaction. Her resistance was wearing thin anyway, and the terror that rocked her core was beginning to surface. With great effort she pushed the tears that threaten to spill out back and swallowed hard. She worked with great effort to school her features into a defiant glare. It didn't feel natural and more than likely didn't look that way either.

Be strong, the weird inner voice told her. *Stall him*, but stall him from what? There was no one around. There were no street lights or traffic and all the nearby shops were closed.

She wished he would just get it over with. The thought of what he might be planning made her shudder. She didn't want him to touch her. Unfortunately, she was a whopping hundred and twenty pounds and generally speaking, small in stature. What kind of damage could she really do? Besides that, she had never even been in a physical fight with a sibling. She didn't even have any siblings. Her thoughts weren't even making sense to her anymore. She had no idea what to do in a real fight even if it was for her own life. She was sure not much time had passed, but her mind raced on for what seemed like forever.

"This is ridiculous!" His firm voice broke into the inner babble going on inside her and she jumped a little at the unexpected change of emotion. When he spoke again she could hear the sneer return. "See, now that's a normal reaction. I was beginning to think you were wrong in the head and I felt guilty about our little game. Now my little mouse we can continue." Without further hesitation he gave her shoulder a hard shove and knocked her flat on her back. Just as quick he was on her cutting off whatever air she had left in her burning lungs.

2

"Please stop! You can't do this. I'm meeting my ride at the corner and when I don't come they'll look for me." Her pathetic voice squeaked as she panted trying to struggle free. She of course didn't really have a ride coming, but she figured it might buy her some time or scare him off.

"Silence!" He growled. "This doesn't have to be bad or even painful just relax and enjoy the ride."

"Please," Emily desperately begged. "I've never done this before. Don't do this!" Her heart was beating out of her chest so hard she thought it might burst. She opened her mouth to scream again and again, nothing came out but a defeated whimper.

"I don't believe that." He whispered in her ear. "My kind has been in this pathetic little town for weeks. You're too alluring. No matter, even if you're not lying it only makes this sweeter. I love being the first." He stretched the last word out like he was purring. He brought his face to hers and kissed her cheek. "Don't worry you're going to love this as much as I do, I promise. Just relax. It's not what you think…. It's better." His voice was husky and only made him sound more fierce and hungry.

What a monster, she thought disgusted. Different… yeah right, he was just like every other psychotic freak out there. He got his jollies by taking advantage of innocent girls. It clearly thrilled him to watch her panic. Unfortunately, she didn't disappoint him in that department. Her mind and body was set in a high panic mode, with no signs of relenting any time soon.

She turned her head trying to dodge his mouth. Instead of allowing her to avoid him, he responded by aggressively grabbing her chin and forcing her to face him. After kissing her harshly on the lips, his mouth moved down and his teeth grazed her neck. At their touch her skin went cold and rigid. They felt like tips of a wicked sharp knife at the base of her throat.

They were the sharpest teeth she had ever felt. They were more like needles than teeth. They pressed on her flesh threatening to break the tender skin. Why couldn't she just wake up from this nightmare? That's what this felt like... a nightmare, only it wasn't, this was reality.

The hem of her shirt had come up exposing her stomach. Emily couldn't feel the chill of the night air on her bare skin though. The jerks shirt was some kind of wool material and it scratched her, but kept her somewhat protected from the cool breeze. It felt like someone was giving her midriff an intense Indian burn. The rocks under her back were sending sharp piercing pains into her flesh. And the entire time that nagging clenching of her abdomen was increasing with every second that passed. It felt like someone was grabbing all of her internal organs and trying to flip them inside out and then into a bite sized pretzel. It was as though the entire world had stopped and began moving in slow motion. Every movement, every pain seemed to last longer than it should have. Her heart was pounding in her ears and she thought she was going to throw up. She didn't deserve this, no one did. She just wanted to go home, with the safety of locked doors and windows. Fear for her life kept her squirming even though it was a useless effort.

Emily opened her mouth to scream again finding her voice, but he quickly covered it with his own. She sickeningly tasted the booze on his breath and had to stifle a gag from exploding out. His kiss was hard, fury and desire pulsed through it like the steady beat of a drum. She tried to squirm out of his clutches with everything inside her. Her attempts were futile. His weight was just too much for her.

Traces of the scent hit her nose again stimulating her senses, sending them into over drive. Was it booze on his breath? The more she thought about it, the odor didn't smell like he had been drinking at all. In fact, the more the scent entangled her senses, the more it intoxicated her. It was as though his pheromones were wrapping around her until she was enveloped in the warmth that they offered. It made her woozy and maybe even a little sleepy. She tried to cling to her awareness. There was no way that the overwhelming feeling that his touch was a *good* thing, was her own idea. It was becoming harder and harder to convince herself that she was in danger. What was this guy and what did he mean by his kind?

He pulled his lips from hers long enough to say, "Now now, don't make this harder than it has to be. Just be quiet." "It won't be long now and you will feel nothing except bliss. Are you as excited as I am?" He said with mock enthusiasm.

He brought her arm to his mouth and kissed the underside of it. Out of nowhere a sharp pinch stung her wrist. Then his tongue snaked out and licked where her arm burned. Oddly, it soothed the sting turning it into a dull ache.

"Simply divine," he purred.

Emily was seriously grossed out. Not only was this pervert attacking her, he was licking her to? She tried wiggling free again, but he was just too massive above her. His mouth moved to her neck hungrily as if searching for food.

A sharp stinging sensation made her whole body tense even harder. It felt like he actually broke through the skin this time. His mouth lingered over the bite mark as he sucked. What was he doing? The pain was unbearable at first. It felt like all of her organs were being pulled from the small puncture. After a minute though, it turned numb. The woozy feeling was starting to take over again. What was he doing? The question was there, but it was getting harder to stay focused.

Even though it was cold outside, she knew the newly formed goose flesh wasn't from the weather. A cramp in her stomach made her cry out. Instead of pausing what he was doing it made him more aggressive. He took it as a green light that she was into it. That was far from the truth. Every fiber of Emily's being was writhing in utter terror. She had a stunningly clear realization that tonight would be her last on this earth. If she had ever thought of her own death, it surely wasn't like this. It wasn't supposed to be this way.

"Please God don't do this," Emily begged again. Her breath was coming in hyperventilating little gasps now and her voice was a hoarse attempt at a yell. Her throat was so dry that she probably couldn't have gotten a scream out that was loud enough for anyone to hear.

Don't move! You will only make it worse. The voice in her head was back again. Emily listened to it obediently. She let the words replay in her mind over and over. She tried to focus everything she had on those words. Somehow, they made her feel not so alone.

The strangely pleasant haziness was taking over more and more of her mind. She knew what was happening was wrong somehow. On the other hand, she was beginning to see what the monster was talking about, as much as she didn't want to admit it. Whatever he was doing, did feel good. She almost didn't care what was happening anymore. Everything was starting to go fuzzy around the edges. It was like-

BAM!!!

At the sound, the monster released a gasp and crumpled to the ground beside her. Emily was jolted back to reality and things were immediately clear again. She let out a breath that she didn't even realize she was holding. Emily was thankful to have the terrorizing weight off her body. Instinctively she sensed the new danger and hurried to her feet preparing to run. She hadn't even made it a foot when she ran smack into a brick wall.

Wait, that was no wall, it was a big broad chest. It wasn't just broad, it was rock hard. She started to scream her best horror movie scream, when a large hand clamped over her mouth. There wasn't even time for a little squeak.

"Be quiet. You might wake him up." The voice was hushed and barely audible.

After what had just happened, she couldn't bring herself to trust him. Part of her wanted to be thankful that he had gotten the monster off of her. Her heart knew he had just saved her from something that could have had a very tragic ending. Her head was still skeptical. What if this was the monsters friend?

His voice regained her attention. "If I take my hand off, will you promise to be quiet?"

Emily nodded slowly fighting back sobs. Even still, she could feel tears sliding down her cheeks disappearing into the stranger's hand. Just when she thought she had a chance, the possibility of her death loomed its ugly head again.

The hand moved off of her face but lingered about an inch away as if waiting for the returned scream and broken promise. She could smell the sweet rugged smell of his hand as it lingered a moment longer, before he dropped it all together. It reminded her vaguely of warm spices.

With a slight clicking sound she saw a small beam of light on the ground at their feet. She was suddenly aware that she was only wearing one shoe. Crap. She must have lost it in the struggle. Stupid slip on shoes she thought. From now on she would wear thick heavy boots. As if hearing her idea, his foot moved across the gravel drawing her attention to his shoes. They were thick soled black boots, exactly the type she had been thinking about for herself. His feet were of course quite larger than hers but he was considerably larger than her in general.

A noise from behind them broke into the silence. As quick as she heard it, her protector had her moved behind him. After a moment, Emily realized the noise wasn't from her attacker. He apparently wasn't going to move anymore, for now anyway. It just so happened that the noise was from a passing car on Main Street. Figures, one would drive by now. Where were they when she was getting shoved into the alley in the first place?

The alleged protector gave her a nudge towards some dumpsters a few yards away. When he motioned for her to go behind them she hesitated, not understanding why she couldn't just run straight home. He gently nudged again slightly harder than the last time. "I need to finish this… it's important that you trust me. I won't hurt you I promise." He whispered.

Emily could hear the reassuring tone, making her relax slightly. She felt like she could trust him. There was just something about his presence that comforted her. She crouched down behind the dumpster as quietly as she could. Unfortunately, there was some sort of debris behind them and her weight on it made a loud crunching sound. Part of her wanted to whisper an apology into the air between them, but somehow that didn't seem appropriate.

The stranger disappeared from her side. He moved so quietly she couldn't even hear a single rock scuff the ground. Emily heard an odd snapping sound and a groan and then nothing. What was happening? She waited frozen for what seemed to be at least forever and still nothing. Was he just watching her attacker, waiting for him to regain consciousness? Whatever it was that he was finishing didn't make a sound.

Creeped out, she listened carefully for any clue but still, there was nothing. Then, someone cleared their throat and she heard footsteps coming towards her. What if it wasn't the good one? Even though he may not be the savior she hoped he was she didn't care. He was being nice to her and he didn't seem at all like that other *thing*. Should she try and run?

Don't be afraid, the unknown voice in her head told her. Great, Emily thought. She was still hearing voices. She hoped that was just due to the trauma she had experienced tonight and not some symptom of a developing mental illness or something. That was just what she needed as if her life wasn't complicated enough, without having to add a therapy bill to the list.

"It's okay, you can come out now." He no longer spoke in a whisper and the concern was much more noticeable.

She felt a hand on her arm and automatically flinched back. His voice sounded kind of like the one in her head. Emily quickly did a mental comparison of the two. Clearly this theory was ridiculous. Obviously they couldn't be the same voices. God, she needed help.

"It's alright. I'm just trying to help you so you don't trip on the siding you're standing on." His voice was apologetic now. He realized he had frightened her and seemed like he was trying to be careful.

As she thought about if she could truly trust him, she glanced down at the siding he spoke of. She could tell by the feel under her bare foot that it was wood, but she couldn't see that it was siding and she had good vision. The night was black and very cloudy so there wasn't a visible star in the sky. This guy must have night vision or something. He repositioned the hand on her arm to help support her through the discarded mess. After both her feet were back on the gravel he lifted her arm and put something in Emily's hand. Her shoe, he had found her shoe. She was grateful; the rocks under her bare foot were murderous. The irony of what she had just gone through, versus the rocks being what she would call murderous caused a slightly hysterical giggle to bubble up her throat before she could stop it. She immediately clamped her lips shut like a vise. It definitely wasn't the time or place for her moronic weirdness.

"What do you find so funny?" He sounded much smoother now, almost fluid somehow.

"Nothing." That's all she could manage? He probably thought she was nuts. She decided not to elaborate and instead bent to put her shoe back on. They really weren't the cutest shoes but they were comfortable for work. Her work attire would never make the what's hot list in a fashion magazine, that's for sure. His attractive voice interrupted her thoughts again.

"Here, take this and rub it where you were bitten." He didn't give her a chance to ask questions. He just put an object into her hand and moved away.

Emily lifted her hand and tried to get a look at what the small object was. It was a tiny cylinder shaped thing. "What's this?" Her fingers probed the cylinder trying to make it out. It reminded her of a Chap Stick or lip gloss tube, only much smaller.

"It's...medicine. It's like Neosporin. It will help close any wound left from the bite." He turned his back as he spoke. "I'll just give you some privacy."

Emily couldn't help a smile at his politeness. "I don't need privacy." She said with equal consideration. "It's just on my neck." With that she began applying the mystery ointment to the wound at her throat. It felt nice. It had a sort of soothing quality to it. It evaporated the flames that were licking up her neck, to just under her chin.

He cleared his throat. "I know, but all the same..." He trailed off. "Just let me know when you're finished. Oh and don't forget the one on your wrist."

Emily swallowed and felt the blood rushing to her face making it instantly hot. How did he know where she had been bitten? She wondered exactly how long he had been in the alley. It was possible that he had seen the entire thing take place. Emily couldn't figure out why he wouldn't have stepped in sooner if that was the case. The feeling was immediately squelched by her common sense. What was important was that she wasn't being attacked anymore. Besides, it wasn't like he was confessing to seeing her naked or something.

She wanted to ask the stranger if he knew what that monster was doing to her. He must have had some knowledge on the subject. Why else would he carry around some kind of bite kit? No matter how hard she tried, she couldn't seem to make her lips form the words.

Instead, she finished applying the medicine and then paused in the act of clicking the cap into place. Emily brought the tube up to her nose and attempted a nonchalant sniff at the foreign substance. Oddly, it almost smelled like blueberries. Huh. Without another thought, Emily pushed up her sleeve and rubbed the medicine over the wound that was no longer numb. It was flaming hot now. Well at least it was until the blueberry substance touched it. It simmered to a tingle and then felt like nothing. Wow, this stuff is wonderful she thought as she repositioned her shirt and snapped the lid back on the tube.

Responding to the click of the lid, the guy turned around back to face Emily again. "Well miss, we should get you home." His words sounded formal and polite.

The use of the word miss almost made her laugh again. He didn't sound like he could be much older than her, if at all. She wondered what was with the formalities. He was probably still trying to reassure her that he wasn't going to take over the job of killing her. Quite considerate of the stranger really, she thought absently.

He led Emily out of the alley the same way she had been pushed in. She could tell they were in the same general vicinity of where she had been laying. She could feel the nearness of the back of the building to her left. When they reached the dip indicating the road he pushed on her arm to the right. How did he know which way she needed to go? It was more than likely just a coincidence, a perfect one at that.

What happened to her attacker? Shouldn't they have run into him? Stepped over him? Maybe they hadn't walked in the same area. No, that's not right, she knew they did and she never heard him being moved. Her muscles were tight and she felt exhausted. Her mind blurred with questions, but she couldn't seem to stay focused on one thought for long.

When they got to the corner, her whole body relaxed under the welcoming blaze of the street light. She smiled to herself at the sight of cars driving by. They were witnesses in case the guy changed his mind. Emily wondered how much time had passed since she left Blake's. She glanced up at the man who had saved her, still not totally sure that he wasn't leading her to yet another location where death awaited.

Her breath literally caught in her throat. This guy seriously had to be the absolute hottest guy she had ever seen. She made an effort not to stare that didn't work out so well. He didn't seem to notice anyway, thank God, his eyes were too focused on the walk sign on the other side of the street. Lucky for her, this intersection had a very long light that gave her a chance to covertly examine him further. He had blonde hair with a slight wave to it. It was neatly kept, not at all like those loser surfer wannabee guys she always saw loping around. She never understood why guys assumed it was cute to look like they just crawled out of bed. His skin was tanned perfectly. The cerulean blue of his eyes was dazzling. Even his nose was perfection. His lips were full, almost pouty. They looked smooth and very kissable.

Wait… kissable? What was she thinking? This man might be planning to make her disappear off the face of the earth and she's drooling over his pouty lips? She looked away quickly feeling foolish. Absently, she watched the cars speeding by pondering whether or not she should jump in front of one at an attempt at rescue. Honestly she still didn't feel like she was in danger. He seemed strong but harmless. Emily felt silly about the worry that nagged at the back of her mind. She was just being paranoid, at least she hoped. This was a public street after all. They were walking in the direction of her own house. Clearly she wasn't in danger. This was the same guy that saved her life not long before. If he planned to do her harm, he had a chance to do so discreetly back in the alley. There would be no point in the theatrics of posing as a knight in shining armor.

Helplessly she found her eyes drifting back to stare at him again. He was almost a head taller than her and broad shouldered. He wore a tight fitting long sleeved knit shirt so she could see that his chest was very well-defined. Emily looked away again mortified. My God, she thought. What was wrong with her? Where was her sense of self-preservation? She apparently had a deep seeded death wish. Just then the light changed and the sign across from where they stood switched to walk.

He nudged her elbow and they started off the curb. Once across, he walked up another block and turned left. Where was he going? She wanted to ask but again, she couldn't make her mouth cooperate.

He was walking with a smooth confident stride, that didn't at all give her any sense of menace. It seemed as though he was heading toward where she lived. That wasn't possible, she had never seen this person before in her life. He couldn't know who she was, let alone where she lived.

She knew she should say something, anything. Instead she just kept walking. Emily felt so ridiculous. He saved her life back there, she could say thank you even if nothing else. Well, either that or she could at least attempt to decipher where it was they were going.

Even though he held on to her arm tightly, she didn't feel trapped. It seemed he was doing so just to hold her up, which was nice. Her body felt as though it weighed four hundred pounds. In addition to that, it seemed like there were heavy sand bags in her shoes. Fatigue overwhelmed her and yet, she was wide awake.

At that moment Emily realized her entire body was trembling. She must be in shock, that's why she couldn't speak. She did feel cold. However, she had figured that was just the temperature outside and not her body's reaction to the trauma.

What exactly had happened? Her memory was starting to feel fuzzy, something bad happened. He saved her, but what had he saved her from? She barely had time to gasp when she stumbled clumsily over a crack in the sidewalk. He stiffened his hold and she never lost a step. Great, now he was saving her from herself.

After walking what seemed like forever, they were turning down elm Street. She had lived on this road her entire life. He couldn't know that could he? Maybe he lives nearby. It was possible that he had seen her around or something. Without a pause, he walked three doors down and to the left.

Emily's house looked creepy in the dark. Some of the faded white paint was chipping and the yard needed a good mowing. Her dad usually kept it short although lately, had been slacking off immensely. As he directed her up the path to the front door she noticed no porch lights were on. Good, her dad wasn't home yet. That meant she had time to throw something together for dinner, before he had time to lose it.

Finally, he spoke, "Here you are safe and sound. If you are able to recall anything from tonight, be sure not to tell anyone. It's less complicated that way I assure you." He peered down at her intently conveying the importance of what he was saying.

If I'm able, she thought. The memories were already fading without her permission. Somewhere inside her she knew that wasn't normal, she just couldn't muster enough worry to care. "Why?" She asked confused. "Shouldn't I call the police?" How could she not tell the police or Sam that she was attacked? That was just madness, crimes should be reported.

His face grew hard as stone. "Absolutely not," he said firmly. "That won't do you any good." Emily started to protest but he cut her off with a wave of his hand. "Look. There are things at work here that the police can't fix." His beautiful eyes softened a fraction. "I need you to promise you won't tell. I can't explain now, but it's important."

It was always necessary to report an attack like this to the police. Emily knew that. The mantra kept replaying in her ears over and over again. Even though she knew it, she found herself nodding stupidly up at him. She wasn't a weak person. No way was she one of those girls that were easily persuaded by a guy's power of manipulation. There was just something about him that made her confident that this time; this one was speaking the truth. She wondered idly if he was part of some crazy conspiracy.

His answering smile cleared that right up. "Good." He turned to walk away and Emily realized she didn't even know his name.

She turned back to ask and he wasn't there. He must have run. Man, maybe he was a ghost sent down to rescue her. At this point nothing would surprise her. She turned back to the door fishing her key out of her purse. Once the key was in the lock, the door flew open revealing darkness. All she had time for was a squeak before she was abruptly pulled in the house by her shirt. The door slammed shut and locked behind her with a clank of sliding metal.

3

The intruder threw Emily across the room, sliding her body into the wall. She curled in on herself waiting for the next onslaught of pain. She soon realized what wall she must of hit. She was right by the entrance to the kitchen. There were knives in there. She didn't know if she could get to them in time, but she had to try. As she scrambled up to her hands and knees the overhead light of the living room came on. She started to hurry to the other room when movement caught the corner of her eye. Impulsively Emily turned her head to see the distraction.

"Dad!" Emily let out a sigh at the site of her father Sam standing across the room from her. It was a massive relief that it was just him, instead of a mass murderer, or her savior guy gone bad. He must have parked in the garage which was odd she thought. His cold rock hard face replaced her good feeling with another that she recognized to well. His eyes were glassy and his graying hair tousled. The red button down flannel shirt he wore was open to reveal his stained white undershirt. His average sized body swayed slightly as she watched him. Her anxiety returned with every one of those sways.

"What do you think you were doing?" He might have spoken a simple question, though it shot out at Emily *execution style*.

What was she supposed to say? Oh gee dad I was attacked and the guy bit me. Don't worry, just in the nick of time some hot stranger made the bad guy disappear, probably killing him and then after walking me home, he disappeared as well. So how was your day? No, that probably wasn't a good plan. Besides, she would sound completely delusional and he already thought everything out of her mouth was a lie anyway. Not to mention, she still couldn't recall the events perfectly. It seemed the more time passed, the less she could remember.

Emily gulped. "Sorry dad I got held up at the store with inventory…"

Sam closed the distance between them in four wobbly strides. "Don't lie to me girl!" He hauled her to her feet and slapped her face. The blow was so hard she almost lost her balance. "Your hair's a mess and your clothes are all wrinkled."

"I'm not dad I swear." Emily squeaked fighting back tears, that would only show him weakness and he hated that more than anything.

"Damn it Emily!" He struck her again this time with the back of his hand.

Emily fell to the floor. She hit her head on the old ratty couch and stayed put where she landed. It was a fairly old piece of furniture so the wood was solid. A blast of pain shot through her head at the spot that had impacted. It wasn't hard enough for a concussion at least that was something. At that point it wouldn't have been wise for her to respond, so she said nothing. Her face felt hot and painful where he had struck her. As she watched him she pressed a hand to her cheek willing the pain to dull.

"I've been watching for you. Figured I'd find out you were up to God knows what. So I set myself up at the window. Sure enough, you come strolling up with a deadbeat." Sam didn't slur very much when he was drunk, but his hand gestures were all over the place. He talked with his hands when he was sober and after drinking the movements became totally erratic.

He was quieter now but she knew better than to test her luck. "Dad there was a weird guy lurking around the alley so a nice man offered to walk me home. I've never met him before-"

"LIES!" he interrupted. "The worst thing is that you were with one of… them." The words were colored with so much distain and disgust it made her flinch expecting another blow. "I don't ever want to see you with that thing again do I make myself clear?" He didn't give her a chance to answer before he continued. "Go to bed. I was going to surprise you thought I'd be nice I ate at the tavern so you're off duty tonight." His words came out in a furious slur that was hard to focus on completely.

Saying nothing, Emily gave him a defeated nod and collected herself off the hard wood floor. There was no point in trying to talk sense into him when he was drunk. She hurried passed him and down the hall to her room.

The family pictures that lined the wall on either side of her were no longer a comfort. They hadn't been for a long time. All they were was a constant reminder that her "happy little family" was gone and never coming back. The year her mom died they had taken a family photo at the lake. To look at that picture of her dad by contrast to the way he looked now five years later was alarming. If someone hadn't known him back then they probably wouldn't have even believed it was him.

Once Emily was in her room with the door closed and locked, a mild feeling of comfort spread through her. Things could have been a lot worse. Sam could have forced her to stay out there with him. That would have been a fate far more tragic then what she had already endured. This night royally sucked. Emily couldn't imagine what else could possibly have gone wrong.

She would have to wait to shower until after he went to sleep. Well, passed out would be the more operative word for the situation she guessed. Emily started for the dresser where her bright orange iPod was charging and quickly changed her mind. Any other time she had a bad day and was upset she would use the iPod as a distraction. The blaring music was a wonderful way of drowning out all the negative thoughts in her head. Sometimes she would even sing along when the song fit her mood, but not tonight. She had too much to think about. Emily had to remember exactly what happened. She knew she couldn't go to the police they'd commit her for sure. Besides that, she promised she wouldn't.

She went to her bed and sat down curling her sore legs up hugging her knees. The pains that gripped her muscles were pure agony that made her eyes sting fiercely with unshed tears. With all the chaos tonight she hadn't had much chance to take inventory of the damage. The muscles in her legs screamed in protest as she felt her knees and calves. She rolled her shoulders and arched her back. Immediately she winced as she felt what had to be a bruise forming in between her shoulder blades. Judging by the amount of pain, it was a very large bruise or perhaps several. She raised her hand to the sting on her left cheek. It was scraped from the gravel in the alley or maybe from her dad's affections earlier. Either option was possible.

Emily stopped her examination and lay down on her side, drawing her legs into a fetal position. She moved slowly, it hurt too badly to straighten them. She let her eyes close and her mind drift back to the events of the evening. Her memory was fuzzy, but the fear was there behind her lids.

She knew she had been pushed down, though she couldn't remember where. Someone attacked her. It could have been much worse, only that other guy had stopped it. While he seemed nice, she couldn't get a clear picture of what he looked like. The details were there, though out of focus and dark around the edges. Did the good guy kill the bad one? She couldn't remember, if he did, the body couldn't have just disappeared. Was she just blocking out that part along with the others? Also, after she got to her door how did that guy leave so fast? Her mind flashed from one image to the next. It was trying to decipher any code her memory might give her.

Then there was her dad's odd reaction to the protector. It was definitely more than just a dad being worried about his daughter getting a boyfriend. Emily was sure of that. Her dad had a habit of raging for ridiculous reasons when he was belligerently drunk, but that was something else. In her mind's eye she could see his face right after he turned the light on. His eyes were narrowed into slits and his leathery skin was tight against his set jaw. Despite the anger, was that a hint of fear in his eyes? What could make him so afraid that he morphed it into outrage, so strong that he would look at her with such hatred? He almost acted as though she had betrayed him. He had already eaten at the bar, so she knew this had nothing to do with dinner not being on the table when he arrived. She used the sleeve of her shirt to wipe the tears that ran down her face streaking her cheeks. Pain flashed again when she touched her face and she clenched her teeth to fight against it.

The entire situation was just too weird, but there was no time to feel sorry for herself. She knew she had to figure everything out one way or another. Luckily, all of her problems would be waiting for her after she got some rest. That was a prospect she really wasn't looking forward to in the least.

It probably had been enough time; Sam should be deep into his drunken coma for sure. She should be safe to venture to the shower.

Emily got up and cracked her door and listened intently for the welcoming chain saw snoring. The drunker he got the worse he snored. Sure enough, it only took a second to hear the deep sounds of his nights end billowing down the hall to where she now stood.

She hurried back to her dresser to grab clean clothes. The bottom drawer was filled with pajamas that her mother had bought for her. Sorting through them, Emily opted for a shorts and camisole set in a deep purple. They were a soft satin material. They were comfy and after everything that had happened, she could use a little comfort.

After that, she tiptoed to the hall closet to retrieve a towel and then was off to the privacy of the bathroom where she could relax the pain indented deep into her bones. The thought of the hot water and steam was so enticing, she practically ran into the bathroom. The feel of the linoleum under her bare feet was shockingly cold.

The mirror above the sink frightened Emily. It showed the reflection of a girl who appeared to have not slept in days. There were dark circles under her eyes and her complexion was paler than usual. The hair that was normally smooth and shiny, was ratty and dirty. She did see one plus though. The scrape along her cheek didn't look bad enough to leave a scar. In fact, it looked more irritated than anything else. She hoped that the appearance meant that it would heal quickly.

The hot steamy water was a Godsend. She could feel it unwinding the knots in her back slowly. It stung against her cheek, but it had to be cleaned in case dirt got into the scrape. It didn't take long for all of her muscles to unwind. She was still sore but it was understandable, after what she had been through.

She couldn't seem to get the picture of the man that protected her out of her mind. There was just something about him. Even in that short time Emily could tell he wasn't like anyone else in this God forsaken town. She didn't think that was a bad thing either. He was mysterious, strong and gentle. He had a very warm presence about him too. He wouldn't give her straight answers though and that just proved he had something to hide. Realistically she couldn't hold that against him. Everyone has bones rattling in their closets. Emily knew that better than anyone else she knew or had ever known for that matter. The hinges have been blown off all the closet doors in her house on more than one occasion. Regardless of what he was hiding he must be a good guy his actions tonight showed that. He obviously was just a savior he never tried to hurt her. He was so gorgeous even the memory of his face made her heart thud. Her stomach fluttered with butterflies through the relentless hunger. Her abdomen suddenly growled up at her demanding refueling.

Crap, she hadn't eaten all day. With work and everything else that happened during the evening, food had just slipped her mind. Sam probably wouldn't have let her in the kitchen anyway, even if she had thought about it. It was pretty clear that her bedroom would be her only sanctuary for the night.

After her shower she would grab a bagel or something. If she was careful, it shouldn't wake him up from his slumber on the springy, uncomfortable couch. It never used to be so dilapidated, but sleeping on it for the past five years religiously, wore it down. It must be too hard for him to sleep in the bed he once shared with her mom alone. He would of course never admit that though, heaven forbid he show weakness. Emily's mother Melissa had always told her that the ability to show weakness gives the ability to embrace strength.

After Melissa died, the drinking got worse too. He's always been a drinker, but it didn't become a form of self-medication until that horrible night. Sam was a brick wall when it came to Emily long before her mother's death though. She was supposed to be a boy and he regretted that she wasn't her whole life. He of course loves her, he's her father, it's required. He just doesn't say so or show it in an outright expressive way like some "daddies" do.

He was different with her mother though. Melissa had always had a way of keeping him in check. He might not have showered her with flowers, candy and romance, but it was evident to anyone who observed that she was his main purpose on this earth.

As the water and steam relaxed the rest of her body, Emily thought about how the drinking had become increasingly worse in the last few weeks. She wondered why that was. Knowing Sam, she would never know. He's not exactly an open book, more like a locked diary that never had a key to start with. Living in the Jameson house taught Emily to keep to herself and her mouth shut. She wished things were different, yet knew there wasn't anything she could do about it. She has just resigned herself to learning how to deal and count down the days until she gets to leave for school. The water was starting to run cold so she unwillingly turned off the blissful shower.

The process of getting dressed was rushed. Her stomach had gone from a slight growl, to full fledge conversations. She prepared herself to go to the kitchen in stealth mode, so not to disturb the grizzly's hibernation. Emily had done this so many times, she had the activity down to an art.

Once in front of the fridge, she propped the door with her hip and pushed the button for the light with her left hand. With her right she quietly removed the lid from the milk placing it on the rack. She grabbed the full gallon of milk from its place on the shelf and began guzzling. The milk did wonders for her scratchy throat. The feel of it traveling into her empty stomach was amazing. Hey, maybe milk really did do a body good, she thought picturing the "Got Milk" commercials. Her hand weakly shook under the weight of the jug until it was finely returned to the shelf. Okay so it may do a body good but she needed to lift some weights or something. The minuscule weight of a milk jug shouldn't make her arms shake. No doubt though that the nights events hadn't done much for her muscle stamina and endurance. That had to be it because she knew she was stronger than that.

There weren't a whole lot of options for food. A trip to the grocery store would have to be carried out soon. Lord knew Sam wouldn't do it so that task was usually left up to Emily. The only store he ever entered was the liquor store. She went to the counter grabbed a bagel and headed back to her room pleased with her OO7 sneaking skills.

Man, she hadn't totally realized how starving she was until she had closed her bedroom door and stuffed the last bite in her mouth. Maybe she should have gotten two. Oh well, she was too tired to care.

The bed seemed to beckon to her, calling her name in sweet purring whispers. She responded obediently and crawled in her comfy full size bed pulling the covers up around her neck. The comforter that warmed her was old but she loved it. It was black with orange poke-a-dots. She even had orange curtains to match with black sheers underneath. As she nestled in, she willed herself not to think about any of the day's drama. She made a silent promise that she wouldn't let herself think about it. It could all be dealt with tomorrow. It would be the only way sleep would take over and she desperately needed sleep. Her self-proclaimed promise was broken but even still it didn't take long for her lids to droop and she willingly gave in to her exhaustion.

4

The next morning Emily felt much more refreshed. She even woke up before her alarm went off, which was definitely a rare occurrence. The first thing she noticed was that her pillowcase was stiff from drool. That's weird. She never drooled, what was that? Anyway, no time to worry about that she had to get to work.

She got up and dressed in record time. She had to get to Blake's before boss man or he'd have her neck for leaving that last box un-stocked. Snatching her hair brush off the dresser, she stood in front of the mirror hanging on the back of her bedroom door. As she ran the brush through her nasty bed head she stared at her reflection appraisingly. The eyes looking back at her weren't familiar. They were still blue like hers, but the whites were invaded with bloodshot lines as if she had been sobbing. Had she cried in her sleep? She didn't remember dreaming or anything. Her mind flashed to her stiff pillow observation. Huh.

Now that she thought about it, it was sort of strange that she didn't recall dreaming. She always knew what she had dreamed from the moment she woke up. Emily couldn't think of a single morning where she didn't know exactly what she had dreamed about. In fact, often some of her best stories had been written from dreams. Emily kept a notebook in the drawer of her bed side table for that very purpose. She would wake up inspired and race to scribble it all down before she could forget a single detail. Her mother used to make fun of how vivid her dreams were. She would say Emily was so animated when telling the story that it was next to impossible to tell it wasn't real. Sometimes, Emily had to admit she wasn't so sure herself. Not all her dreams were noteworthy though. She did have the occasional dreams that seemed more like science fiction or a bad cartoon comedy. Those ones were always good for a laugh if nothing else.

The scratch on her cheek was red, but didn't look too bad this morning. Emily could remember Sam hitting her when she got home. The reason why was a little trickier. He wasn't a regular abuser or anything. In fact, it was really pretty rare for him to raise a hand to her. It had only happened a few times in her entire life. It had never been like last night though. Despite how drunk he was, that was ridiculous even for him. Emily dug through her memories of last night trying to piece it together. Nothing became clear, it was strange that she couldn't remember. Maybe she hit her head when she hit the wall. She stared at her reflection intently, willing herself to recall even the smallest detail. No matter how hard she tried the night before was still a blank. She shrugged her shoulders and sighed. The thought of George's wrath was more frightening right now.

She finished her hair and tossed the brush back on the dresser. A glance at the black and silver clock on her wall kicked Emily into overdrive. Without any further preamble she hurried out the door. She could see the morning sun pouring into the living room at the end of the hall. It wasn't like Sam to open the curtains. That was one of Emily's self-delegated tasks. He would be perfectly happy living in a dark cave for the rest of his life.

To her surprise, Sam was still sawing logs on the couch as hard as last night. He was supposed to be at work. The courteous thing to do would probably be to wake him gently and rush him off. She shrugged her shoulders with a sigh and hurried out the door. There wasn't time to deal with the repercussions. Sam wasn't a morning person, especially when he was hung over. Nine chances out of ten, he would wake up swinging. With her luck, he had taken a floater and was supposed to be right where he was. Or better yet, for as long as it took to sleep off the hangover. She would have to worry about that later.

Outside the weather was crisp with just a hint of morning fog. The sky was grey but showed sure signs of clearing. Birds sang their good morning songs in all the trees down the street. At first glance, it was a beautiful summer morning and everything seemed perfect. Of course though, things aren't always what they seem. Emily was beginning to realize that fact all too well lately.

As she walked down the streets of her small town, her mind drifted to the way things used to be. Things had gotten so weird around Lakeview. People still did the usual things, but their demeanor was different. The first time she had noticed it was roughly a few weeks ago. Gosh, maybe over a month. Not everyone seemed to have changed, just some of them. Lakeview was a town that's population had never been above eight thousand until Mayor Bradshaw came to office that is. His goal was to give their quiet town a shove into the future. He wanted tourist sites, shopping malls and anything else that would increase the prophet margin. Some of his ideas were implemented but others haven't gotten very far. Even with the "improvements" he put into action, the town remained quaint. Everyone knew everyone and their business was public record. Kids could play safely outside without parents having to worry. With some exception, the crime rate was down and the jail never full.

Once things started changing, they turned full circle. The only muggings this town has ever seen have all been within the last month. Kids seemed to stick to the safety of their backyards, instead of exploring the neighborhoods. Some of the people that normally would be out mowing their lawns on a day like today, were nowhere in sight. Instead, they let their yards grow passed ankle high. That sort of thing might be trivial, but it's unheard of in Lakeview. Most everyone kept their yards neat and tidy like a golf course even if their house was subpar.

Others walked quickly down the side walk to their destinations with their heads down. Normally, they would look around at familiar faces and cars waving and exchanging greeting and small talk as they passed. The ones who weren't staring at their feet were like walking zombies. There were even a few shop owners that changed their hours. They made excuses that business was going well enough that they didn't need to stay open into the evening or something like that.

The prospect didn't seem very likely to Emily. Most of the privately owned stores didn't get much business except for the loyal customers opposing big box stores. Most everyone flocked to the convenience of one stop shopping at bargain prices as soon as they arrived in Lakeview. Everyone knew the small businesses tended to have higher prices. They couldn't afford to compete with the big boys. Granted, there wasn't much in the way of big box stores yet, but there was now a WinCo, Wal-Mart and talk had spread about a Ross coming to town. The main objective was to try to convert Lakeview from its small town ways to overcrowded big city. Truth be told, it didn't really seem to be going well.

When Emily moved her gaze straight ahead, her eyes widened in surprise at what was in front of her. There was a woman speeding down the sidewalk directly in Emily's path. Mrs. Cleary was headed right for her and didn't seem to notice the potential head on collision. The middle aged woman's head was down. It looked like her chin might bore a hole into her collar bone. Her shoulder length hair was falling down around her face like a ball of fluff, obscuring her face completely. Emily had to laugh a little. It made her look like a frizzed out version of Cousin It from The Adam's Family. She was coming at Emily fast.

"Good morning Mrs. Cleary." Emily greeted brightly still giggling. Stupidly she even gave her a little wave. The other woman wasn't even looking at her so the gesture was pretty pointless.

Mrs. Cleary jumped back so hard, Emily thought she'd fall in the road for sure. Her breath caught and she was watching Emily with sheer panic plain on her face. She looked like a deer caught in the headlights. After a few moments recognition seemed to finally dawn on her.

"Oh, hi Emily. I didn't see you."

The smile that she plastered across her face looked false, not like her at all. It was one of those smiles like in a tooth paste add. The ones where you think for sure the model's cheeks might burst with the pressure of their toothy grin. Honestly, it looked painful. Great, she's apparently become one of the Stepford Wives.

Mrs. Cleary's head whipped around and back down again. "Well... if you'll excuse me. I've got to get... home." Without another word the stout older woman squeezed passed Emily on the sidewalk and regained her speed around the corner until she was out of sight.

That was different, Emily thought shaking her head as she resumed her own path. Maybe she's got something going on in her family. Emily figured it must be bad because she was known as the gossip of the block. Mrs. Cleary had no trouble telling anyone everyone else's business even her own. For her not to chatter away to everyone she meets is like telling her not to breathe. Emily shuddered inwardly at the latest thought bouncing around in her mind. The choppy discourse had nothing to do with family problems. Mrs. Cleary had been recruited into the odd behavior club that seemed to be taking over the town.

Emily crossed the street directly in front of Blake's Books and half jogged to the door. The blinds were already open, displaying the big OPEN sign in the window with bold block lettering. Crap! He opened early today, which of course meant he had seen her laziness. She could actually picture him behind the counter with a scowl etched into his stone cold face. His eyes were probably boring holes into the door awaiting Emily's arrival.

When she stepped in, she was pleasantly surprised to see George's bubbly daughter behind the counter in his place. Emily let out a huge sigh of relief and her shoulders instantly relaxed. Lucy was her best friend. If Emily was honest with herself, she would have to admit that Lucy was her only real friend.

Lucy was Emily's age. She has always attended a blind school out of town, so many of the kids their age didn't know her well. They see Lucy all the time and still treat her like she has the plague, usually giving her a wide birth as she passed. The thought made Emily roll her eyes heavenward. Small towns are so ridiculous. It's not like blindness was contagious. Emily wished they would just get over it. Unfortunately, that wasn't likely.

Her mind drifted back to when they were little. Lucy's mom used to set up play dates with other kids around her daughter's age. She wanted to give Lucy a chance to feel normal and allow the other kids to get to know her better. No chance of that in this town of course. Heaven forbid they put into practice the all famous rule of not judging a book by its cover.

The kids would act like they couldn't wait for their parents to get back the whole time. When they weren't doing that the jerks would purposefully play games that would only in essence tease Lucy without them having to actually do the teasing out loud. This way if they were called out on their trickery they could just blame ignorance. The fact that Lucy couldn't easily play their games just had never occurred to them... yeah right. They played things like

Marco Polo but kept their eyes open. The worst was when they would all go outside and say they wanted to play tag. Everyone would whoop and holler, having a blast. Poor Lucy couldn't keep up and would end up sitting in the grass by herself until Emily came by.

It didn't take long for the two of them to become good friends. Lucy was great and so funny. She had a quality about her that was much more valuable than any of those other kids. When the others saw that Emily was Lucy's friend, some of them figured she must not be carrying the plague and would try and play with her too. It never lasted long after the novelty wore off though. They all just went back to thinking Lucy was an inconvenience to be around. Anger swelled inside of Emily with the memory. She allowed herself to return to the present and tucked the past away in a vault at the back of her mind.

If Lucy was up front, that meant that George was more than likely in back plotting Emily's punishment. Emily took a deep breath and started toward the counter. The smell of books enveloped her senses and she breathed in deeper. The smell of paper had always soothed her. It was pleasant and hinted at new uncharted worlds that were waiting to be discovered. A new book was something to relish and appreciate. Emily's love of books was something she had acquired when she was barely old enough to read. The fact that she worked at a book store was perfect, even if her boss did leave something to be desired. He wasn't really that bad for the most part though. Good old George was challenging but tolerable.

There were only a few customers browsing and they didn't appear to need help. Emily smiled and nodded hello to the ones that glanced up as she passed. Only two of the customers smiled back. The other two that she saw, were apparently suffering from the Invasion of the Body Snatchers syndrome.

"Hey Emily. Dad's been waiting for you and he doesn't sound happy." Lucy was always so friendly, even when her news was not. Her bright cheery nature was always infectious.

Emily couldn't ever seem to help being surprised when her friend recognized the sound of her footsteps. Lucy couldn't do this with everyone, just those she knew. Once known to her, it only took her one or two meetings before she had your mannerisms down to a science. "Hey Luce what's up?" Emily tried ignoring the comments about George without much success.

"Not a lot. Same old mostly." Her words grew softer. "Mr. Scott is over there." She pointed a short slim finger to the right. "He's been browsing the Travel section since we opened the door. I mean literally he was waiting on the curb when we got here." Lucy was leaning across the counter over to Emily.

"Maybe he likes books about far off places. Your dad has been getting more and more in stock." Emily mechanically replied with a shrug. A customer's browsing habits didn't really seem like a big deal.

"Yeah but he's one of those… ones." She maintained her low level of volume in case someone came up Emily guessed. This made her smile a little because no one could get in ear shot of Lucy without her knowing about it. She always knew how close people were in comparison to her hushed voice.

"What are you talking about?" Lucy surprised her. Did she know something that Emily didn't?

"Nothing I guess," she shrugged a shoulder. "I just get a weird feeling about him. I can't explain it."

"I think you're just paranoid. I'm sure it's nothing." Emily tried to sound nonchalant, even though she had noticed the same thing in the past. He too was one of the ones Emily more recently began referring to as the pod people.

"Emily!" George's voice bellowed from the back room. "Is that you I hear out there? Get back here there's work to be done. I don't pay you to sit and visit." His rough deep voice was the absolute pinnacle of annoyance.

"It's alright dad… I stopped her to talk," Lucy called clearly trying to help. She shot Emily a sympathetic glance as she spoke.

"Now, Emily!" George's voice thundered from his office.

Lucy raised her hands in defeat. "Sorry Em." Lucy's dark brown eyes softened. It always bothered her when her father talked down to Emily.

"Don't worry about it." Emily whispered to her, as she hurriedly made her way around the counter to the overcrowded room George grumpily occupied. "He's all bark and no bite." Emily knew this was far from the truth but she hated showing anyone weakness, even her best friend.

"Yeah right." Lucy said sarcastically as Emily passed her.

The back room was cluttered and dusty. As power hungry as the old man was, he had no patience or concern with being orderly. He was a total pack rat. The room was dimly lit by a single light fixture that dangled away from the ceiling by a cord that looked like it would turn to dust at any given moment. It swayed slightly from the breeze from the ventilation system. Any books that didn't sell after a period of time never got discarded or put into a bargain bin. In fact, at Blake's there was no such thing as a bargain bin. The sinful word was taboo to George. He didn't do discount.

After clearing the threshold into the time warp, she saw the familiar floor to ceiling shelves that housed the old neglected titles that she was sure dated back to the beginning of time. There were also tables all around the room that held stacks of books covered in dust. Some of the piles looked to be about ten books high. Underneath the tables were boxes of yet more out of print editions or unwanted books.

George figured someday someone would come in looking for a title they had been seeking out for years. Of course he would have it stored in the back and would mark up the price under the statute of supply and demand. He wouldn't tell the customer that of course he would instead call it a classic and explain the price was for quality of good literature. Emily had actually seen him do this a time or two. She also knew that his vast knowledge of literary works allowed the customers to trust him implicitly. This was despite the fact that he was just blowing smoke to inflate his profit margin. Secrets of the trade, Emily guessed.

She couldn't help but eye the door to the back of the room between the shelves. There was a table in front of it implying it was unused. She always wondered what George kept in there. She tried once to turn the knob, but it was locked. It even had a deadbolt further securing its mystery. She had asked George once what was in there and he never answered. Lucy said it was her dad's secret book collection. Luce had never been in there either, which is why she sarcastically called it secret. She even put air quotes around the word showing her irritation whenever the subject came up. Her rant about it was hilarious. She didn't understand why her dad wouldn't even let her in there because it wasn't like she could see anything anyway. Well, maybe he just had a bunch of valuable first editions in there and didn't want anyone to have a chance to case the joint. He was greedy like that. That or it's where he planned for world domination. Either option seemed likely.

Emily turned to the right and entered the office to the side where George's desk, and probably plans to take over the universe were located. As always, he was deeply frowning at the entrance awaiting her passage into his lair. On the corner of his desk was the box she didn't get a chance to stock on the shelves. He gave it a disgusted glance and then turned his narrowed eyes back to her.

"Emily even though I find your work to be mediocre, you do normally get the job done. The lack of responsibility however, makes me question your present employment status." He spit as he patted the box as if she needed reminding of her wrong doing.

Never mind the fact that Emily never left work undone. Never mind the fact that she always stayed longer then her shift required. With George it didn't matter how loyal an employee you were. It was all or nothing with good old George. Emily pushed aside the fury that was boiling up inside her. "I'm sorry George. It was getting late last night and I had to get home. I figured-" He interrupted her so abruptly she jumped.

"You figured you could sneak in before me this morning and get it done before I could see the work you had neglected to do," he hissed through clenched teeth.

"I'm really sorry. I figured it wouldn't be that big of a deal." She apologized meekly and bit her lip.

He glared at her over the frames of his glasses. "Well missy you figured wrong. You could have cost me money this morning. What if someone came in wanting the books you deemed to be unimportant?" His eyes told her there was no winning. She had lost before she even got to work.

She unwillingly nodded in defeat, shoulders sagging. "Sorry George it won't happen again."

He started to grumble further lecturing words at her but Lucy cut him off. "Daddy there's a man on the phone wanting to know if we have the latest James Patterson."

He stood, "well, as a matter of fact, we do." Giving Emily a quick glare he dug through the box on his desk where apparently the title was located. With a grunt of satisfaction he plucked the new copy of what he was looking for out of the box and smacked it against his hand. As he Moved passed them to get to the phone, he pushed against Emily's shoulder and patted Lucy lovingly on the head. "Such a good girl," he crooned.

After he left Lucy broke into hysterical giggles. "You can thank me now." She grinned up at Emily mischievously as she tucked her short black hair behind her ear.

"Huh?" Emily gave her a curious look, not understanding.

"There's no one on the phone I just put it on hold to make him think there was. I figured it would get him off your back. After all, he's not paying you to sit around and talk." Lucy giggled again.

Emily snorted. "Oh. Well thanks," Emily said, laughing now too. "What would I do without you?"

"You'd probably be living on the unemployment line," Lucy responded sweetly. "Well really I just wanted to talk to you. I figured we could put the price tags on the books in the box so daddy won't bug us too much." While she conspired her chocolate brown eyes gleamed like a child in a candy store. Emily's friend was always at her happiest when she was up to something.

Lucy's excitement was infectious. It was impossible for someone's mood to be down when she was around. Emily moved to the desk and hoisted the large box onto her hip and waited for Lucy to move to the stock room. She practically dropped the heavy load onto the only empty table. It was always kept cleared for this very purpose. Emily could tell Lucy was waiting for her to get everything unloaded and situated, before she started in on whatever gossip she overheard working the counter.

After Emily pulled the last book out of the box and put it on the table, she reached to the shelf behind it where the price labels were. It was nice to have Lucy there to help break up the monotony of the task. It never failed to crack her up when Lucy helps her with pricing. Realistically she mostly just hands Emily various books to put the right price tag on them. She let Lucy do the labeling for some of them a few times and some ended up with the wrong price. Others had upside down labels put on the wrong side of the book. This wasn't a very big deal since the labels are made especially for books. They can be removed easily for the readers who don't like them cluttering up their covers. Lucy liked leaving some of them messed up for her father to find. Once he found out it was Lucy's doing, all hints of anger evaporated into a surprisingly gentle smile and another pat on her head.

"Okay I'm ready for ya. You want your usual chair?" Emily asked knowing Lucy would, so she had already slid it out to ready it for her. It really wasn't a necessary gesture. Lucy was a very independent person and could handle finding a seat for herself. Even so, it was hard for Emily not to try and help her.

"Thank you," she cheerily responded as she quickly took her seat. "You're such a gentleman," Lucy chortled. As she sat down, she folded up her cane and set it on the table.

Emily followed suit and waited for the first novel to price. "Ha Ha dork."

For a while they worked in silence. Emily thought maybe her friend had forgotten what she wanted to tell her. That more than likely wasn't the case though, Lucy loved nothing more than to tell a good story. From out in the store Emily heard George greeting a customer. A man with a booming voice told him they were looking for a particular cookbook. George led him off to help him find what he was looking for. It was always interesting to see the interactions between George and his customers. He definitely knew how to put on the Mr. Nice Guy persona.

About then Lucy broke through Emily's distraction. "Okay, so here goes," Lucy started dramatically as she leaned in closer to Emily. "I've been getting some seriously weird vibes from some of the people around here. Some of the people that usually chat with me about school or tell me about whatever they've got going on, don't say anything other than trivial hellos and thank you's. Some don't even come in here anymore at all." Lucy stopped talking abruptly and sat back in her chair expectantly with her arms folded.

Emily took that as her cue for rebuttal. "Luce, I don't know, maybe they're just busy. It's really not that big of a deal." Emily spoke absently while she worked hoping Lucy wouldn't notice her hesitation.

She couldn't shake the feeling something was going on either, only she couldn't put her finger on it. Emily had always been pretty intuitive about things. Something deep inside her gut told her that something wasn't right. It just wasn't clear what that something was. From an outsider's prospective, things would probably appear pretty typical for the most part. The difference was that Emily had lived in Lakeview her whole life and knew the way things usually worked. Whatever was happening wasn't normal.

Leave it alone, a voice in her mind told her. What the…? What was that? It was like her subconscious but it wasn't Emily's voice.

Without warning, the words released a flash flood of images in her head. Oh God! Last night… That voice… The attack… Suddenly, broken memories started flashing before her eyes like a flip book. Holy Crap, last night, how could she have forgotten? The soreness had been minimal when she woke up. She had just chalked up any residual ache to her run in with Sam. Somehow the rest of the night's events must have slipped her mind. How could something like that slip a person's mind? You get attacked, at least you think you did, and rescued by a God like mystery man and you just forget it all? Really was that even possible? She tried to recall her attacker's face but for some reason that detail was blank. That's strange, last night his face was all she could see behind her lids now she can't even recall the color of his eyes. Actually, the more she thought about it she couldn't really remember the details of the attack either.

Absently her hand rose to brush across the scrape on her cheek. Yep, still there. It felt stupid to need that reassurance. She had seen the mark this morning in the mirror. Now, she wasn't so sure it had been Sam that had put it there.

Emily felt like such a moron. Logically she should file a police report. It *should* have been done last night. Even though she didn't remember the bad guys face, the incident should still be turned in to make a paper trail in case something happens to someone else. What was she supposed to do? She couldn't just march in there and be like, um yeah I was attacked last night. I have no idea by whom and I can't tell you where it happened, just that it did. Oh yeah, and some guy swooped in and saved the day, only I don't remember how or what he looked like either. So gee, you think you can help me? Yeah right, like that was going to happen. She would be institutionalized in like half a second. On the other hand, that would get her out of her house. That's one positive at least.

Lucy's voice broke into Emily's fast moving train of thought. "Let's just say I get really strong feelings about people and my surroundings. Just trust me Em, I'm not crazy. I guess you could call it extremely intuitive. I've never told anyone before. No one. So you can't say anything to anybody. Promise?" She stared at Emily modestly but there was an imperative tone to her voice Emily had never heard before.

Emily focused back on the conversation. She would just have to deal with last night later. "I promise Luce but…" Emily swallowed hard. "You're sort of creeping me out," she admitted. She felt like such a coward. It wasn't like Lucy was telling her she could talk to ghosts or something. She was just saying she was aware of her surroundings. Somehow though, Emily felt like there was more to the story Lucy wasn't telling her. "How have you never told me this before?"

Was it really possible that sweet little Lucy was some kind of psychic? The thought boggled Emily's mind. There was no way. That garbage was just hype and propaganda. Emily had seen all the late night commercials. They were just phony fortune tellers trying to suck in the gullible. The only ones who believe in that crap are the ones who lacked good purchase judgment thanks to sleep deprivation. She had always thought that psychics were far reaching and sometimes, good guessers at best. Was it possible though that her best friend had some supernatural power? This new knowledge made Emily look at her friend in an entirely new light.

Suddenly, Lucy's dark hair that framed her face like a flowing curtain seemed mysterious. The silky smooth complexion of her fair skin seemed to glow mystically in the illumination of the room. Lucy's deep chocolate brown eyes seemed to burn deep into Emily's, trying to convey a message with her stare alone. Emily shook her head as though she could toss the theory to the floor. This is just silly. It's Lucy for crap's sake.

Truth be told, it frequently wierded Emily out that Lucy always seem to manage to stare directly into people's eyes. It was as though she could see them. Emily once saw a guy actually accuse her of lying about being blind. He told her it was a cruel joke to make fun of the handicapped. He absurdly waggled a finger at her and said that she should be ashamed of herself. Shockingly, Lucy didn't get discouraged even a little bit. Well, if she did she sure didn't show it.

Seriously, if it were Emily she probably would have told him where he could shove that finger. Not to mention the fact that she would have shattered the bone in that stupid finger before giving the jerk the directions. Lucy might not have seen the finger, but Emily was sure she felt the air from the movement or something like that with her heightened senses. He did it right in her face. She simply laughed, and told him she was just a people person. That allowed her to find their eyes without seeing them. Before he stalked off angrily, she made sure to include the fact that she was not handicapped she was blind and that he should look up the difference before attempting to fight a cause he knew nothing about.

Emily had always admired her friend's conviction and her never down attitude toward life. She never let anything upset her day. Sometimes she was just bubbling over with happiness. With George as a father, it just didn't make sense. Even though she was Emily's best friend it did get on her nerves sometimes. She didn't see how someone could be that happy all the time. You would think it would make their cheeks crack or something.

The dim florescent light above them flickered eerily, as if to dramatize their conversation. After Emily put the last of the labeled books back into the box, she stood to take them to their places out in the store. Lucy went out front first. She took her usual place back at the counter. Thank God she went out when she did, the phone was wailing relentlessly. George was sure to have an aneurism.

Picking up the load of freshly priced books, Emily headed out to reclaim her duties of stocking. That's me, she thought dryly. Literary goddess bringing the great works to the masses. As she wandered to the first section, her mind drifted back to Lucy. Her thoughts of her friend being just paranoid had broken away, leaving behind the rightness of what Lucy was saying. Emily didn't know why but she believed Lucy and she still had a feeling that this was going to mean more than just simple intuition.

5

After work, Emily remembered that she had to get a few things from the store. Okay, so there were reasons why she never took the bus. It was more than a few hours into the afternoon so riding the bus would cut her travel time in half. The prospect of walking across town and back before dark wasn't thrilling. Try as she might, she couldn't help but regret that choice when it came to this particular occasion. For the most part she walked everywhere. Lakeview was small so it really wasn't a problem. Sometimes though, she would be lazy and turn to public transportation.

It was inevitable that a variety of people rode on Lakeview's public transit system. That being said, this was still too much. Emily got how the busses main rider population was from the low income community due to its cheap rates, but really? Come on, just because a person is low income, doesn't mean they have to be a weirdo. Emily knew plenty of low income people that were perfectly normal, herself included.

Upon walking up the bus steps through the automatic door a nasty B.O smell overwhelmed her senses. Instantly her nose wrinkled up at the stench. It was seriously disgusting. The owner of that smell needed to be washed down with a fire hose immediately. The reek of the bus permeating to where she stood on the steps almost made her turn around. It would have almost been worth the extended trip to not have to be anywhere near that smell. The prospect of being out after dark was the only thing that kept her from bolting. She turned her head away from the bus and sucked in a deep cleansing breath of clean air, before being submerged in the nasty.

There were no seats near the front where it was typically safer, so she had to make her way through the thin narrow aisle. The bus was overly crowded. The aisle way was cluttered with feet and bags. She tried really hard not to step on anyone but it was like an obstacle course. Every time she touched someone's ankle, she half expected a buzzer to go off like in the board game Operation. Out of the several that Emily passed, only a couple moved out of her way so she could get by.

Movement caught her eye from the back and she looked up in time to see a skanky looking girl slide into her assumed boyfriends lap so they could make out. They were really going at it. They looked like they were going to swallow each other's tongues or something. Okay gross, even in private that kind of kissing is unacceptable. Emily wondered why the driver allowed this kissing fest to go on. Then it occurred to her, he was a middle aged sweaty guy who was probably enjoying the free show. How disgusting. Where was that girl's self-respect? Didn't she know how completely wrong it was to give free peep shows on a public bus?

Forcing her eyes to avert from the couple, she glanced around hoping to find a seat by some of the half way normal people. Finally, three rows from the back she spotted one. Luckily the seat next to it was empty too. Emily hurried to it and tossed her backpack down on the seat. She sat down quickly as the bus revved its engine before it headed off to the next stop.

The majority of the riders were relatively quiet. A young teenage boy sat nearby, completely enthralled in the gross couples exploits. Emily sighed and rolled her eyes. Well isn't that just sweet, nothing like the city bus giving children a real sex education? Watching the kid drool after them made Emily want to go and smack the couple until they stopped.

The bus came to a halt for the next stop and Emily's body jerked forward. She planted her feet firmly to the slick floor to steady herself. The elderly woman in front of her groaned and clutched her tan suitcase sized granny bag closer to her body. After the doors opened, quite a few people got off. They were in one of the residential parts of town.

The people that entered the bus next were interesting to say the least. Most were dressed in tattered looking clothes that had been passed around from way to many garage sales. The two women that now occupied the seats across from Emily reminded her of old time TV commercials for a bingo parlor. One was wearing faded black sweat pants and an oversized man's T-shirt with the phrase "Get'er dun" across the chest. Emily could tell the woman clearly wasn't wearing a bra and desperately needed one. The other was more conventional in an old pair of jeans and fitted red top but she wore way to much make up. Her red lips matched the color of her shirt, vaguely reminding Emily of a circus clown.

The... gentleman in front of them was very obviously a mechanic she guessed. His hands and clothes were covered in grease. His hair looked as though it had been covered by a hat most of the day and he had been combing it back out of his eyes to much with his oil stained hands. He had very nice eyes though and his skin was that pretty mocha tone. It looked creamy and rich somehow, despite the grease. He was actually kind of cute in a rough sort of way.

Emily wasn't trying to act all high and mighty or anything. There was nothing wrong with jeans and a T-shirt. She had many in her own closet. Either way, there was still a right and wrong way of doing things. Certain clothes just don't look right no matter what a person looks like. Emily had nothing against them what so ever. They were all probably very nice people. She even recognized a lot of them as patrons of Blake's Books. As she peered around the rest of the bus feeling guilty for her judgments, her mouth dropped with an audible pop.

There were two of the most beautiful people she had ever seen in real life sitting behind the driver. She didn't know how she could have ever missed them. The couple looked as though they were on their way to a red carpet event. The woman was model tall and stick thin. Even sitting on the bouncy seat of the bus, she looked graceful. The man definitely belonged on the big screen or in Calvin Klein underwear ads. His face looked like a flawlessly chiseled statue. They were both dressed in sleek black clothing, except for the deep plum under shirt the woman wore beneath a V-neck nit top. They had a sort of timeless quality and Emily couldn't help staring at them open mouthed. It was obvious they weren't anywhere near her age, but they still looked young.

They couldn't have been from anywhere around Lakeview, which, Emily thought, would explain why they were on the bus in the first place. Perhaps they were taking a tour of the city. There really wasn't much to see but maybe they were investors scouting new business locations or something. The mayor did say he wanted to bring in more businesses. Emily glanced at the other passengers to see if they seemed to notice them too.

Out of nowhere it hit her with a jolt. Her stomach tightened into a ball of double knots and her hands involuntarily rolled into clenched fists. She quickly turned around to stare out the back window biting her lip against the agony. The grimace of pain was etched into her face with deep lines of agony. She didn't want anyone to see her like that. Letting her eyes shift slightly, she concluded no one would have even noticed if she had danced down the aisle singing show tunes at the top of her lungs.

Every single person on the entire bus wore the same mask on their faces. Those masks were designed in the same frozen expression of pure and utter terror. The gut wrenching kind you would expect to see after a plane had just been hijacked. It appeared that they were all looking at the same thing as if frozen in time. Emily followed their horrified stares to see what she had missed. As she had expected though, she hadn't missed a thing. They were all staring at the strange out of town couple. Only they didn't watch with wondering admiration like she had.

Looking back at the couple in black she saw that they were obviously noticing the looks and not at all troubled by them. Their faces wore no expression at all. The interesting thing was that their eyes board holes into those of the people that were so focused on them. What was going on? They looked normal, rich maybe but normal. Definitely way over dressed for Lakeview, which really wasn't a big deal.

At the next stop no one moved. Instead, two people got on. It was a young woman with her small child. She was quite pretty in a natural sort of way. Emily couldn't help but watch her as she sat across from the couple to see if she gave them the same reaction as the others.

The small boy tried wiggling out of her arms causing the woman to hold him more firmly to her chest. It was easy to see that she held her body more confidently then the rest. The newest passenger still eyed the pair with confusion that quickly transformed into worry. Her brows slightly rose creasing her forehead. Her eyes were wide and lips pursed in a firm line. If Emily hadn't have been so engrossed in the scene playing out in front of her she wouldn't have even noticed the man's movement. With the rest of his body completely still, he gave the newest rider an almost imperceptible nod. His eyes then shifted to his friend, jutting his chin slightly in the direction of the mom and her son. The young girl noticed too and her whole body flinched and then tensed. Her motherly embrace on the boy abruptly turned to that of iron bars locked around him with no sign of release.

Why was everyone except for Emily riddled with paralyzing fear at the sight of these people? Even the gross make out couple sat upright in their seats. Making out apparently held no importance for them anymore. The knots in her stomach clenched spasmodically as if reminding her of their presence as if she could forget. If it wasn't for being scared of drawing attention, she would have cried out in pain.

As if reading her mind, the man's head turned to Emily and he watched her appraisingly. At first he gave her a slow languid smile revealing a perfect set of pearly white teeth. Soon though, his smile dissolved into a look that seemed confused and frustrated. His eyes moved to the teenage boy near her and the kid immediately cringed. His frustration turned to satisfaction and then back again once he regained focus on Emily.

It must have caught the beautiful woman's attention because she turned her emerald eyes to Emily now as well. How odd that they both have the exact same color of eyes, Emily thought. They must be siblings or something. The porcelain Goddess also looked annoyed. The annoyance quickly morphed into fury. Her eyes blazed and narrowed at Emily so intently that she couldn't help but stare right back. Emily's head just kept darting back from the man's face to the furious woman's over and over again. What was their problem? Did they think because they were high society everyone should bow down and be afraid of them. As far as Emily was concerned, that was crap. If they were such high society why couldn't they have sprung for an expensive rental car? Clearly they were posers.

The bus stopped again breaking into their seemingly impenetrable stare down. Her body lunged forward causing her to clutch the seat in front of her so she didn't go sprawling into the aisle. The couple's heads nodded in the direction of the young mom, the teenage boy and then hesitantly at the mechanic. At first they recoiled in their seats as though they wanted to hide. Then, as if cattle prodded they rose to their feet and followed the couple down the steep steps to the busses folding doors. When the couple passed they gave the driver a tight smile and he nervously nodded back.

Before the couple descended all the way down the bus steps, he flashed a murderous look back at Emily. It only lasted a few seconds but time seemed to stand still during the exchange. Emily couldn't tear her eyes away. The man's expression softened, his eyebrows rose slightly and then he was gone. Emily stood to get a better look out of the windows on the other side. She watched to see where the group was headed and saw they were all going to the same place.

They were in the outskirts of town now in the heart of the under classed. The houses were falling apart. Most of the yards were knee high with garbage piled outside. A few had old dilapidated cars propped up on jacks in the center of their yards as if displaying a classic. At the center of the dead end though there was a brand new house that had apparently just been built. Emily would have remembered something like that in this neighborhood. It was a big two story house with vinyl siding that was so dark grey that it was practically black. The yard was elaborately landscaped and all the large picture windows had their fancy thick curtains drawn. What was a house like that doing on a street like this? It was gorgeous but eerie at the same time which totally didn't make sense. It only took Emily a few moments to recognize the home. She remembered attending a birthday party there when she was a kid. It wasn't as nice back then that's for sure. The strange couple must have done a serious over hall of the place.

The fear stricken passengers followed after the couple up the front walk and on to a large porch that stretched across the entire front of the house. Without pause, they all filed after the leaders like baby ducks. Well, baby ducks that looked like they were about to be punished for stepping out of line. Emily was frozen with complete and utter bewilderment. She couldn't figure out why on earth those people went with the couple even though they seemed like they were absolutely terrified of them. It just didn't make any sense.

Before the last person was lost inside the darkness of the home, the bus engine growled and was moving again. She craned her head behind her trying to see anything else. There was nothing to see, the door was now closed. The people left on the bus still looked afraid. They seemed more relaxed but still shaken. It didn't seem to matter that the weirdness was over. The gross make out duo was still in the back. They still hadn't resumed the activity of sucking face. Emily carefully turned her body to them. She didn't want to come off overly anxious. She was though, totally chomping at the bit.

"What just happened?" Emily tried to speak low but that was next to impossible over the roar of the loud engine.

The two of them jumped practically out of their seats. Evidently she had startled them right out of their deep concentration. They looked at each other and then back at Emily curiously. The girl cocked her head to the side as she looked at Emily as if considering something. "Don't you know?"

"No," Emily retorted perplexed. "I don't mean to pry um…I'm just confused." She really was too. More than that, she was concerned. Even though what just happened was a mystery, everything about it was wrong, she was sure of that.

The teen girl shot her boyfriend a questioning look. For an answer, he shook his head furiously at her. "I don't know what you're talking about," she insisted with finality. Both of them turned to look out the side window away from Emily. Everything about their rigid posture made it perfectly clear they weren't going to budge on the subject even an inch. It was also equally clear they did in fact know what was going on. They acted as though they were brain washed or something.

She was going to make a second attempt when an alarmed voice sounded in her head. *Leave…it…alone!* Emily shuddered. The voice said the words slowly with barely suppressed anger. Confused, she returned to a frontward position. Like before, the voice wasn't her own. It was almost like her subconscious, only the voice was male. Weirder still, she seemed to recognize it even though she had no memory of ever hearing it before. It was a low voice deep with warning. Her mind flashed a picture of eyes, amazing deep blue eyes that were like the sky on a cloudless day. Emily knew those eyes but she couldn't place how. Oh great. So now apparently on top of the weird bus episode, the development of schizophrenia and delusions could be added to the list. Part of her wanted to yell back at the voice. She wanted to ask him or it, how they were doing that. It would have been totally easy to freak out, if she hadn't been occupied trying to remember whose words those were. Maybe it belonged to the same person who owned the gorgeous eyes.

What a horrible day this was turning out to be. All she wanted to do was go to work, then take a normal bus ride to Wal-Mart to pick up shampoo and razors. This day had turned drastically wrong from the start. That was becoming more of a pattern lately. She wished she could take a vacation far off somewhere remote. That would be total heaven. Maybe she could go somewhere hot and beautiful. She could really use some R and R. Unfortunately though, that would never happen. For one, she didn't have enough money. For another, as much as she didn't want to admit it and he wouldn't either, her dad needed her.

The familiar blue Wal-Mart sign came into view. Emily breathed a sigh of relief. She didn't want to be on the bus anymore and was thankful when none of the remaining passengers got off with her. That would hopefully mean they would be to their destinations when she caught the bus back home. The trek across the parking lot would give her time to clear her head. This was just all too freak show for Emily. Absently, she longed for days of normalcy. Well, at least what she classified as normal.

When Emily crossed through the automatic doors, the greeter bombarded her and was way too cheery for her taste. She was in absolutely no mood for pleasantries. This was a get in and get out mission. It would be getting dark soon and she only had so long before the bus came back through again.

6

The sight of twilight approaching was in full view when she made her way out of the store with her two bags. Crap, she had taken too long. Her cell had died and that's her usual way of telling time. She had gotten caught up browsing through the bargain book bin. They were having a two for one sale which never happened, ever. She purchased a whole bag of books. I am such a trader to George, she thought with a sarcastic smirk. She was going to Hell for sure. At least she'd have something to read during her damnation. It really wasn't her fault. She's never had a lot of money but has always had a ridiculous addiction for books. Besides, George doesn't even like her. So why should she be loyal to his greediness? Also, what good old George didn't know wouldn't hurt him… or her.

After asking a nearby man what time it was, she was in a mild state of panic. It was seven. Hurrying was essential, the last bus of the day would be leaving in like two minutes. Emily quickly put both shopping bags into her backpack and started off at a dead run across the parking lot. When she got closer to the back of the bus stop shelter she heard the familiar snarl of the big bus engine.

"No!" Emily called. "Wait!" Right about the time her hand smacked the doors the driver flipped the gear shift and pulled away from the curb leaving her abandoned and very angry. Damn it! Why did they have to be so strict? Technically, she was there before the doors were closed. They should really be more compassionate. Her passage does increase their day's prophet for crap's sake. With a disgruntled sigh Emily moved to the crosswalk. There was no point in delaying the inevitable. Her phone was dead so no one to call. No one to call meant no possible ride.

As Emily traveled the blocks in record time, an odd sense of Déjà vu enveloped. Every time she passed a dark alley her heart thudded rapidly in her chest. It was obvious they were empty and pitch black, so where did this fear stem from? Was it just her, or did the darkness seem not so dark tonight? Things appeared much clearer then they should for as dark as it was.

Somewhere distant in her mind's eye she caught a fast glimpse of herself lying on the gravel ground on her stomach. At first she thought she was just remembering a fall she must have had or something. That honestly wasn't that surprising thanks to her unfortunate clumsiness. Dipping down on the entrance to the next alley, Emily froze when her foot slid slightly across the rocks. The sound brought back a picture of someone's boot. What was it about these alleys? She knew there were things she had blocked out from that night. The details were still very cloudy. She tried desperately to break the memories free.

Just then, her mind suddenly sharpened to an intense brightness that only lasted for a second. Emily squinted against the light as if it were actually in front of her and not just in her head. It was like someone snapped a flash bulb at point blank range except, there were no cameras around. There was just her newly formed recollection of the fact that she had defied death in an alley just like the one she stood in. The memories were coming in fast bursts of vivid clarity that left her breathless.

She could recall the crushing weight of her attacker lying on top of her and his intoxicating scent. Also, the gorgeous guy that rescued her, hiding behind the dumpster and the bad guy vanishing. She remembered thinking the man that had saved her must be a guardian angel, but then he vanished too. Then there was the look in her father's eyes when he told her to stay away from that *thing*. OH MY GOD! She screamed the words in her head. At least she hoped it was in her head. Emily probably wouldn't have even noticed either way to be honest. She couldn't see or hear anything now. The memories were holding her prisoner as they replayed over and over again. How could she have repressed something so horrible?

Emily vaguely remembered hearing something about that. It was an article online about people who experienced a traumatic event and then blocked it afterward. At the time, she thought it was kind of screwy. Anything remotely traumatic she had ever been through was right there in her memory bank to torture her whenever she didn't want it to.

When Emily finally got a grip on reality, she was overwhelmed by an outpouring of emotion. She fell to her knees with tears falling like a down pour of rain. The alligator sized tears had already begun to stain her light blue shirt in big wet blotches. Without thinking about it she brought her hand came up to feel her neck where she had been bitten. It didn't feel like there was anything there. There was no trace of a puncture mark or anything. Her neck was smooth and blemish free.

Realizing where she had collapsed in total breakdown mode, she scrambled to her feet. The last thing she wanted to do was to hang out in another alley. All she wanted was to go home. Suddenly the darkness seemed to be pulsing with things lurking in the shadows, everywhere she looked. The night was pressing down on her like a heavy weight on her chest, making it hard to breathe. She had to get out of there.

Emily broke into a run then, completely forgetting to pay attention to her surroundings. She was moving too fast to worry about where she was going. The air hit her chest, making the wetness from her tears frost her skin. Her eyes felt swollen from crying and she didn't care. The wind whipped her hair behind her so hard, that it felt like it was being pulled. The remaining moisture on her cheeks mingled with the wind stung like needles as she ran. Her heart was violently hammering inside her in a way that shouldn't be possible for anyone. She couldn't stop. Emily had a long way to go and couldn't get passed the fear that now gripped her whole body.

I'm not going to let anything hurt you, the voice in her head commented reassuringly. Through her steady pace she could recall this voice from the bus and back at Blake's. With all the memories intact now she connected the most recent ones with the one from that terrifying night. Instead of feeling crazy this time, Emily allowed herself to be comforted no matter how irrational that comfort might be. Somehow, it made her not feel so alone when in reality that's exactly what Emily was, alone.

She was running too fast and it was too dark. Emily didn't see the lip in the sidewalk and her body went down like a ton of bricks. Reacting surprisingly quickly, she caught herself with her outreached hands. She grunted in pain as she hit the ground with a skidding thump. Agony immediately followed as a sharp burning sensation ripped at her palms and knees. They were on fire. She briefly envisioned the road rash that would surely accompany the pain. For a second she just lay there trying to collect herself grateful there didn't seem to be any cars thinking she was a speed bump.

Despite her lingering fear, Emily willed her breathing to relax. It really wouldn't do her any good to hyperventilate. Getting to the safety of home was still the top priority. The urgency of that need could not be ignored. Her mind worked frantically as she started pulling herself up from the ground.

A strong hand gripped her arm and hauled her to her feet. Startled, Emily automatically jumped back however, the grip stayed firm. She could have sworn she was out on the darkened street alone. There had been no warning sound of footsteps approaching. She had gone from seeing nothing but sidewalk, to looking up at the night sky with clusters of stars that normally would have comforted her. Tonight there was no comfort though. The torrent of memories left her in a fog.

Her attention was brought down abruptly by the person still holding her up. "Don't be frightened child," the unfamiliar voice sounded accented but Emily couldn't tell its dissent. He spoke slow and careful in an eerie sort of way.

The hairs on the back of her neck rose and goose bumps formed on her forearms. That awful nagging stomach clenching was taking over her midsection again. It felt as though it would tear her in two any minute. Her body's fight or flight mechanism was screaming at her to move, only the call went unanswered. It was as though her feet were formed into the concrete, trapping her where she stood. Mentally she shook her head against the unwillingness to move to no avail. The next course of action was putting on a brave face. The problem with that was, he probably wouldn't buy it.

Emily swallowed. "Um… thanks." She hurried and slung her fallen backpack over her shoulder. "Have a good night." She said in an awkward rush as she started to move passed him.

"No need to hurry. I'd be happy to offer a lovely girl such as yourself a ride, to anywhere your heart desired." His hand found purchase on her arm again, clenching just a bit tighter than before.

What a creepy guy. His warm friendly voice was a mocking contrast, compared to the grip that was cutting off her circulation. A hand shaped bruise would surely follow later when she got home. "Oh that's okay. I like the walk." Emily shrugged off his touch and started off quicker now towards the next street light. She tried to act oblivious to Mr. Creepy's terrifying charm even though her normal disposition was wearing thin fast.

She sprinted to the corner in a flash. There were cars driving passed, so she had to stop and wait. The bright sight of their headlights was comforting, because that meant she was in plain sight of several passing by witnesses. Hopefully they would come to her aid if the situation came to that. This man hadn't done anything overtly threatening, but still. His words definitely carried an ominous undertone, and made her skin crawl. She was just about to flag someone down with a dramatic flail of her arms and a scream, when she was stopped short.

Creepy guy caught up to her and reclaimed his grip on her arm, forcefully spinning her around to face him. "You're being very rude. I just want to get to know you. I'm new in town that's all." He said with mock pain coloring his inflection.

Emily couldn't say anything in response. She just stood there like a helpless idiot without the courage to even bat an eye lash in his direction. Completely disappointed in herself, she imagined that if he wasn't holding her there she would probably drop into the fetal position crying and rocking back and forth like those stupid girls in the movies. She had always been told what to do when faced with an attack. Apparently she should have studied up more on the bravery and carry out of the counter assault.

When she looked up at creepy guys face, she involuntarily sucked in a breath. He stared down, piercing her with his green eyes. She immediately recognized them. Well, maybe not his exactly, although the color was disturbingly familiar. They were the same dazzling emerald as the couple from the bus. He wasn't the same man from the bus however, that much was clear. The only similarity between the two was the eyes and the chalky pallor of both men's skin.

The main and most frightening difference was that this man's emerald irises were bordered with an outline of red. Emily opened her mouth to scream, except nothing came out but a pathetic squeak. Her throat was too dry from all the running earlier. She tried once more and got the same result. There was seriously something wrong with this guy. That just wasn't normal. In all her life no matter how short, she had never ever seen eyes like those. People with hints of two colors or flecks of gold... yes. Green outlined in bright ass red... never.

Another memory tried to break into the forefront of her mind. It wasn't as clear as the others though. There was something she was forgetting. It was right there at the edge of her consciousness, teasing her just out of reach. It was something to do with the red. As fast as the memory presented itself, the picture floated away, completely lost to her.

Sensing her alarm, he attempted to soften his demeanor. "Don't be afraid child. I just want to be friends. My name is Luke." His words were friendly but they came out husky and low. He ended with an attempt at a smile that resulted in a sickening grimace displaying very sharp teeth. There was something very different about those teeth. They made him look like a predator somehow.

Even through the expression, there was no doubt this person reminded her of the couple on the bus. He looked different, yet had the same features. He was unbelievably beautiful coupled with a heavy dose of sickeningly intimidating. There wasn't anything reassuring about him. Nothing about the display did much for the friend inquiry he had just presented.

He smelled kind of weird too. It wasn't bad, but it wasn't good either. Somehow it seemed to whirl around Emily, almost intoxicating her like the night in the alley. On one hand she wanted to run and on the other she wanted to be closer to him. She knew the latter option was crazy and still couldn't help the pull towards him.

The longer she stared at him, the stronger the pain in her stomach pulsed. That pain was the only thread to her true feelings. Emily started to struggle free so she could find help from a passing car. As if by magic, there wasn't a single car left driving by. Seriously, a minute before there were practically a steady stream of cars and now, nothing. A quick glance over her shoulder showed her there wasn't even one coming off in the distance. Suddenly it was like town of the dreaded sundown or something. Talk about rotten freaking luck. She struggled harder anyway. She had to get out of there.

Remembering she had a load of books in her backpack, she brought her arm back and then swung it towards him with everything she had. Luke released her other arm seeming surprised but simply laughed humorlessly. He didn't even budge. In fact, it seemed to have absolutely no effect on him what so ever. It was a good blow too. She knew a blow like that would have sent her sprawling. It would have even knocked Sam back a few steps. What was this guy made out of? It was like he was made of stone or something.

"Go ahead and try and run. No matter how fast you go I'll match that stride and then some." The smile never left his face and his glowing eyes never left hers.

His eerie soothing tone began to relax her somehow. She knew his words were meant to be threatening but she was starting to feel fuzzy as she watched him. Try as she might, Emily's resolve was fading fast. Suddenly, getting away didn't seem so important.

The glow of his stare seemed to pulse with each word he spoke. Even with the red his eyes were pretty. She couldn't seem to stop staring into them. A small part of her wanted to try and run. It wasn't going to happen. His gaze still had her feet locked to the cement with an extreme force that paralyzed her. The other part of her could think of nothing she'd rather do then stand there with him.

From the back of her mind came a panicked voice. It was Emily's voice this time and it was telling her to *move*. Despite the advice, she just gazed right back at him like a star struck teenager. She wanted to run her fingers through his beautiful main of black hair. She wanted to feel his strong arms around her never releasing. Desire burned inside her that felt like an exciting wild fire. Those eyes were mesmerizing she couldn't look away. She was lost in the alluring depths of them. Somewhere inside her she knew that she was supposed to be afraid, the emotion just wouldn't take shape. The world seemed to swirl in a blur around her. It was as if all the houses around them disappeared leaving nothing behind except for the two of them.

Emily was about to tell him to come closer to her, but her desire was interrupted by a growl off in the distance. Before she realized what was going on, she was just angry that she had lost Luke's attention. It never occurred to her to worry about the possibility of new danger. It also never occurred to her, that the feeling that had enveloped her wasn't her own. She was absolutely furious at whatever had broken the moment the two of them had been sharing.

Her insides were screaming at her, but the intoxication seemed to wrap around her entire brain making it difficult to think straight.

The emotion that took over next, was a furious jealousy that made her think like the predator instead of the defenseless prey that she so obviously was. Violent thoughts were flooding her mind like a tsunami. She could for just a minute, actually picture what she wanted to do to whoever was stealing his attention away from her. She wanted, no needed that attention and would do anything to get it back.

From the alley behind them Emily heard another low rumbling growl. Her attention was broken from Luke to seek out the noise. When he completely released his stare hold on her the terror crashed back down on her like a freight train. Her knees wobbled uncontrollably. She felt dazed and confused.

Oh my God, Emily thought wildly. What just happened? That guy had her in a… well, trance like thing. She shook her head fiercely trying to dissolve any residual fog that clouded her mind. The pain in her abdomen was more intense than ever. There was no time to think about that now though. She had to get out of there. Her palms were clammy. The moisture stung the road rash reminding her more caution when she ran was imperative. She gave a quick mental groan of pain immediately thankful that the sound didn't escape from her lips. Whatever he could do there was apparently someone nearby that could do the same, or maybe even worse. It was crucial that attention didn't transfer back to her.

Luke spun around and gave the anonymous owner of the growl a snarl of his own. It sounded feral and terrifyingly menacing. The wrenching of her stomach was becoming more insistent. He lost all focus on Emily and retreated to find the intruder. She stood wide eyed and gaping as she watched him speed off into the mouth of the alley around the house they were in front of. What he did really couldn't even be called running. It was faster than Emily had ever seen anything move. Really, it was more of a blur than anything else. One second he was with her searching for the source of the growl. And the next, he was gone. There was no sound from his departure just total nothingness. There wasn't even the sound of a single footstep to mark his passage.

Emily felt very weak as if she had just woken up. Her knees were like rubbery Jell-O and her neck didn't seem strong enough to hold up her head for even a moment longer. As if still partially under whatever spell Luke had her under she took a few wobbly steps toward the alley where he had vanished. There wasn't a clear view of the alley's opening but the threatening blackness. The blindness of the abyss made her dizzy with fright. Still, she slowly trudged on after Luke.

A fierce snarl tore into the night and was quickly answered by one matching its anger and verbosity. She had a flash of two ferocious tigers going at it on Animal Planet, fighting to the death. Emily could hear scuffling and powerful blows, before responding crashes invaded the peace of the night. The sounds were like a slap in the face. Any after affects Luke had on her mind, melted away. So much for the nothingness. He must be fighting something. Whatever it was, it didn't sound human. It sounded like an animal was ripping into him. Or, maybe it was Luke doing the ripping.

She should go get help. Wait, what was she thinking that guy was going to kill her. Something within his eyes, told her just how true that fact was. It just wasn't in her nature to allow something like that to take place. She couldn't help but wonder where her sense of self-preservation was.

Emily heard the noise of violence seem to calm slightly. The thought that one of them could soon be coming to get her, sent her body into action, death was not an option. She turned to run, completely forgetting about the curb that was behind her. Her foot came down on the empty air that should have been sidewalk and she felt herself going down into the street. It all happened so fast and yet, she felt as if she were in slow motion. Her body was about to come to a crashing halt, but her mind traveled on. Note to self, not careful enough…

7

In her dream, she was walking down a long dimly lit corridor. It wasn't scary but instead sort of… well, dreamy. The only lighting came from sconces hung at far apart intervals down the long hall. The light fixtures were old fashioned and the small bulbs gave the effect of tiny intimate flames. It was a very pretty affect actually. The walls were a rich cream color with doors spread out along either side. The floor was a marbled ruby with silver flecks that gleamed like sparkles even in the mild lighting.

The first door she came to was locked. She knocked lightly and waited. Nothing. The next door held the same result. Sensing a pattern, she ignored the rest and continued on down the hall. The only sound that could be heard was the faint echo of her shoes on the marble floor.

It was very cold in her dream. There were no vents for an air conditioning system anywhere in sight. Even so, the air in the hall was chilly. It was too much for Emily's taste. She had always preferred the heat though, so she was kind of a baby. She rubbed her hands on her forearms hoping the friction would warm her up.

A second hall came into view, peaking her curiosity to the max. It turned sharply to the left. Timidly, she peered around the corner to see where it led. It was a shorter hall that mirrored the one she was already in, except there were fewer doors that were closer together. At the end, the hall opened up to a large room with an amazing antique looking wooden archway. Whatever was passed the arch was lit slightly better than the hallways.

With a deep breath, she turned the corner and started towards the opening. It was just a dream after all. There was nothing to truly be afraid of. It was moderately unsettling how aware she seemed to be that she was in a dream and not reality. Usually she didn't know an event was a dream until her eyes opened and she discovered the comfort of her familiar room.

Passing through the archway, she was amazed at the sight before her. It was so elegant. This room had marble floors too, but they were a glittering cobalt blue. The walls were painted in a muted grey color, which came alive with the affects from the sconce style lighting. Over in the corner, was a beautiful fire place designed with intricate patterns that stretched up the stone to a vaulted ceiling. In front of the fire place, were giant overstuffed black club chairs. The wall directly in front of where she stood held an enormous painting in a gold frame. It was of a cityscape at twilight. She recognized the two largest sky scrapers and realized it was in New York before September eleventh. In front of it was a wide glossy black desk.

The wall to Emily's right, had the most comfy looking couch she had ever seen. It was the same material of the chairs on the other side, but the cushions were giant fluffy pillows that housed golden throw pillows at either end. The end tables on each side were black rod iron with glass tops. The coffee table matched, but on it was only one book. It was a very thick book that from where she stood looked to have an old fashioned tattered leather cover.

A crackling sound brought her attention back to the left side of the room. There now was a roaring fire in the fire place. That wasn't there a second ago. Emily looked around the room, trying to see who could have done it. She was still the room's only occupant. Part of her half expected a troll to jump out of the fire and say boo or something.

"I find a fire to be quite relaxing, don't you?" A soft voice purred from behind her.

Emily jumped and spun around with a shriek.

"I didn't mean to frighten you Emily. I forget how quiet my passage can be."

Standing in front of her only two feet away, was an overwhelmingly handsome man. Although definitely middle aged, Emily sensed a timeless quality to him that made him seem ageless. That's weird. She didn't usually have dreams where she was crushing after an older man, no matter how hot he might be. And he was hot. He had broad shoulders and powerful looking arms. His stance was just as powerful of a presence. His hair was golden, with a hint of silver streaks. His eyes sparkled like perfect sapphires.

"That's okay," Emily replied mechanically, still stricken by his beauty. After responding the fact that this gorgeous man knew her name and she had no idea who he was crept into her awareness. That probably should have freaked her out. Her dream self however, was completely intrigued, confused, but definitely intrigued.

He motioned for her to move to the chairs at the fire place and she did so without speaking. She sat slow and cautious, waiting for a terrifying blob monster to ooze out of the cushions or something. After all, this was one of *her* dreams, which were typically vividly spooky or over the top and unrealistically happy. In fact, she once had a dream where she was running toward a hot guy with open arms across a field of sun flowers. It was seriously like you see in slow motion scenes of movies. Completely corny and pathetic, but apparently that's the sort of things her mind cooked up after she was done running the show for the day.

The man chose the chair across from Emily on the other side of the fire. She noticed that in the illumination made by the fire, he cast no shadow on the nearby wall. She glanced beside her own seat and saw her enlarged shadow, right where it should logically be. How was that possible? She had never seen anything like that before. Honestly, she had never seen anything like this place before either. She gave her imagination a pat on the back, for the detail it had come up with.

"Who are you?" Emily said shakily. For a dream she felt completely lucid. Normally she couldn't tell she was having a dream, but now she seemed way too aware. She was even wearing the same clothes she had on that day. Suddenly she felt totally under dressed for the rich surroundings. The light blue shirt, boot cut jeans and Nike's didn't feel appropriate in a place so lavish.

"Oh I'm terribly sorry, I didn't introduce myself," he apologized sincerely. "I am Alexander and I'm quite pleased to make your acquaintance."

"Well, I'd introduce myself except you seem to already know me." She replied unintentionally curt. "Forgive my rudeness, but would you mind explaining that to me?" As Emily spoke, she caught a small blurry movement out of the corner of her eye. She looked to see what it was and there was nothing there. Emily could have sworn the blur was a person. That couldn't have been what it was since there was no one else in the room. There were also no sounds of footsteps in the outer hall. So what was it?

The man's liquid voice brought Emily back to the conversation. "I do apologize Emily, but I brought you here because I needed to talk to you. Let me get right to the point so you may return to your slumber. It's of the utmost importance that you engrave my words into your mind. I have heard you are concerned with the happenings of your little town. I'm here to tell you not to be concerned with such trivial matters. The situation is completely under control so rest assured my dear girl. And please control any urge to undergo your own form of private investigation. You may not like the repercussions of such findings. It is detrimental to your well-being." He sat back in his chair laying his arms on the large arm rests thoughtfully as if pondering impossible math calculations without a sweat.

"I don't understand, you're gonna have to give me more than that. What situation? Why is it dangerous? And who told you I was concerned when I don't even know what I am concerned about? Also…" Her words were cut off short.

"Trust me dear Emily. I value this town and its surroundings greatly. I will not allow any harm to partake here. Nevertheless, I am not at liberty to discuss the happenings with you." His face was very gentle and sincere as he spoke. "I don't mean disrespect. It's only that you would not yet be able to understand. What you could understand, would frighten and endanger your safety. It is also possible, very possible in fact that such knowledge on your part would mean damage to my family and I refuse to take such chances I'm sure you can understand that. All I will speak of at this time is a few pieces of advice that I hope you bear in mind quite considerably." He finally hesitated long enough for a response but Emily still had a thousand questions.

A key point didn't escape Emily. "Um… yet? What do you mean yet?"

Alexander appeared thoughtful. He pressed his hands together forming a steeple at his mouth. "I can't tell you everything now. I'm sorry for that but that's just the way it is." He removed his hands from his face and looked at her expectantly.

Giving up Emily said, "I guess if that's all you can give, that's all I can take." She figured she shouldn't expect much cooperation from a dream. Emily decided not to push it. Her words were mostly a muttering to herself anyway.

"Good I'm glad we see eye to eye on this matter." Alexander hesitated for a moment and then as if reading her mind he said, "This isn't a dream. You are really here in spirit." He didn't give Emily a chance to question this information, like she wanted to. "My advice to you is simple. Evil danger does not merely remain in the shadows. When ruby borders emeralds, may their prey heed warning. He smoothly stood finalizing their conversation.

Emily sighed deeply," "I don't understand any of that. It makes no sense to me." She stood, following him to the entry into the hall. As she walked, fury radiated from her. She hated riddles, especially when they sounded like a fortune cookie. She had never been good at them. The advice he gave sounded like nonsense to Emily, nothing but gibberish.

Alexander turned briefly to face her as he spoke. "The answers will come to you with time my dear. I do humbly apologize, but as I have previously stated, this is all the knowledge I can afford to bare at this time. Honestly, you should feel privileged that I have divulged as much as I have." He turned back and moved just passed the wooden archway. "Now you must get some rest. Don't worry, we will meet again. Let the journey take you back to once you came child, may you go in peace forever more."

As she passed through the archway into the hall, she turned to ask him just one more question. He wasn't behind her anymore. She peeked back into the big room to see if he returned to the chairs. That scan turned up empty too. God, that was frustrating! Was everyone she met from now on going to have that power? She started down the hall, hoping it wasn't the part of the dream where something jumped out of one of those locked doors to scare her awake.

She didn't understand how she was supposedly only there in spirit. An idea sparked, and she pressed her hand on her arm. It felt solid enough to her, so she gave it a good pinch. OUCH! She rubbed her arm furiously willing the pain away. This was all so confusing. For one thing, weren't spirits supposed to be transparent? Also, when she pinched herself, she should have woken up, that never happened of course. As she passed the doors her view of the dream seemed to fade more and more until there was nothing left but blackness. Great, Emily thought drowsily. Now what?

When she opened her eyes, Emily shot straight up in her bed. How had she gotten home? The last thing she could remember is falling into the street. Remembering she had hit her head her hand reflexively rose to probe the spot and she winced. While there wasn't an open wound, there was a goose egg that reminded her vaguely of a third eye. Did her dad find her?

The clock on her bedside table said ten O'clock pm. Sam usually isn't even home yet. He gets off around seven but occupies his usual stool at the bar till eleven at the earliest. Sam was nothing if not routine. She stretched her muscles and got up to see if any damage control was necessary.

She peeked out her door, but couldn't hear any sound that indicated he was home. He wasn't capable of making no noise, even when just watching TV. Silence was always broken by the sound of crushing beer cans, feet hitting the coffee table and him rummaging for something in the kitchen. There was also her personal favorite, the sound of him thanking the beer Gods by releasing a roaring belch before cracking open another can. Not to mention, the TV was so typically blaring loud she could hear his shows perfectly from the comfort of her room.

There were none of these things out there, so she decided to see for herself. Walking down the hall, she realized belatedly that she was still in her regular clothes. That's weird, she thought quizzically. It wasn't normal for her to not put pajamas on before going to bed. Even when she was dog tired she at least took off her jeans. She had never been able to stand sleeping in jeans, no matter what the circumstances were. Even if she passed out that still didn't explain everything. How did she get home, and who put her in her bed and tucked her in?

The house was dark with not a single light on. The front door was locked and her black backpack sat beside it like usual. She went to the window and pushed back the curtains. Sam's truck wasn't on the street. It could be in the garage but he normally doesn't park it in there except for on his days off. It wasn't the type of vehicle you needed to worry about securely hiding in a locked garage at night to avoid damage or theft. Well it might have been once before his intoxication and carelessness got a hold of it.

Emily went to check his room but it was empty. The bed was still made. In fact, she could tell it was still made from when she had done it forever ago. She got tired of seeing an unused bed looking rumpled and recently vacated. Emily's mom always kept the bed made neatly every day without fail. The crisp clean sheets had to be tucked in tight and the decorative pillows in perfect position.

The only sign of Sam living in the room was his dirty clothes strewn about on the floor. His Romeos lay tossed by the bedside table. She highly doubted Sam sat there to take them off. He never let so much as a fingertip touch that bed, at least not that she ever saw. She knew why this was so she didn't need to ask. It was of course because it was the bed he shared with her mother once upon a time. Even if she had wanted to talk to Sam, he wasn't exactly an open book. In his world, things are better off unsaid.

She was still really tired, she guessed she should just go back to bed. The whole way back to her room, Emily's mind raced thinking of how she had gotten back to her house. It wasn't reasonable to assume that she had gotten herself home, tucked herself into bed, and just forgotten about it. The night after the first run in, the memories had been repressed, or temporarily erased. In a weird way, she wished these memories would disappear too. At least then, the mental stress that pressed on every corner of her brain would melt away.

When she curled up under the sheets she shivered but not from the cold. Luke's green and red eyes burned in Emily's memory like flames engulfing all they touched imprinting themselves forever.

Those eyes were something out of a sci-fi movie. She's never even seen something like that in scary movies. She cringed remembering how petrified she was at first and then how her mind and body longed for him, as if under a spell. *When ruby borders emeralds, may their prey heed warning.* The words of her dream scrolled through her mind. Maybe that's why she had dreamed of Alexander and that beautiful place. Her imagination ran wild with the mark Luke's eyes had left on her

Alexander didn't seem like a dream and neither did that place. Emily had felt completely aware and in control during it. He said that she was actually there in spirit and it really did hurt when she had pinched her arm. She turned her arm over to look and she was not surprised to see that there was a small bruise on her skin. The only part that remotely seemed dreamlike was when everything faded away to darkness. What else had Alexander said?

Evil danger doesn't merely stay hidden in the shadows. She guessed evil danger hidden in the shadow, could have been referring to Luke and her attacker from the other night. However, they came out in the dark, so in a way they were still shadowed. Luke had followed her under the street light and didn't seem to mind the cars driving by that witnessed their little meeting. As Emily toyed with the theories that were utterly ridiculous, she slowly felt herself giving into unconsciousness until she was left with what she hoped was a peaceful sleep.

8

The next day at work seemed to pass in a blur. Emily spent the morning running the register and helping customers. She knew the inventory at Blake's backwards and forwards so it was a fairly mindless task. No matter what she did though, her mind was still stuck on last night. She tried to ignore it, but it just kept slipping back in.

In a matter of just a few days she had been attacked twice. The attacks themselves were bad enough. Though the monsters who delivered the attacks, were what plagued her the most. There was just something so different about them. The one called Luke, didn't even try and hurt her. Granted, he probably would have, if it hadn't been for whatever was in that alley. Both times they put her under some kind of spell. That couldn't be what actually happened, there was no such thing as magic, was there? Either way, there was something very wrong with this picture. Every time she closed her eyes, glowing red burned behind her lids. It was as though the image of those eyes was imprinted there with the sole purpose of torturing her.

The other ginormous problem was that more of the residents seemed to be lost to the pod people too. Well, maybe the numbers hadn't necessarily increased. More of them were coming out to be counted, that's all. They were like Lakeview's personal version of Stepford wives or something. Most didn't even purchase anything. They just seem to wander around the store aimlessly. They were talking more today, despite the underlying fear that still lingered behind their put on facades. Well, she guessed she shouldn't say they were talking, per say. It was more like the freaky pod people spoke in hushed whispers to each other and no one else. They kept scanning the room every few minutes. It was like they were expecting something bad to happen.

When they caught her eyeing them from behind the counter, the huddle would disperse like scared little mice that were being hunted. When Emily would ask them if they needed something, they smiled quickly and just walked out of the store without saying anything. What was that? It wasn't like she smelled. Whether she was distracted or not, Emily knew she had been pleasant. The group acted as though they had been caught doing something embarrassing. That was the type of reaction that had been going on all day and she almost couldn't help but take it personally.

Unfortunately, Lucy wasn't in today. She was supposed to be according to the schedule. Hopefully she wasn't sick or something. Emily wished desperately that her friend had been there. She wanted to confide in her about everything that had been happening. Trusting Lucy was as easy as breathing. Plus, she wouldn't think Emily's theories were insane like everyone else surely would. That knowledge was comforting. Lucy thrived on weird. She loved all things unexplainable or impossible.

A book slammed down on the counter, interrupting her reverie making her jump. "Hey I've been standing here forever. You think you might return to this planet long enough to ring me up?" The guy's voice was sarcastic and his expression was extremely annoyed.

Man, how long had he been there, she thought. Her face flushed with hot embarrassment. "Oh sorry, guess I'm sort of out of it today. " Emily grabbed his book so she could scan it. As she did the title caught her eye, Supernatural Hunters. Huh. She had never seen that book before. Oh well, she thought as she flipped it over for the bar code.

"There's no tag on this. Was it in science fiction or paranormal?" Emily gazed up at the guys face expectantly. He couldn't have been much older than her if even at all. She thought he looked familiar but she really wasn't very good with names.

"Neither. I was looking in the self-help section for something for my mom. I was gonna go over there for something for me and fate just brought what I wanted to me." He smiled a crooked smile that gave him an air of arrogant boyish charm.

George came trudging out of the back room, eyed the customer with money in his hand and instantly softened. "Is there a problem?" His question was directed at the man but his glare was definitely meant for Emily.

"Hey George this guy wants this book." Emily held up the novel as evidence. "There is no tag and it's not in the computer. I've never seen it before."

Before she even started to hand him the book, he shrugged it away. "No matter just punch it in the computer and charge the suggested price." He moved passed her and around the counter. "I've got to go. Emily you'll need to close up and I won't be in tomorrow." Without a second glance, or a response from Emily that tomorrow was supposed to be her day off, he was gone.

Man, he was sure in a hurry she thought as she watched him disappear out the door. It wasn't like George to not have time to worry about what a customer is charged. She figured he would take the lack of tag as a golden opportunity to mark up the price. If nothing else, he should have lectured Emily on the fact that the book wasn't marked. Normally he would take great satisfaction in such activities.

Sensing the annoyance in the other guy's posture, she quickly punched in the book and searched for a price to charge. There wasn't one, so she put in a logical price for a book of its size and genre and then slipped it into a bag. "Here ya go. Sorry about all the trouble." She smiled warmly trying to soften the tension.

He dropped a bill on the counter and when Emily tried to get his change, he told her to keep it. He appraised her for a moment, smiled and then left the counter without another word. When he got to the door he paused with his hand on the knob and turned and looked back at Emily. She matched his stare with one of her own. They seemed locked into a contest for what seemed like forever. Then, the door flew open startling her staring partner back a few steps, immediately breaking them from their trance. A customer stood just within the doorway, looking impatient. They got around each other leaving the door way empty and the bell still ringing announcing the new comer.

Why was that guy watching her like that? The look he gave her wasn't an admiring one. Even though she didn't have much experience in that department, she knew what it looked like when a guy was into a girl. He had looked like he was trying to delve into the deepest contents of her brain. It wasn't frightening or anything. He just seemed curious. Emily wondered idly if he was new in town. He didn't look like one of the construction workers that were working on the new developments. Really she didn't think he could have been far from her age.

Lakeview was a small hole in the wall town, which no one really cared about. People Emily's age didn't usually come flocking into town voluntarily. It's not like the community college was a treasure. They strived to follow the policy of mediocre education, at rock bottom prices. Even if the price lured student's, community colleges were a dime a dozen, they wouldn't need to come to Lakeview.

The guy was definitely good looking, in a shaggy sort of way. He wore a white T-shirt with faded jeans that rode low on his hips. They were the kind that was supposed to be that way. He wasn't like the gang banger wanna-be's that like to show off half their assets and oversized boxers. He had a casual demeanor that still radiated determination. In other words, he was a walking contradiction. On one hand, he appeared to be a gentle giant, and on the other, seemed like a sarcastic pain in the butt. Like he didn't have a care in the world, yet displayed an obvious impatience and distaste for everything.

It wasn't very common for her to take such a strong notice of a guy like that. Emily had never really had a boyfriend before. She didn't have time nor the desire to put up with the drama a guy in her life would bring. Even still, she knew what her type was. Even if she didn't plan on dating there was no harm in admiring the merchandise. It's not that she didn't want a boyfriend. She had always wanted to be kissed and feel the security of someone's strong arms around her. Feelings like that would only get her in trouble though. Getting out of Lakeview was imperative and a boyfriend would only complicate the plans that have been made since her mother died.

Not to mention the fact that her beast of a father would have to sit at home and clean his gun all night. Sam wouldn't stop there. He would have no fear in *using* those guns to get his point across. He didn't even really like Emily to bring regular friends home, but a boyfriend? Yeah right! That would be like giving the poor guy a death warrant before he even walked into the door. Maybe throwing him to a pack of wolves would be a better analogy.

There had been boys that had shown interest in Emily, the feeling was just never mutual. Most of the bottom feeder boys that went to the high school with her weren't worth anyone's time. The college didn't seem to produce a wide selection of winners either. It wasn't that Emily was a snob or anything, because she wasn't. Certain standards were just necessary for survival.

The rest of the day was slow. She decided to close up early, no one would even notice anyway. She had now had two run-ins with jerk guys after dark. Emily wasn't about to give an open invitation for a third. Besides, it wasn't too early. The worst George would do was doc her pay. As much as she needed the money she could live without it.

The decision was already made, even while she was still contemplating. Unconsciously making preparations, she had already shut down the register and turned off most of the lights. She grabbed her backpack and keys. Not giving herself time to second guess calling someone for a ride, she headed out to the street alone.

Emily thought about calling a friend to see if they wanted to go to a movie later. An estrogen rush would probably be just what the doctor ordered. It didn't really even matter what the activity was. Emily was just really over all the drama that had been going on lately. Since she had been going to college, she had lost touch with a lot of her friends. Some of them did go to the local college too but they weren't really in the same classes. Working didn't leave much time for a social life either especially since she started picking up extra shifts.

If she was being completely honest with herself, she didn't really have close friends in high school either. There were acquaintances that she spoke to at school, but never after the school day was done. Lucy was really the closest thing Emily had to a real friend and that was saying something. The two of them rarely got to see each other anymore. Emily had always had other priorities in her choice of after school activities. Luce was always busy with her various blind studies and her martial arts training.

To anyone else it may have seemed odd that her blind friend was a black belt, but Emily just always thought it was super cool. It really helped heighten Lucy's senses to epic proportions. Also, who better to learn to defend themselves than the blind community? After all, they were practically walking targets. Her friend wasn't a victim though and never would be.

The party scene wasn't really Emily's cup of tea either. Alcohol and her DNA didn't seem to mesh well, judging by her father's life. She never wanted to take the chance she would be susceptible. That lifestyle wasn't good for anyone and that was doubly true for her. There were more important things to worry about. Most of the kids from her high school and a lot who now go to college with her were on a drink now study later game plan. Most of the people that choose Lakeview Community college for their choice of further education weren't planning to transfer to better more prominent Universities.

Emily reached into her pocket and grabbed her cell phone. She looked up Lucy's number in the contact list and hit send. Maybe Luce wasn't sick and would feel like hanging out. Plus she really wanted to talk to her about all the drama trauma going on lately.

"Hey Em what's up?" Lucy's voice sounded cheerful as always.

"I closed the shop early and wanted to hang out. I really need to talk to you Luce, it's kinda important."

"Awww…I'm not in town. I came back early so I could get going on studying up for finals. I'll be back in a few days though. What's wrong Em?" Lucy sounded concerned by Emily's request.

Recognizing her friend's concern, Emily tried to eliminate any false note to her voice before speaking. "Oh, nothing. I just miss you is all. We haven't got to hang much ya know?"

Lucy didn't buy it. "Sure, whatever you say Em. How about I call you tonight, so we can talk more about whatever it is you can't tell me now, k?"

"Sure sure, sounds good," Emily sighed. There was no point in arguing. Lucy had always been able to read Emily like a book.

"If you don't call or text I'm calling you." Lucy scolded in her mom voice.

Emily sighed again, "Alright I get it. I promise I'll talk to you later. There is stuff I need to talk to you about." Emily stressed the last sentence, hopefully conveying the necessity of their talk. Everything was pressing down on her shoulders like the weight of a grand piano.

"K good. I'll be waiting for your call babe so don't bail on me," Lucy scolded again. This time though, it was obvious that she was returning to her perky self.

"Alright mom I'll talk to you later." Emily laughed.

When Emily hung up she felt better about the situation. She hadn't actually told Lucy what was going on, but at least it was out that she needed to. She shoved her phone back in her pocket and finished locking up the store. Even if Lucy didn't have any answers, she would probably be able to help her figure everything out.

Luckily, when she started home there were still people out on the sidewalks, all along Main Street. Emily heard whistling and looked in the direction of the sound. It was coming from outside Flora's Flowers next door. Flora was outside watering her hanging plants outside her shop. Emily smiled as she recognized the tune *Zippidy Doo Da* coming from the shop owners lips. No matter the season people could always count on a jungle of plants or flowers outside the middle aged woman's store. The scent from the hanging plants was totally intoxicating. Emily took in a deep breath letting the smell envelop her senses. The light breeze rustled the plants branches and the spray from the hose misted Emily's face. Despite the breeze the cool water felt nice.

Flora smiled and waved when she saw Emily watching. She was the nicest woman and a serious expert at her craft. Her thumb was the greenest in town. She could turn a simple flower arrangement into a masterpiece worthy of appearance in a magazine. Emily always wondered why she didn't take her business to a bigger city where she could make better money.

On the other side of George's place, was a comic book store. All in all, it seemed to do pretty good business with the kids. The owner of the store was a young guy that had taken over when his father died. Emily had never really been into comics although, to each his own right? Even though they were supposedly graphic novels, she personally didn't buy it. It just didn't seem logical that something with brightly colored pictures and word bubbles could be called novels.

There was a dog across the street digging at the insides of a box left outside the bakery. Maybe there were discarded pastries inside. Emily couldn't help but giggle. The pretty retriever was pawing at the box savagely. As she got closer she could see its pink studded collar so she obviously had a home. She had never seen her before Emily hoped the dog wasn't lost. She debated crossing the street so she could check her tag. If the dog lived on her way she could take her back to her owners. The animal shelter would already be closed for the night. So if it was a stray there was always her house. At least the pup would have somewhere to sleep for the night. Sam wouldn't notice anyway. As long as Emily kept her in the bedroom and tried to keep the barking down to a minimum it wouldn't be too big of a deal.

She was so lost in her mental preparations, that she didn't pay attention to the path right in front of her.   She ran smack dab into a person. Thankfully, a strong person so they didn't fall. The force of it though knocked Emily back a few steps. Whoever it was, they were solid. It was so sudden that it startled Emily badly, making her gasp loudly as she brought her hand up to her chest willing herself not to have a heart attack.

Breathing hard, Emily collected herself enough to speak. "I'm so sorry," She stammered. "I didn't see you I was watching the dog over there." Emily pointed awkwardly in the retriever's direction.

"It's no problem. I stopped to watch the feast too." His voice was like velvet.

Her mind swayed with recognition.   She knew that voice, but from where? She brought her eyes up to see him for the first time. A picture flashed into her mind. His ocean blue eyes seemed to wake her memory out of a deep sleep. It was her rescuer from the night in the alley. "It's you." What a dumb thing to say, she thought feeling incredibly stupid. She could have come up with something more intelligent. The last time she saw him she at least had an excuse for acting like an incoherent moron.

"Yes. And it's you. I was wondering how you were after the other night." His sentence ended in the most magnificent smile Emily had ever seen.

"I'm fine. Thank you by the way…for saving me I mean." Well, at least she half way managed a full sentence, sort of. It was ridiculous, but she couldn't stop gazing at him like a pathetic little school girl. She felt like the Retriever, just before it pounced on the pastry box. It was incredibly easy to get lost in his amazing eyes. It felt as though she was somehow swimming in the endless deep blue of them.

He seemed to notice and it made his grin grow cockier. "Don't mention it. I've always been a sucker for damsels in distress. I just happened to be in the right place at the wrong time.

"Well either way, I really appreciate it. I owe you one," she said with a tremendous amount of gratitude. It suddenly dawned on her where they were standing. The now not so dark alley she had been jumped in was directly to their right. Her heart began to pound furiously at the sight of it.

His eyes followed her glance. "Well apparently, this has become a meeting place for us. Were you trying to relive a moment?" He said with mock disgust.

A hysterical giggle burst from Emily's lips without permission. "No definitely not." Emily cleared her throat trying to quiet her moronic nervous laughter. "I could do without this place. I only come passed here because it's on my way home from work." She made a gesture behind them toward the front of Blake's. "I work at the book store," she babbled idiotically.

"Would you like some company?" He asked, sounding as if it didn't matter to him either way.

"Um, what?" Emily said totally surprised. She could feel the flames licking up her cheeks and here this guy was standing there all casual as if he was completely unaffected by their odd situation.

"I thought you might like me to walk you home. Maybe it's not the best idea." He began to walk around her in the opposite direction. As he did, he gave her a very guy like nod.

Crap, Emily thought. He must have misunderstood her reaction. She couldn't let him go. There were still so many questions about the other night. The morbid details may have felt very fresh but she still didn't have all the answers. The chance to get those answers was trying to walk away. "Wait." Emily said hastily. She put a hand up as though she could stop him. "I'd like it if you walked me home. That is if the offer is still there…" She let her voice trail off hoping he would pick up the thread and accept her request.

He took a deep breath and turned back around to face her. "Of course, the offer still remains Emily." Without another word, he started off down the side walk leaving her behind him a few steps.

The mysterious hottie walked about as fast as Emily jogged. She had to scramble to catch up. The awkwardness made her feel very inept. Her anxiousness allowed her to catch up quickly though.

How strange. He was sweetly walking her home but acting all arrogant at the same time. Emily wondered if this cool bad boy persona was just an act for her benefit. The thought quickly squelched though however as she remembered him battling her attacker effortlessly with no hint of apprehension. He was obviously a bad boy. The mysteriousness that radiated off of him was electric.

As she glanced at him periodically, she noticed that his face was wiped clean of any emotion. It was impossible to get a read off him at all. The silence was driving her insane. She had to get him explaining, or it would be too late. The distance to Emily's house wasn't far.

"How do you know my name? And how did you know where I lived the other night? Where did that guy go in the alley? Did you do something to him?" The questions shot out of her mouth like bullets from a machine gun but she couldn't help herself. Once the words got started they had a mind of their own. It was as though she had no control of her mouth what so ever. He probably thought she was nuts. That would be understandable, she thought she was nuts too.

An almost imperceptible smile tugged at the corners of his mouth. "My my, so many inquiries, so little time. So you have a strong recollection of the other nights events do you?" He almost seemed surprised. It was clear he was trying to not let it show but it was still there.

That wasn't a normal reaction. There was definitely something more behind his words, some hidden meaning that one way or another, Emily *had* to get to the bottom of. The surprise on his face was confusing. Why wouldn't she have her memory? It's not like he could have known she had blocked it out at first.

"Well… I didn't at first." Emily shrugged. "I guess it just came back to me." She watched closely for the expression to change, though it stayed in perfect control.

"You must have a strong mind to have repressed such terror and then regain it so quickly." He grabbed her elbow helping her off the curb across the street.

She hated realizing it, but they had already crossed several blocks. It seemed like they had only been walking seconds and not the several minutes it had to have been. She had to get him talking. Time was running out and he would be gone again. "You still haven't answered my questions." She pressed, hopefully encouraging him to explain things further. Apparently, he wasn't going to offer up any information without a bit of prodding from her part.

When they reached the next street, he promptly dropped her arm as if he had been burned. Geez, it's not like she had a disease or something. It wasn't like he was obligated to be all gentlemanly in the first place. Emily knew how to walk just fine by herself. The sting on her ego was blazing like a raging wild fire. She knew she shouldn't care, but the feeling of not being good enough coursed deep within her core. Thanks to Sam, that was planted that seed long ago.

"You're right, I haven't answered." He retorted sharply. He said nothing else as if his words were answer enough.

That just wasn't enough for Emily. She deserved answers and was going to get them one way or another. Suddenly, bravery settled in. All hints of shyness melted away with every step.

"And then?" Emily pushed harder. If he would just look at her, he would see the look on her face was fierce and smoky. At least that was the look she was going for anyway. Knowing him, it would probably hold no intimidation at all.

It was at least another block before he said anything. "I've been in the bookstore before. One of the employees said she had a co-worker named Emily. When you said that you worked there, I guess I just made the connection." He looked casual but his voice faltered.

He was lying. "Um no. You knew my name that night. You just found out I worked there today. Not to mention the fact that I don't work for a girl." She shot back shooting him an equally cold side long glance.

"Alright calm down. No need to get angry. So you caught me. Let's just say… I'm very observant to my surroundings. I've seen you around." He did sound apologetic, even though he was still obviously lying.

It was crystal clear that she was going to get nothing else from him on that subject. She'd let it go for now. There were more important things to worry about then her name anyway. Plus, he seriously made the simmer down motion with his hands when he told her to calm down. That was completely unexpectedly cute and annoying at the same time. Emily hated the affect he was having on her. She wasn't really sure what that affect that was but didn't really want to know either. There was no time in her life for complications.

"And the jackass from the other night? What happened to him?" Emily's thinly lined brow rose fiercely with her accusing glare. She tried to sound tough so he would take her seriously. This honestly wasn't hard since she really was getting aggravated.

"I simply encouraged him to take his business, elsewhere," he said the last word slowly as if to display its double meaning.

"Which means? Emily was feeling annoyed at his evasions it's not like she was asking him to recite the Battle Hymn of the Republic backwards or something. Which for future reference, probably wasn't a good idea, since Emily didn't even know it forwards.

"Alright alright. I used just a bit of force but under the circumstances, I had to do what was necessary. He hurt you I wasn't just going to give him a lesson in politeness and manners."

They turned the corner onto her street. Her time was running out. It was annoying that the conversation really wasn't going anywhere. Although, he had just admitted to fighting for her honor, so maybe it could be excused. That was kind of sweet really.

When they reached her driveway she looked up to the garage. Oh thank God, she thought relieved. The garbage can she had strategically placed partially in front of the door was still in place. That meant Sam wasn't home. The placement was something she did often. Emily wanted fare warning he was home in case he tried to be sneaky and park in the garage.

She stared at the driveway for a moment trying to think of her next question. It would have to be carefully chosen if she had any hope at an actual answer. Absently, she noticed the driveway was getting some pretty dangerous looking cracks. They would need to repave soon. It was totally weird that she would think of that right then but the cracks really were a serious tripping hazard

"Who are you really?" I've never seen you around here before and I have lived here my whole life." There was that short time she and her dad were out of town after her mom died, that didn't really seem relevant though.

"I haven't lived here very long but I have gotten to know my way around fairly easily. It's not like Lakeview is a big city. I read maps well." He was still evading her questions. His answers were vague as if getting to know Emily would be horrible or something.

Fine, if that was the way he wanted it, she didn't need to be his friend. It's not like she cared if he didn't want to exchange friendship bracelets or anything. No point in getting close to anyone anyway she would just be leaving for school. She didn't have time for personal relationships platonic or otherwise. Emily had distanced herself from her family and friends after her mom had died. She had inadvertently severed all ties not wanting to strengthen any bonds that may break leaving her alone again. She missed her mother so much it was hard to breathe sometimes. She couldn't bear the thought of losing another person that was close to her. That problem in her life was at least easy to solve. Don't want to get hurt then don't get close enough to be hurt. The only problem with that was that it left her spending an awful lot of time by herself.

"Oh, and to answer your other question, my name is Sebastian." As he spoke he gave her a slight bow as if in formal introduction to a Queen.

Did he really just do that? What time warp did he come out of? Well, she guessed it was kind of cute in a dorky sort of way. "Well Sebastian it's nice to meet you. Thanks again for helping me the other night with the…" What was she supposed to call her attacker? Should she reveal her suspicions to this guy? No way. She hardly knew him he would think she was nuts. "Uh, thanks. Ya know, for helping with that guy the other night." Giving Sebastian no further chance of getting under her skin she turned and headed up the walk. When she glanced back to tell him goodbye more politely he was already gone. Damn it! He did it again.

How does he do that? Whatever, she thought as she turned back to go inside. He was a very frustrating person, who seemed to be quite self-assured. Emily hated arrogant conceited people. It's great when people have confidence as long as they understood there were boundaries. Her mom always said that no one person is better than the next and that had always stuck with her. Logically she couldn't be too mad at him though. Technically, she had turned from him first trying to immaturely gain the upper hand. Somehow even in doing that, he still managed to one up her. Emily couldn't figure out what it was about him that drove her so crazy. He seemed to bring out a competitive drive in her that had never been awakened before. It was so maddeningly annoying, yet for some reason she liked it.

9

The kitchen in her house was bright and cheery. There was a large fluorescent light fixture overhead, but that wasn't what brightened up the room. Its main color was a pale blue. It wasn't dull, and it wasn't so annoyingly bright it hurt your eyes. It gave it a real homey feel. Honestly it was kind of adorable, in a cheesy kind of way. The scalloped white lace curtains were homemade. Emily's mother never thought it was a good idea to purchase curtains from a store. Melissa always said with the right sale at the fabric store someone could purchase the perfect material for curtains and let their own personal flare shine.

As much as it may have seemed like it, her mother wasn't cheap. Or at least she didn't have to be. Back then Sam didn't drink that much, so they had plenty of money. Her mom just figured if they cut corners that would leave them money to do other things. One of those things was a college fund for Emily. Between medical bills for her mom's hospital stay, funeral costs and Sam's binges, it was totally deflated. Emily knew her mom would roll over in her grave at the thought of the savings fund that was no more.

The big pot was in the top cupboard where of course, she couldn't reach. She had to use a stool her father had made for that very purpose for her mom. Melissa was not graced with a models height, that's for sure. Unfortunately, Emily was stuck with the same vertically challenged fate.

She had decided on making spaghetti for dinner. It was easy enough. Sam would return home from his busy day at the bar totally inebriated. That meant he wouldn't notice if she didn't make a gourmet sauce. The jar kind would have to do. Once the meat was simmering and the noodles on boil she got to work cleaning out the fridge. It hadn't been done in a while. If she didn't do it they would surely have months old leftovers in there growing more mold than there was food.

The jingling of keys sounded outside from the back door. Why on earth was he coming in the back? She never even heard the sound of the garage door rolling up. It was old and partially rusted so it made its presence known quite loudly. Emily liked to think of it as its own personal alarm system. Even in her bedroom she could be woken from a dead sleep when her dad came stumbling in late.

Boots clomping on the hard wood floor broke into her thoughts. "Hi Em...ily..." He slurred and then his voice faded out. Sam gave her a sloppy version of a warm smile that made Emily nervous.

Sam was never in a good mood after a whole day at Moody's Tavern. He would normally consume enough liquor to kill an army. Maybe Janice convinced him somehow to take a cab, which would have been a miracle. It had always scared Emily to think of her father driving home so intoxicated but it did her no good to say anything about it. As he would say, *acting like his mommy would only get her a fat lip.* Her lips were to thin, but that wasn't the way she wanted to make them full and pouty. She plopped a big helping of pasta for Sam on a plate and sat it down in front of him.

Her dad looked at the meal in front of him and asked, "What's for dinner?"

"Steak and potatoes dad, if that's okay," she replied sarcastically. She tossed the towel she used to keep his plate from burning her hands onto her shoulder as she grabbed her soda. Pepsi was truly the greatest beverage ever invented. The caffeine was speaking to her from within the confinement of the can.

"That's good darling I love spaghetti."

He shoveled a bite in his mouth so big, Emily thought for sure he'd gag. It was kind of evil, but she figured at least if he did, then he might pass out early. She didn't feel like babysitting him and it was only a matter of time before his temper reared its ugly head.

"How was your day Em?" Sam still slurred, though he managed to speak in between bites.

What is this? Since when does he care about her day, or anything about her life in general for that matter? She noticed a single bead of sweat drip down her dad's forehead. Whisky always made him sweaty. His body's probably trying to purge out his overconsumption of poison, *yuck.*

As they ate, she found herself staring at the lines of her father's face. Sure he was middle aged, but the years since her mom died have been etched into his skin like several grief tattoos. There were permanent creases on his forehead. Lines fanned out on the outside of each of his eyes like spider legs. Instead of smile lines, his were indented into a grimace. Sam was still handsome in his own way, but his face definitely was whether beaten. He has acquired an unattractive spare tire that hung over his pants. Even still, she could see the lines of his muscles along his chest and arms. With every raise of the fork his forearm muscles rippled slightly as though trying futilely to wake up. She normally didn't make it a habit to gawk at her dad's physical appearance. It just pained her to see how much he had let himself go. Plus, usually Emily couldn't look at him for long because he would get paranoid and think she was plotting some conspiracy against him or something. He was a very paranoid man who thought there was a reason for everything and in his mind that reason was never good.

Breaking into her mind babble he said, "Baby I need to talk to you."

Seriously that's two terms of endearment in one sitting. She didn't think she could take much more. Somewhere along the line the shoe was about to drop. "Um, sure dad what's up?" She hedged timidly.

"Well it's about that boy…" Sam's voice trailed off. His face was reddening, but Emily couldn't tell if it was embarrassment or anger.

Seriously was he going to give her the birds and the bees lecture? She couldn't believe this was happening to her. Besides, he was late mom had already told her about that. Plus she did go to public school. Where did this interest in being a parent come from, because however it got there Emily wanted to kill it.

"Dad I told you, I don't even know him. He just offered to walk me home so I wasn't alone that's all. I promise."

"No no, I believe that you just need to stay away from him I mean it." Sam shoved another bite into his mouth.

He believed that? Daddy dearest sure didn't seem to believe that the other night when he was smacking her around. She would sure hate to see what would happen if he didn't believe her, she thought while she chewed hiding her annoyance. He didn't even ask about the marks on her face. If he even remembered he could have said sorry but that wasn't his style she supposed. If he didn't remember, he could have at least shown some concern. Isn't that what a typical parent would do? That's what her mom would have done. He's so paranoid about everything and everyone, she's surprised he didn't try and get a mob of town folk together with flaming torches to start a riot. Then again, that would show he cared which up until tonight, just didn't happen.

"Dad really, I don't even know the guy…"

"Damn it Emily, I'm serious! He's dangerous. All of them things are, you don't understand and I hope you never do." He interrupted aggressively.

She started to respond, but Sam didn't notice he just kept right on talking.

"There are forces at work in this world that are alien to you. Not everything is peaches and cream and the Brady Bunch little girl."

That's funny, Emily thought. She didn't think there was such a thing as peaches and cream in the real world. If there were dads out there like Mike Brady, then she got ripped off royally. Except didn't Mike have an alcohol problem in real life? Also, she thought she remembered hearing something about Greg and Marsha doing it behind the scenes. Clearly even the Brady's had drama.

Her dad's voice rose and regained her attention. "Will you focus?" His slur turned into great steady conviction. He slammed his fist down on the table so hard it shuddered under his blow. "There are killers in this town, probably everywhere. It's not like in the books and movies either. What you would normally expect isn't always the rules."

"Dad you're not making any sense." Unintentionally, her voice came out sarcastic.

"Good. It's time you see the truth and don't believe in the fairytale cuz that's just not the way it works. I'd tell you not to go out after dark, except that doesn't seem to make a difference all the time. Not that you would listen to me anyway, you never do. I couldn't fix things for your mom. I'll be dead before I sit back and watch the same thing happen twice." He didn't yell for once, which made him sound all business. When he mentioned Melissa, his eyes took on a distant star struck quality. It genuinely softened his features.

Here we go, Emily thought as she gave a mental eye roll. The alcohol must have been kicking in again. No one killed her mom. She had gotten pneumonia and her body became too weak and couldn't fight anymore. He always thought there were other factors involved. Though he had never came out and said what those factors were.

Switching gears completely Sam said, "I got you something in town today. I had to special order it." Sam took a little black rectangular box out of his pocket and slid it across the table. "Go on, open it."

Emily did as instructed. When she lifted off the lid, her mouth dropped open with an audible snap. So much actually, that she thought her chin banged on the table. In her whole life, her dad had never personally gotten her anything that would constitute as a gift. Well, there was last Christmas when he bought her a pack of socks from the thrift shop in town. Oh, and she couldn't forget how they were repackaged in a Ziploc bag and the zip part was broken. Second hand stores in Lakeview spare no expense on their value finds, that's for sure.

Laying inside the box on white padding, was a necklace. It was a silver cross that appeared to have silver rope braded around the inside corners, with her birth stone in the middle. It was the most beautiful thing she had ever seen. The fact that he had given it to her only made it that much prettier. She felt her eyes sting and well up with tears that threatened to spill over at any moment.

"Thank you. I…don't know what to say. It's… beautiful." She wiped at her eyes to catch the tears before they betrayed her. Emily worked hard to gulp down the baseball sized lump in her throat.

Sam didn't even seem to notice her barely contained flood of emotion. "Now Emily, I want you to wear that always. No matter what. It's very important that you take this as the one time in your life that you listen to your old man."

Emily couldn't remember her dad ever being religious. In fact, after her mom Melissa died he threw away their Bible. It wasn't like he just casually dropped it in either. He threw it in with everything he had. Emily had to fish it out of the trash after he fell asleep. He had said no God would take such a wonderful woman before her time, so there must not be one. Emily's mom always told her when someone died, it was because God needed them for a greater purpose than their work on Earth. Personally, she liked that idea much better. It helped her to know there was something bigger out there than the Hell on this Earth. She may have been angry with God when her mom died, but like with the unbearable agony of grief, that too passed.

"Okay dad. I will I promise." She felt she was telling the truth. The moment of generosity would never be taken for granted, no matter what his reasoning might have been. She wouldn't ask either, she thought as she clasped it around her slender neck. The answer might not be as nice as the one made up by her imagination.

After she was done doing the dinner dishes her cell phone chimed, signaling that she had received a text. When she flipped it open to check she saw that it was from Lucy. Big surprise, she wasn't even going to give Emily a chance to call.

Lucy's text read, I'm *patiently waiting for your call... NOT! lol.*

She's such a pain in the butt, Emily thought as she typed a message back. *I'll call in a sec*, Emily replied. Shutting her phone, she grabbed the trash from under the counter. "Be back in a minute dad. I'm gonna take the trash out and get some laundry started," Emily called to Sam.

From the other room, the only response was a grumble. So much for the quality bonding over dinner. That moment was evidently long gone. Oh well, back to reality.

Once in the garage, she got her phone back out and dialed Lucy's number. Noticing the mountain of laundry that was piling up, she let out a loud exasperated groan. It would probably be a good idea to throw a load of towels in the ancient washing machine while she waited for Lucy to answer. Emily seriously detested doing laundry. If it wasn't for the fact that it was considered unacceptable to walk around naked, she would never do it. Lord knows Sam wasn't about to break up his trend and clean anything.

"Finally!" Lucy's voice sounded frantic into Emily's ear. "So, what's up? Spill it girl."

Emily wasn't really sure where to start. "Well, I had a bit of a run in with a guy in the alley the other night and then with another guy last night." Emily paused a moment and waited for the explosion on the other end.

"Wait, what? Start from the beginning. What do you mean you had a run in? With who?"" Lucy didn't wait for a response before continuing. "Em were you like mugged or something?"

"Luce, calm down. I'm okay. No harm, no foul and all that. Yes I was attacked, but someone saved me." Emily's voice sounded strained as she bent to dig through the hamper for the rest of the towels. How on earth did her friend know to go there? Anyone else might have interpreted Emily's words as *hey I met two different guys and got their numbers. We're going out next Saturday.* Not good old Luce. She was nothing if not observant.

"Oh my God Em! Who saved you? Did you call the cops? Oh my God!" Lucy's words were panicked and more than a little worried.

"Hey just stop a minute and breathe. Here me out okay? Let me get it all out before the interrogation begins." Emily started the wash and then hopped up on the machine to prepare for the onslaught of questions.

Lucy sighed. "Okay I'm listening, no more interruptions I promise."

Emily swallowed deep then went for it. "Okay, so I don't know who attacked me. He pushed me down in the alley and it was dark, so I didn't get a look at him. Before he could really hurt me, someone came out of nowhere and saved me. He got rid of the guy, I mean literally the bad guy disappeared and I have no idea what happened to him. I didn't go to the cops because there's something weird about it Luce. I mean seriously, like with the pod people. I'm not sure why, but I'm pretty sure that it's all connected somehow. I saw more of the pod thing on the bus yesterday. There was this couple… who kinda seemed to be controlling some of them. A bunch of the passengers followed them off the bus. I tried to ask someone what was going on, but they wouldn't answer me and then started ignoring me all together." Emily sighed with the release of all that information in such a short time.

Lucy took the breath as an opportunity. "Wow Em. This is some kind of Twilight Zone script or something! Are you okay? Oh, and what about the second attack?"

"No I'm fine I swear. A few scrapes and bruises, but nothing permanent." Except for her sanity, Emily thought to herself. Absently, she hoped it wasn't that weird voice again. It didn't seem to be. Thinking about that voice, reminded her oddly of Sebastian. That was ridiculous. It wasn't like he was talking to her in her mind or something else equally disturbing. That kind of stuff only happened in the movies. "Anyway," Emily finally continued. "The other attack was a different guy I'm pretty sure. I was walking home from Wal-Mart…"

"Why were you walking home from Wal-Mart?" Lucy interrupted angrily. "That's a long walk back to your house."

"I know mom, I know," Emily responded sarcastically. "Anyway," she continued with more emphasis. "On the way home I fell and this guy helped me up. Nice right?" Emily answered her own question. "Nope, not at all. Dude turned out to be a total creeper. Oh and Luce, here's more of the weird part. His eyes were a bright green, but that's not the weird part. Around the green was a ring of bright red. Seriously, like Kool-Aid red and when he got mad they glowed even brighter. It was freaky."

"Oh My God!" Lucy sounded stunned.

Emily took a second to be utterly relieved that as usual, her friend didn't doubt her. As crazy as the eye thing sounded, she showed no sign that she didn't believe her. "I know right? The other thing is that he almost seemed to put me under some kind of trance thing. Seriously, I knew it was wrong, but I wanted to be near him even though not more than two minutes before, I thought he was going to kill me." Before Lucy could freak Emily said, "Don't worry, nothing happened. Something growled at him and he took off after it. I took the opportunity and got out of there as fast as I could." Emily's words sped up as she got more into her tale. "Like a clumsy idiot, I totally tripped over the curb and cracked my head. I passed out and somehow I ended up at home in my bed. When I was out, I had some crazy dream about this gorgeous place, where this old guy gave me advice." She finally took a breath, it felt amazing. It usually was Lucy that talked ninety miles an hour.

For a while there was silence until Lucy finally regained her thoughts. "Um... I don't even know what to say."

"Oh, and I've run into the guy that saved me a few times now. His name is Sebastian and he is totally gorgeous. His eyes are deep blue like the ocean. He's totally mysterious. I also think he knows something about the weird stuff going on around here." Emily sighed. "He's not really a plethora of information though. Well he might be, but he doesn't offer any to me." Emily blew out a big breath glad to have most of it all out in the open. "You believe me right Luce? You don't think I'm crazy or anything right?"

Lucy laughed. "Of course I think you're crazy. I still believe you. I know you wouldn't screw with me when it comes to paranormal stuff. You would never tease me like that. That would be cruel."

"Paranormal stuff?" Emily asked confused by the reference.

"Well yeah, paranormal stuff," Lucy replied. Her tone added in an unspoken but clearly evident, duh. "Think about it. People disappearing and showing up out of nowhere? Eyes outlined with bright ass red? Trance like states…" Lucy ticked down the list, supporting the theory.

"Emily!" Sam's booming voice called from somewhere near the house.

"Ugh," Emily sighed. "Sorry Luce gotta cut this short. Sam's looking for me," she apologized regretfully.

"No problem. Don't worry Em, I'm on the case. I'll do some research on this. Be careful okay?"

"Emily!" Sam's voice was getting much louder and more insistent.

"Crap! He's yelling again. K Luce I'll be careful. Gotta go, bye." Emily quickly hung up the phone and hopped off the washer. "Coming dad!" Emily yelled, hopefully keeping him from releasing the search dogs. It would make things so much easier if their house had a garage that was attached to the house.

By the time she returned inside the house, Sam had retaken his usual position on the couch in front of the television. Their eyes met, and then his returned to the game that was on. Well alright then, he apparently was just checking to see that she hadn't run off and joined the circus or something. Whatever.

Later on that night after her blissful shower, Emily lay wide awake in bed. She couldn't help but think about her father's gift. She clutched the cross that hung just below her collar bone while she thought about the day, and what a weird day it was. Sam's gift was a gesture that she would have never expected in a million years. Even when he wasn't being impossible, he could never be considered the sentimental type. No matter what his motives were, the thought was totally sweet.

Before she knew it, her mind drifted yet again to Sebastian. His drop dead gorgeous face kept sneaking passed herself made wall like it was nothing. She didn't want to think about him. He kind of seemed like a jerk. Plus, for whatever reason her dad seemed quite adamant about his distaste for him. In Sebastian's defense, who knew if she could take what her father said seriously. He was kind of crazy most days and it might just be that he was afraid of his little girl getting deflowered. Whether he liked her or not, that is every dad's nightmare.

The flower metaphor never really made sense to her. It was a known freaking fact with evidence and everything that there were no flowers in the female anatomy. Why can't people just call things what they were? She wasn't condoning vulgarity by any means. It was just incomprehensible why people couldn't use technical terms at least.

She couldn't believe Sam with his not wanting her to go out after dark business. What was that? Does he think girls only date at night? Things aren't how they used to be. Even if they were, she wasn't dating anyone anyway. It had never been a priority. Sure she has thought guys were cute, hot even. Regardless, the superficial didn't matter much in the big scheme of things. Soon she would be leaving, so attachments would have to be severed anyway. She didn't plan on coming back once she got out of Lakeview's wretched clutches.

It wasn't like she had a model example to follow. Her parents had been sublimely happy. In the end it didn't matter, look at what her mother's death had done to Sam. Going through something like that would be unbearably horrendous to say the least. And she would never bring kids into this world for fear their *daddy* might someday turn out to be like hers. She loved Sam but she refused to marry a carbon copy. If it ever came to that, becoming a Nun would be a much more viable choice.

As her hands massaged the braids on the cross a light clicked on in her brain like a camera's flashbulb. Pieces of the terrifying puzzle seemed to be falling into place right before her eyes. Her mind became a dizzying blur of thoughts that were almost indecipherable. Her dad bought her a *silver* cross. He didn't want her to go out at night because there were things out there she apparently wouldn't understand. Sebastian knew way too much and it seemed impossible.

She didn't really know exactly how that fit in, but somehow she just knew it did. The man that tried talking to her on the sidewalk under the street light had that red glow thing going on... OH MY GOSH! Her mind suddenly exploded.

In the *dream*, that Alexander guy who had told her that there was danger when *ruby bordered emeralds*. That man's eyes were *green* and when he got angry, she swore that the *red* in them was real. There was no way it was just a weird reflection of the light. Sebastian's eyes were blue and so were Alexander's. She thought that meant something too but what? Sebastian could somehow disappear or at least run really fast. He avoided talking with her and was vague and mysterious.

Emily's mind spiraled out of control, working fiercely to make some sort of connection, when it hit her with a jolt. Holy Hell! Was her dad trying to tell her there really is such thing as...? No that can't be possible, it goes against everything she believed in. Emily couldn't bring herself to even think the word. It was just crazy. The people in town must be right about her father. They all think he's crazy. Melissa's death knocked him off his rocker, that was the way most of them put it.

He couldn't have been trying to say... There was just no way something like *that* could really be out there. Could it? It would sort of explain what had happened on the bus. The fear that radiated from those people was tangible, absolutely not her imagination. The couple that was weirdly too perfect and scarily intimidating, was highly unusual. The pallor of their skin looked, as though they had never seen a single day of sunlight. Their movements were so controlled and precise, as if they had been planned out. They were definitely attractive, but there was something very *off* about the couple.

As her mind raced on, she avoided the possible conclusion she had already come up with. There must be a better explanation than that, but nothing gelled. No idea became solid and nothing else made sense. Just as her mind was utterly defeated, it froze on the original theory. Her dad hadn't been warning her about *sex*. He hadn't even been talking about rapist or serial killers. He was trying to tell her that she... Emily Marie Jameson, was living amongst vampires.

10

The next day at Blake's was fairly uneventful, weekends usually were though. Emily wished Lucy was there. At least it would help pass the time. They could play cards or something. Lucy had these awesome playing cards that had Braille labels on them, but print for sighted people. Creepy Lucy had always wanted Braille Tarot cards. Emily didn't think they even made such things but if so, stranger things had happened. Thinking of her friend made her smile. She really didn't understand how someone as wonderful as Lucy could come from someone as terrible as George.

The perpetually cranky owner of Blake's Books wasn't always nasty, just most of the time as far as Emily could tell anyway. The only time there was an exception was when he was talking to Lucy or customers, of course. She didn't think you could really count customers though, since most of the time he was trying to scam them for higher prices. Maybe something happened to him that made him so cranky. She guessed it was possible that maybe he didn't get hugged enough when he was a kid or something. Emily used to think that she could crack his hard shell and get to the soft caramel inside, but so far she hasn't had much luck. Anytime George even suspected she was getting too personal, he conjured up some reason to scold her.

Emily was starting to feel completely drained by boredom. She had already vacuumed, dusted, straightened up shelves and cleaned the windows. She reached down under the counter and grabbed a paperback she had in there in case she decided to ride the bus. After the last excursion however, that wouldn't be happening any time soon. She really wasn't supposed to read while on the clock but in her opinion it was just good advertising. It was a book store for crap's sake. It wasn't like she would ignore the customers or make them wait until she finished a chapter before she rang them up. George really needed to lighten up.

Emily really enjoyed authors that always gave a happy ending, or at least left the reader feeling good about the book. She really wasn't a Harlequin Romance kind of girl, though she did like love stories. Crime novels weren't too bad, as long as it was solved and not a cold case. Unsolved mysteries creeped her out because they make her imagination run wild and that can sometimes be worse than reality. They imply that crimes happen and the bad guys don't get caught. Although that was probably true, that didn't mean she had to read about it. Currently, Emily was reading a book by Nicholas Sparks. His books are so easy to get lost in, for hours at a time without even noticing.

She was just starting to dig into a chapter, when the bell clanged against the door letting her know a customer was coming in. She quickly finished the paragraph she was on and tossed the book on the counter.

"Don't stop reading on my account." A liquid voice spoke from behind the shelves. The store had row after row of book shelves that stood about six foot high.

Emily craned her neck around but couldn't see where the voice came from. They had to be behind one of the shelves.   It almost sounded like Sebastian. He said he never came in Blake's though. "That's okay… I don't mind," Emily replied hesitantly.

Then, he was there. Standing at the end of the book case to her left was Sebastian. It should seriously be illegal to look that good. He wore blue jeans with a skin tight black T-shirt. His hair was short and spiked but preppy not punk. Light reflected off his watch and what little she could see of a silver chain that hung around his neck.

"Oh, I'm just browsing." He stared at her for a long appraising second.

Her face flushed at his words. Before speaking she cleared her throat nervously. "Well, if you change your mind let me know." What an idiot she thought. There was no one else in the store. There would probably not be a better chance to talk to Sebastian and pick his brain. She was seriously blowing it. As she gave him an equally appraising look, she couldn't see how something that looked so angelic could be as evil as a vampire. There was just no way blood had ever tainted the beauty of those lips.

Sebastian came back around the corner then with a paper back in his hand. He held it up by his chest, cover facing out, but she couldn't look away from his eyes. Her heart was pounding in her chest. If he really was a vampire he could very easily kill her without anyone ever knowing. Vampires probably have ways of making a victim disappear. She squelched the thought as soon as it took form. That was just silly. There was no such thing as vampires and her dad was just crazy, which was no surprise whatsoever.

She let her eyes fall to the book Sebastian was holding. In the hands of the big muscled model slash possible vampire, was a novel by Danielle Steel. She couldn't help the escape of hysterical giggle at the irony of the situation. She tried to stop but she couldn't help herself. Crap, she was being rude she thought. He might really like romance stories. It was wrong of her to pigeon hole him like that. She clamped her lips together halting the laughter. Well, at least sort of.

"Can I help you find something?" Emily asked mechanically. She was supposed to say that after all. Granted, he had clearly already found something, but that was beside the point.

"Do you have this in a hard back?"

His voice was so serious Emily almost burst out laughing again. "Well, if it's not by the paperback copy then we must be out." As Emily spoke she had to choke back another escaping giggle.

Sebastian raised his eyebrows at her. "What's so funny? You don't like romance?" He gave her a look that pretended to be offended.

Despite her wariness of him, the innocence of the look made her dizzy. "No, romance is good. You just don't strike me as the fairytale romance kinda guy, that's all." Emily said trying to back track.

This time she got only a single raised brow. "Oh? What type am I then?" He asked expectantly.

Emily blushed. "Oh, I just meant…"She felt like a total idiot.

He waved away her explanation. Her blundering seemed to amuse him. "The world would be a lot more peaceful if they used romance novels for a guide book ya know. Besides, didn't you hear? All the fairy tales are true."

Emily noticed that while he spoke his eye lashes fluttered like a butterfly's wings. Stop it, she scolded herself. If her theory was true, the guy could seriously jump over the counter at any moment and suck the lifeblood right out of her. Even so, she couldn't help but notice the overwhelming sense of calm that flowed over her entire body as he watched her. It was like she had known him her whole life. He didn't seem like a monster. And Emily wasn't one of those girls who flocked to the bad boy type. She was the annoying girl no one wanted to watch movies with, she was constantly yelling for the stupid girl to run. She knew herself, or at least she thought she did. She was normally a very good judge of character. Sebastian just didn't seem like the Dracula type.

"Are you still there?" Sebastian asked as he waved a hand in front of Emily's face, trying to get her attention.

"Oh. Sorry I guess I spaced. What did you say?" Emily's face grew hot with embarrassment, *again*.

"I guess I shouldn't have said anything then." Sebastian said, averting his eyes from hers.

"Why?" Emily asked curiously. What was that supposed to mean?

"Well…" Sebastian let out a long sigh. "I was admitting that while I'm not opposed to this author, it's not really what I came here for." Sebastian's head bowed hiding his expression.

"So, why did you come then? Were you really looking for a hunting magazine or something?" Emily asked sarcastically. It was a weak attempt at regaining some cool points. "If so you should know George doesn't carry magazines in here. He thinks they're junk."

Sebastian chuckled. "Nope nothing like that ironically." His laughter seemed to be at an inside joke that apparently she wasn't privy to.

Emily gave him a questioning look. He said nothing in response. The only sign he even saw the gesture was that his laughter stopped short. He cleared his throat awkwardly and turned mildly sheepish.

After a long pause he finally said, "Sorry, I guess you had to be there."

"Maybe you'll fill me in some day."

Sebastian's face grew immediately serious. "Something's are better left unsaid. You know, secrets of the trade and all that?" He turned around and walked back to the other side of the shelves again, leaving Emily clueless.

What was that? Emily could respect a good inside joke as much as the next person. Usually there's at least a hint of humor behind the words even to the unaware, letting them know a joke is in progress. When there's not, it can leave you feeling like you've missed something. In Sebastian's case, he just sounded obtuse and sarcastic. And what did the information might be necessary mean? She wished he would just talk straight with her. He didn't have to make cryptic remarks all the time.

Just then, he came back around this time with empty hands and a controlled smile. "Sorry about that. I figured I better put the book back, since I'm not going to be purchasing it today." He stood in front of the counter now. His hands rested on it casually and he was watching her again.

Emily had never been around someone before that was so… silent. Lucy was her best friend and all, but she never shut up most of the time. There was George, except he was only silent with her. He always chatted up the customers. Sam was always blathering on and on about something or another too.

What was he doing? Those blue eyes of his seemed to be scorching her under their powerful stare. Did he know what he was doing? It was like he was a car enthusiast sizing up a new purchase. Or, a hunter with his prey… *Stop it*, she scolded herself again. He wasn't a monster. There was no such thing as monsters, not the kind Sam had implied anyway. There was just no possible way her father was right. He was rarely right about anything so why should this time be any different?

"So… anything else? You never said what you came for." She asked sheepishly under his gaze.

Sebastian seemed to be thinking about his answer for a long while. "I came to see you of course.

Emily's breath stopped and her heart began to pound rapidly. He came here to see her? Why? She wasn't saying she wasn't an attractive girl. She just wasn't anywhere near his league.

As if he could read her mind and knew she was battling with herself doubt, his eyebrows rose ever so slightly. That was crazy though, it wasn't possible for someone to hear another person's thoughts. His eyes held a very well-defined question mark in them.

Emily knew she should say something, anything. No matter how hard she tried, she couldn't get her mouth to work properly.

"I… can leave though if you are too busy to talk…" He sounded unsure. There was a hint of hurt in his eyes that he masked quickly.

Standing from her stool abruptly she blurted, "oh no!" Emily cleared her throat embarrassed by her eagerness. "I mean… you don't have to go anywhere. Stay," she continued frantically and then immediately regretted her enthusiasm.

He didn't seem to mind though. Instead, it seemed to be the exact opposite. In fact, his answering smile lit up his whole face and in turn the entire room, making her a little breathless. Dizziness began to overtake her again. The butterfly's that had been in her stomach before, took a vacation making room for the giant birds that now flew in there. She was also very aware that if she didn't get a handle on her heart rate, it would be a good thing he was there. He would have the pleasure of calling the ambulance.

After she collected herself, Emily slid a stool around the counter to him so he could get more comfortable. He started to protest, but she did it anyway and he eventually sat. Time went by in a blur. They talked for the remainder of her shift. They talked about everything; books, movies, family, Lucy, school and God knew what else. Emily couldn't believe it, but before she knew it, it was closing time. No one else had come in the shop, thank goodness.

The only problem was, she couldn't seem to gather enough courage to ask him more about the night in the alley. She could mostly remember it all now. There were some blank spots but from what she could tell, that was fine by her. That night would be starring in her nightmares for the rest of her life.

After Emily locked up, they walked together down the block. She wondered if he would walk her home again. Before she could ask they were halted by a person storming out of one of the buildings. He seemed to come from one of the stairwells that led to the apartments above the shops. When he saw that they were in his path he stopped on a dime. Good thing he did, because he was moving as fast as a bowling ball. Unfortunately, that would have made Emily and Sebastian the pins in that equation. Ouch!

"Sorry," the bowling ball said panting slightly. "I'm just in a hurry."

"Hey! You're that guy that came in the book store the other day." Emily said as recognition dawned. He didn't respond so she continued. "You know, you bought that book that didn't have a tag… I'm the one that rang you up." Her eyes widened as if to say, *duh am I that forgettable jerk?*

His expression morphed into one of understanding. "Oh yeah, that's right. Sorry I guess I forgot." He offered an apologetic smile that made his eyes crinkle.

"My name's Emily, and this is Sebastian." She gestured between the two of them. She had never really known the protocol for extending a hand or not. She decided against it.

Sebastian gave him no greeting except a manly nod. Emily wasn't sure, but it looked as though Sebastian wasn't pleased to have the interruption. He actually kind of looked like he wanted to bolt. Part of her wondered if maybe he had a jealous streak. The smarter more rational part knew that was stupid. He would have no reason or claim to be jealous and she really needed to stop jumping to conclusions.

"Yeah, I'm Tyler. Tyler Simms."

Emily searched her memory banks, but couldn't call up any recollection of that name. "Are you new to Lakeview? I've never seen you around here." Of course she had seen him at Blake's, though she didn't think that counted.

Tyler nodded as he scuffed a foot impatiently on the sidewalk. "Yeah I've been here a few weeks. I live up there," he gestured vaguely to the building he had burst out of. "Well it was nice to meet you, but I gotta go." He gave Emily an awkward smile and a quick nod to Sebastian. Tyler didn't wait for any goodbyes to be exchanged. He just set off behind them back at a sprint.

"He seemed…" Emily's voice trailed off as she struggled with the right word.

"Interesting?" Sebastian supplied helpfully.

"Yeah. Interesting." Emily gave Tyler another second glance. She could just barely make out his shape as he rounded a corner in the distance.

They continued talking the whole rest of the way to her house. She did manage to say goodbye to him before he could vanish this time though, so that was a plus. Emily only allowed him to walk her to the corner. It was possible that Sam could be home from the bar already. If he saw her with Sebastian there would be Hell to pay. She wished she didn't have to say goodbye. She badly wanted to keep talking to him. It was like they had been friends forever. Actually, it was almost like talking to Lucy, only better because he was hot. There was an undeniable connection between the two of them. If only she knew why that was, things would make so much more sense.

Of course, she never got the answers that she wanted. In his defense, she hadn't really worked that hard to get them. Something told her deep in her gut that Sebastian wasn't hiding things for the wrong reasons. There was some kind of method to his madness. Emily got the weird feeling he was trying to protect her.

She had asked him if she would see him again. All he said was that *time would tell, but it probably wasn't for the best*. What on Earth did that mean? She toyed with a million different ideas in theories in her head for a long time. Unfortunately, nothing made more sense than the V word she couldn't even bring herself to say. Just about anything could have been possible. In this case, they all just seemed crazy.

Emily wished she could talk to someone about it. All of the thoughts had built up so much pressure in her head that she felt like a shaken up soda bottle. The only person that would be willing to take her seriously was Lucy but Emily in no way wanted to get that ball rolling. Once her perky pixy like friend got a hold of the information, she would never let it go. Honestly, Lucy was kind of OCD when it came to that kind of stuff. Emily didn't want to be under Lucy's very relentless microscope even if that meant she could have helped Emily sort this out. Also, there wasn't any point in freaking her out. She would just have to go at it alone. Just before Emily walked the rest of the way to her house by herself, Sebastian called out to her.

"Yeah?" She spun back around much too quickly. Man, she must really seem like an over eager little puppy. If she had a tale, it would probably be wagging profusely.

A sort of knowing grin slowly spread across his face. It quickly returned back to serious. "Try not to go out after dark anymore." He stared at her intently. "Especially not alone." Sebastian's eyes flickered slightly as if he were trying to hide something. Not giving any chance for rebuttal he continued. "You take care of yourself and keep your head on straight ok?"

Emily wanted to extend the communication further, to try and get some explanation out of Sebastian. Unfortunately with him, further explanation wasn't the way he worked, no matter how much she wished it to be true. She didn't bother and instead just nodded and walked the rest of the way home.

11

The next morning Emily got up early so she could get the rest of the laundry done. Thanks to her conversation with Lucy, the chore was right in her face screaming at her to get it done. With the washer and dryer located in the garage, it was easy to forget things needed washing until you were out of socks. The pile was getting as high as Everest. That wasn't the top thing on Emily's priority list though. She was bound and determined to try and make heads or tails of her suspicions one way or another. Of course, the prospect of that task wasn't that appealing. Not only were all her theories freakishly absurd, but it was also like finding a needle in a hay stack.

The best solution was to go to the library. Their computer was on the fritz and she didn't want Sam to be able to look at her browsing history anyway. Not that Sam knew much about computers or anything, but it just wasn't worth the risk. She was going to do some research, or at least try and do some research. How does someone look up information about vampires for crap's sake? There would more than likely be a lot of fluff out there. The problem was finding something accurate, that wasn't all propaganda. Maybe there were news stories similar to what had been going on in Lakeview. That would at least if nothing else, tell if anything could be done.

If there was anything that could be done, Emily mused. She pushed that pessimistic thought from her mind as quick as it had entered. That way of thinking would not bring results. Optimism was crucial, even if she didn't believe a word of it. Real life vampires roaming the Earth might have seemed farfetched to Emily, but at this point nothing was off limits. It was clear something was going on. A simple search online at least allowed her to eliminate the halfcocked theory from the list of possibilities.

After she got a couple loads done, she decided that was good enough. At least a small dent had been put into the dirty clothes pile. It may have not been the responsible choice to leave, but she couldn't wait anymore. Anxiousness made her body move like a live wire. She couldn't concentrate on anything while thinking about going to the library. When she looked down at herself she realized that she was still in sweat pants and tank top. Not figuring leaving the house in her pajamas was the best option, she hopped in the shower.

She had gotten dressed fast after bathing and was out the door in no time at all. It was warm outside. Emily had decided to wear jean Capri's with fraying around the bottoms. They were super comfy. Her stark white V-neck tank was one of her favorites. There was a little lace on the neck of the shirt and at the bottom. It wasn't as Emily would call it, skank wear though. No skin was revealed that she didn't want shown. There were three small Hawaiian flowers across the chest in blue. Emily had never been to Hawaii but it was the number one thing on her "Things to do before I die list".

The walk to the library didn't take long. Even though the sun was obscured by big fluffy white clouds, it still took a second for her eyes to adjust to the indoors. As she walked into the poorly lit computer lab she looked around for a free station. She hoped she could find a cubicle that was discrete so no one could read over her shoulder and find out how crazy she had become. Word traveled fast and the last thing she needed was another lecture about what a disappointment she was.

Luckily there was a semiprivate workstation in the back corner. No one worked at the seat next to it, so it was completely perfect. Fearing someone could sense what Emily was there to research, her face grew hotter and hotter the closer she got to the computer. There weren't a lot of people working in the lab but most of them seem to be college age. Maybe they're starting their first round of term papers. She had wanted to take classes summer quarter but she needed the extra shift at work much more.

Sam made good money, but his bank statement would never reflect that fact. Most of the family fortune was drunk away every evening at Moody's Tavern and all day on the weekends. Other than that she had no idea what he spent his money on because it sure wasn't on anything practical. Melissa would be utterly disgusted by the lack of the family funds.

Emily's mom was a penny pincher from way back. Her main pleasure in life had been finding a good bargain to save another dollar. When she went to garage sales she was the type who could talk the seller down from a quarter price sticker to a dime. Melissa definitely had charm and she wasn't afraid to use it. She also knew how to work someone. If she didn't think she'd get the reduced price she was after, she would wait until the last day of the sale to return. By then the seller just wanted to get rid of the junk cluttering their driveway and was willing to give it away. If they weren't, she'd pretend like she wasn't interested either and start to walk away. She had such a presence about her that before she got to her car the seller would be on her heels accepting her low ball offer.

Melissa used to tell her young daughter that the number on the price tag was just a starting point for negotiations. If a seller isn't willing to drop it down they must not really want to get rid of the item. Emily used to marvel at watching her mom work her gifted craft. Even as a little girl Emily was amazed and entranced by watching her mother work. Depending on the type of seller she would bat an eye lash here or toss her hair there. If the seller were an elderly woman her strategy totally changed playing of the woman's compassionate side and practicality. They seemed just as mesmerized by her mom as Emily was and who could blame them. Melissa was flawless.

When Emily sat down at the cubicle the PC was already on, so all she had to do was click on the internet browser. She sat back in her wobbly chair and waited. The lab was connected to high speed, but when too many people were on the server, it was slow to load up. She didn't mind, it gave her time to think of where to start.

If Emily were totally honest with herself, she would have to admit that she had absolutely no idea what she was looking for. If anyone had caught sight of what she was doing, they would probably have her committed. Part of her was beginning to think that were a good idea.

When the Google homepage came to life on the screen Emily leaned forward with her hands ready on the keys. Her posture was rigid. Now what? Well, she might as well start simple, Emily supposed. With a deep regretful sigh her fingers began typing the word Vampire into the search engine.

Her eyes widened in disbelief. Seriously, like a zillion results popped up on the screen. There was everything from myths, books, movies, legends, and clothing. The list went on and on for what seemed like a million pages. She had no idea this was such a popular topic.

There was definitely going to have to be some narrowing done. Without really knowing what to look for, the task was going to be cumbersome. Emily couldn't wrap her head around all the books out there on the subject. The majority appeared to be fiction, but she had never heard of most of the authors, let alone the titles. Working at a book store, she had countless titles at her disposal, she should know about them shouldn't she?

Maybe George didn't care for the topic and that's why he didn't carry them. However, she didn't think he cared much for ghost stories either, and he had all of those on the shelves. She decided to make a mental note to ask him about it. Emily could hardly believe that George would pass up a chance to tap into a new Genre that might bring the shop more revenue.

As corny as it seemed, she decided to type in real vampires. That had to bring up something. Maybe the screen would go black and big letters would scroll across in red telling her she was nuts. That really wouldn't have been that surprising.

Well, it did narrow the amount of results that were found to only like a million. Scrolling through all the results she was astonished at what she saw. Most the headlines were about old world myths from other countries. There were even some blogs done by people who claimed to be real vampires. Emily couldn't help but laugh a little at that.

One headline stood out from the others as she scanned. It read "Today's Urban Vampires Truths, Myths and Protective Measures". The description underneath briefly informed that today's vampires were a force to be reckoned with. It said that the new breed held old ways as well as new at their disposal. The part that really got Emily was "Check out this site for recent news stories that will chill your bones. Emily was just getting ready to click on it when she was interrupted.

A firm hand came down on her shoulder. Emily jumped in surprise. She whirled around in her seat to see a towering male standing in front of her. He was dressed all in black. Upon further examination, she realized who he was. It was the scary man from the bus; the one that was with that icy woman. They were the ones that herded those people into that big house. Instantly Emily saw that she had been right, His eyes *were* the same emerald green as that Luke guy.

He hadn't done anything overtly threatening, but malevolence rolled off him. Emily couldn't speak. She couldn't even move despite the fact that her instincts were screaming at her. The pain in her midsection was agonizing. It was almost impossible not to yell. Emily bit the inside of her cheek against the pain. She had to stop when she could taste blood in her mouth.

Even though she had turned completely around, the man's hand remained on her shoulder. He seemed to be holding her in place. She quickly scanned the room. Not a single person seemed to notice anything was happening. Theoretically, nothing *was* happening. Even still, the growing knots in her stomach told her otherwise. Emily knew deep in her gut there was something very wrong with this man.

Don't panic. The unfamiliar voice in her head warned. *Don't move and don't look him in the eye.*

The reassurance that came from the male voice was calming. It helped her to keep a level head. Freaking out would just make this situation worse, and probably please her captor. More than ever, the voice reminded her of someone. Try as she might, she still couldn't place it. It was right there at the edges of her mind just out of reach. Clicking on the note to self tablet in her mind, she mentally jotted down the words *find out what on Earth that voice was.*

Whether it meant she was crazy or sane, it seemed like good advice so she decided to follow it obediently. Weirdly, she still thought it sounded an awful lot like Sebastian. Obviously, that couldn't be the case though. The comparison was more than likely a product of her wild imagination.

The man cleared his throat. "I don't think it's a good idea for you to look at that."

Look at what? She wasn't really looking at anything. Then, with a start she realized he must be talking about her web surfing.

"Um… I just thought it would be a fun topic to look up." She didn't know why but everything in her gut told her that playing clueless was the way to go. It really wasn't much of a stretch anyway. She was totally clueless.

His eyes widened questioningly as he watched her intently. "Well sometimes little girl the answers you seek aren't always found on the World Wide Web. You children and your… technology, disgust me. I happen to know a lot on the subject though." As he said this, he gave a slight nod to the computer screen that was still loaded with search results. "I may be inclined to share my knowledge for a small… fee."

When he had spoken the word fee he stretched it out with an implied implication that Emily didn't quite understand. Even with the lack of understanding, she was able to pick up on the obvious threat behind his words. Emily gulped. "Oh… Thanks, but this was just for fun. I was just bored is all. I don't really even need to look at the site. Just bored." The words came from Emily's mouth like flowing word vomit. She knew she must sound ridiculous. For all he knew she was just some dumb teenager and that was probably a good thing. Maybe that would allow him to disregard her and move on. Emily suddenly wanted to go home badly. At any moment this whack job could turn her into one of the pod people.

"Have it your way." He gave her a placating smile. "You might find that in the future, it would be wise to be mindful of your research. Too much knowledge can be damning for a person. He lowered his voice to a more secretive tone. "Also, it can become quite dangerous." His face was hard and all business. The tone of his voice was a contradictory melodic that did not match the expression at all.

Emily found her eyes drifting up to his against her will. How could she have ever thought something was wrong with them? Those eyes were beautiful. They seemed to mesmerize Emily, capturing her deep within their depths.

The unfamiliar voice screamed at her to look away and the urgency of it instantly grabbed hold of her attention. In all the times she had heard it, the voice never carried such acid or such volume. It completely broke her concentration on the man standing before her. Emily couldn't help but jump, instantly breaking the stare. "Uh, thanks for the tip. I um, guess I'll be seeing you." She tried to sound strong. Instead, she stuttered uncontrollably.

"Oh yes, you will be seeing me very soon in deed. By the way my lady, you should know I am called Andre." He grabbed Emily's hand and raised it gingerly to his lips.

The action made her stomach contract violently and it churned with nausea. It felt like she would surely flip inside out from the pressure that clamped down on her whole body. His lips weren't cold, yet they definitely weren't warm either. The sensation was like nothing she had ever experienced before. An involuntary shiver came over her with his touch.

Emily quickly, but politely took her hand from Andre's. "Well nice meeting you." Her tone was dismissive she hoped anyway. To further make her point she swiveled back around toward the computer screen.

Without another word she watched the man's departure from the corner of her eye. His steps didn't make a single sound, not a shoe shuffle or noise from the material of his clothes rustling. There was just nothing. As he passed though, she felt a cold breeze follow him. It was like when the wind would pick up after a good snow fell. That type of weather shift wasn't normal in the middle of a computer lab.

Everyone working on a computer still did just that. Their heads never turned to see Andre. There were a few that she could tell upon closer examination, weren't actually working. They simply stared at their screens, most with their hands in their laps clenched into fists. Emily considered asking one of them what they knew of Andre. Figuring she would get the same response as on the bus, Emily kept her mouth shut.

When she turned again towards the computer screen her thoughts weren't on Andre. In all actuality they probably should have been, he was really freaky. Instead, they were on the new unfamiliar voice she had acquired as some sort of conscience. It was a male voice. She knew she had heard it before, and not just in her mind.

She ran through everyone she knew in her head. No one in her life sounded like that. It was stupid anyway. Someone couldn't be talking to her through her mind. Her thoughts stopped on *Sebastian's* face. Could it be?

If he was the "V" word that may very well entitle him to some kind of special power. Except if Andre was one of them as well, why would Sebastian feel compelled to help her? Shouldn't they have some kind of undead solidarity or something? Besides, Sebastian seemed different from Andre and Luke. They had an evil presence that seemed to radiate off of them like a breathing pulse. It pooled around them like a living shadow. Sebastian was mysterious, yes. Was he evil? No, Emily didn't think so.

"Hi Emily. Remember me? Tyler?"

The voice came from behind her making her jump and her breath catch in her throat. God, hadn't she had enough scares for one day? She spun around to face him. Even though she knew who he was, the sight of Tyler didn't calm her nerves.

"Wow, are you okay? You look like you've seen a ghost or something." Tyler sounded worried.

Emily was vaguely aware of the color that had drained from her face. The encounter with Andre had left her feeling numb and very cold. Was it just a coincidence that Tyler would come strolling along right after him? "What are you doing here?" She shot back at him with a little too much acid.

He held his hands up in surrender. "Easy there, I didn't mean to bug you or anything. Sorry."

He began to back up in retreat, when a wave of guilt passed through Emily. "No wait. I'm sorry." Emily held out a hand to him. "You just startled me, that's all. You don't have to go. It's just been one of those days you know?" Emily motioned for him to take the empty chair beside her.

He hesitantly took the chair watching her the whole time. He looked as though he thought Emily might bite him or something. "When I came in it looked like you might need help with something," said Tyler.

"I'm fine," Emily replied. She gestured vaguely at nothing in particular.

Emily let him help you. I summoned him to you. It was the peculiar voice in her head again. It had never been that directly personal before.

Despite the fact that the voice was trying to help her, she wanted to scream. Some part of her knew she wasn't insane and should trust the voice. The other part wanted to reserve her very own room in the psych ward. Emily noted that the more she thought about it, the voice did sound like Sebastian… if that was even possible. Finding him had to be a priority. He was going to answer her questions one way or another. If his was the voice she was hearing, she deserved an explanation as to why he was invading her thoughts. Not to mention he needed to explain how the heck that was even possible.

"Hello? Earth to Emily. You still here?" She realized Tyler had been waving a hand in front of her face trying to get her attention. "You sure space out a lot don't you?" The hesitation was gone from Tyler completely.

"Sorry I just have a lot on my mind," she apologized. Then, her mind sparked with an idea. "Hey Tyler!" She realized she sounded frantic and toned it down a few notches. "Sorry. Did you see the guy I was talking to a minute ago?" Emily stared at him hopefully, praying he could confirm her suspicions.

"What guy? When I came in you were alone." Tyler looked utterly perplexed. He looked around the room as though he could have gotten a glimpse of the mystery man Emily spoke of.

Not wanting to let go of the thread, Emily pressed on. "What about on your way in? Did you see a guy all in black with crazy intense green eyes?" If Tyler saw Andre then maybe he would have some opinion. He totally didn't look like one of the pod people, Stepford Wife combinations. Surely he had to have seen him. Emily bounced her leg impatiently waiting.

Tyler seemed to give the question some real thought. "Nope, I'm a guy." He pointed at his chest and sounded obnoxiously sarcastic. "I try to only pay attention to crazy eye intensity in a hot girl." He gave her a sarcastic smile and winked.

Emily ignored the implication completely and sighed. "Oh well never mind." Emily felt utterly morose. Just when she thought she had someone to talk to about everything too. "Sorry," she apologized again. "Like I said, just a lot on my mind."

"I could see that," he answered dryly. "I think I'm supposed to help you with that."

12

"Huh?" What did that mean? He's supposed to help her with what, her internet search? Emily was incredibly confused. How could someone she didn't even know help her? Maybe he knew something about what was going on in Lakeview. That didn't seem very likely though. Tyler had just moved to town. How could he possibly know what was going on?

Tyler leaned in closer to her before continuing. "I can't explain it. It's just this feeling I get every time I'm around you. I know it's crazy but you've gotta believe me." He spoke in a hushed whisper.

Emily wasn't sure why, but she did. It was true that she really didn't know him. At the same time, that didn't seem to make a difference. For one, with all the weird things happening lately, she couldn't turn a cheek at this even if she wanted to. It sounded normal compared to the other stuff that had been happening. Second, she felt safe with him. It was kind of like the feeling she got when she was with Sebastian. "I believe you," Emily said firmly.

"Really?" Tyler sounded shocked. He leaned back in his chair stunned. "I thought you would think I was nuts, or trying to feed you a line or something." His astonishment was softened with relief.

His expression was kind of cute. "If it was a line, it wouldn't have been a very good one," Emily admitted with a smile.

She allowed herself to look at him more closely. He was quite attractive. Emily had noticed that the first day she saw him in Blake's. Now she could also see that he had high cheek bones and dimples. His eyes even crinkled a little whenever he smiled. They were blue, a very pretty blue. They were the blue of the sky on a cloudless sunny day. They weren't as deep and gorgeous as Sebastian's, but pretty.

Tyler's face grew thoughtful. He cocked his head to the side for a second then shot her an incredulous look. "I think I'm supposed to walk you home." He looked startled by this revelation.

Let him walk you home, it will be safer. The voice she thought might be Sebastian's rang through her head again.

Instead of condemning herself to crazy town for the fact she was hearing voices, she let herself accept it. If nothing else, at least it was giving her sound advice. She wondered if Tyler heard it too. It would surely explain the odd turn this conversation had taken.

"Okay," Emily was unsure, though it would make her feel better to not have to walk home alone. Lord knew where Andre was and she didn't want to find out while she was by herself. Honestly, she didn't want to find out while with Tyler either. At least this way, she wouldn't be alone. She clicked off the web browser and hoisted up her back pack to leave.

It was a pretty long walk home. They had to cross the center of town and then through the residential streets to get to where she lived. Tyler and Emily walked a lot of it in silence. Emily's eyes kept darting around looking for a lurking Andre. Every noise went through her like a gun shot.

The temperature outside had cooled down considerably. A breeze blew around them ruffling the leaves in the trees. Emily wished she had thought to put a hoodie in her backpack.

Without warning she opened her big crazy mouth breaking the silence. Emily began to verbally vomit everything that had happened and she couldn't stop it. Apparently that was becoming a habit. She was going to have to invest herself into making a real effort to use a filter when explaining things. For now it was kind of pointless. She told him about the night in the alley. She didn't leave anything out about Sebastian, Luke, or the bus. The bus flowed into telling him about Andre in the computer lab. Emily even took a chance and told him about her and Lucy's theories of what they were. She never gave Tyler an opportunity to answer. Afraid to even take a breath, she hurried through every sorted detail.

When she finally stopped talking she waited for him to say anything that would indicate that he didn't think she was delusional. Hopefully he wouldn't dismiss the information and just tell her how crazy she already felt. For a while, Tyler didn't say a word. Emily snuck a look at him out of the corner of her eye. It didn't look like he wanted to laugh or anything. He just looked thoughtful, like he was trying to absorb everything that had just poured into his head. Just when Emily started to really worry, Tyler broke into the awkward silence.

"I think I know why I feel like I'm supposed to help you now." Tyler sounded hesitant but calm. There was no trace of mockery or sarcasm in his words.

"Really? Why?" That was all Emily could muster.

He slowed his pace and then stopped altogether to turn toward her. "I came to Lakeview because of one of those feelings. It was sort of like the one I got telling me to help you. I was going through a lot where I lived in Ridgeway and didn't know how to deal with it. Something told me to come here. The thing is, I don't know anyone here and really, had never heard of this town. I think it has something to do with the vampires. " Tyler's voice broke off with an involuntary shudder. "Do you remember the first time I met you in the book store?" He didn't even give Emily a chance to answer before he continued. As he spoke his fingers flexed and unflexed making the tension he felt visible. "I wasn't really looking for a book for my mom. I don't even know who my mother is. Well, not personally anyway. Something told me to go there and where to find that book." He stopped talking and just watched her for a moment.

Emily thought about that. She remembered the title of the book he bought, Supernatural *Hunter*. She shuddered convulsively. If what he was saying were true, that would make sense as to why she had never seen it there before. If some force wanted Tyler to have the book and just brought it and him to a logical place so it could be retrieved… Well never mind, maybe it didn't make perfect sense after all. She just couldn't wrap her head around the idea that some mystical force brought Tyler to Lakeview to aid against the vampires. It just seemed way too *Twilight Zone*.

What did all of it mean? She had to admit, it was a profound relief to release the nonsense that had been cluttering up her mind lately. That Tyler hadn't rejected her afterward was a huge bonus. The new burden of Tyler's information was more than a little overwhelming. It was sort of like getting rid of one problem just to have it replaced by another. His was worse than hers because it was more than just random theories being thrown out into the wind.

Maybe he had thrown his out too, and it was looking like… they stuck.

Tyler took Emily's hand and gave it a gentle squeeze. "I'm gonna need you to trust me. I want to tell you my story but I have to know you trust me first." His blue eyes pleaded with her to understand.

Emily gave him an answering smile of reassurance. "I trust you. I just told you all I knew. So now it's your turn right?"

Tyler took a deep breath in preparation and gripped her hand." I know this all is gonna seem crazy to you. Just let me get it all out before you judge alright?"

Emily gulped. "Can't be much crazier than I've already experienced right? Just spit it out Tyler."

Without any further hesitation Tyler jumped into his tale. "Vampires are real. I know they are. I knew they were before I ever saw one in real life." Tyler swallowed hard. "Well, I guess I've never technically seen one, at least not up close. It's just a feeling I guess." He shrugged a shoulder noncommittally, as though what he was saying was no big deal. "So it's like this, I've lived a totally normal life up until now. I never had my… feelings until the other changes started. When I heard about a crime on the news, I could tell if it was a vampire cover-up or something done by a human. I can't explain it. It just happened one day. The news was talking about a girl's dead body found in a park. Without any hesitation I thought to myself… vampire. I started noticing that my body was beefing up with muscles that had never been there before and I didn't earn by working out either. I started dreaming of fighting strategies, ways to take down the blood suckers. I haven't had any formal training except for the tutelage in my dreams. When I would wake up, I could do the moves I was taught in my sleep. I could run faster, walk quieter and jump seriously crazy heights like they were nothing."

"Are you saying you're psychic?" Emily interrupted.

"I don't know. I just get these weird feelings about things."

Emily was still confused. "How can your dreams teach you to fight?" As she said it she thought of her own dream with Alexander. She still didn't know if that had been real, or was just a figment of her imagination. If it was real, maybe it somehow related to what Tyler was talking about.

"If I knew, I would be telling you. Just let me get this all out before you interrupt again." Tyler gave her hand another squeeze before letting it go.

"Okay I'm sorry, you're right." Emily still needed answers, but locked her lips anyway and waited for him to continue.

He took another deep breath and started in again. "This one day before I left Ridgeway, I found a cat that some neighborhood kids had trapped under an exposed tree root." Tyler's eyes narrowed with the memory. "It was ridiculous. I didn't have anything to tear away the root and the cat was yowling, trying to get loose. All I could think was how helpful a knife would be. Then just like that, I felt a wave of energy and when I looked down at my hand, there was a knife in it." He held up his hand and looked down at it like the knife was still there. "I had never seen it before, but it was sharp... deadly sharp. It was the perfect tool for freeing the cat. I put my hand on the cats head willing it to chill out. The cat didn't budge while I quickly cut him free." Tyler dropped his hand to his side and looked up at Emily. "I know saving a cat doesn't have much to do with vampires, but that's when I discovered I could ask for something in my mind and somehow make it happen. When I got the feeling to come here to Lakeview I knew deep in my core that it was because there were vampires here.

Emily's mouth dropped open. "Wait... just wait. Are you screwing with me? There's no frickin way you can just make a knife appear out of thin air." Her mind was whirling with the possibilities.

"Hey, you said you wouldn't interrupt again." Tyler replied only slightly exasperated. "I know it doesn't sound logical or reasonable. It's true though, I swear." He put a hand on her shoulder. "I'm still not done though, so let me get this all out."

For an answer and apology, Emily said nothing. She just stood there expectantly waiting for the rest. What Tyler had said sounded totally farfetched and not scientifically possible, but she had made a promise. Emily did her best to shut down the analytical part of her mind.

"So... I also find that in the dark my vision sharpens, like I have night vision goggles or something.

Emily wanted badly to ask if maybe he had just said abracadabra and night vision goggles appeared and maybe he had just forgotten about it. That probably wasn't the best thing right then so she kept her sarcasm to herself. She didn't want to be rude and say what she was thinking. It was just that it sounded almost more unbelievable than what she had been through. She mentally chided herself for getting distracted and continued listening.

"In that book I got from your store, I learned ways that passed hunters have killed off the leeches. It's like a time honored tradition or something. The hunter's presence is just as much of a secret as the vampires. Apparently not all vampires are evil though. Some choose to live a modest life refraining from killing human's while feeding. That's just as dangerous, even though it doesn't seem like it would be. I've been watching the ones you have been talking about, that Andre guy and the one that seems to be his girlfriend, or whatever. I think she is called Lina? I haven't seen them kill, but I have seen them bring humans into their house like you have. The weird thing is, that most of them return back out looking unharmed, just a little dazed. I don't know what they are planning but I'm sure it's not good.

That just didn't make any sense. Tyler's words implied that Andre and Lina were amongst the modest vampires. How could that be true if they were also up to something really bad? Emily pondered different ideas, weighing them out in her mind. There was some connection that she wasn't able to put together. It was just out of reach and driving her crazy.

Tyler went on. "Since moving here, I'm more sure that I am destined to be one of these hunters. I wonder if my parents had this ability. They died when I was only two so I don't remember anything about them. My adoptive parents didn't know much either." Tyler's eyes drifted back to Emily and he seemed startled. It was almost as if he had forgotten she was even there with him.

Emily didn't know what to say. It would seem that all of her horrifying suspicions were now confirmed. In one conversation Tyler had turned her entire world upside down forever. The question now wasn't if she was crazy, but why this was happening and how it could be stopped. Emily just stood there like an idiot, not knowing what the next logical step should be.

She looked around at the houses that surrounded them. The streets of Lakeview were once a peaceful safe haven. A person in need could knock on any of the doors and ask for help and in turn be given the aid that would make them whole again. On the corner across the street she saw where one of her childhood friends had once lived. Now it was owned by a young couple starting a new home. They had made several renovations to the home refreshing its look to something similar to Emily's memories.

The sun was lowering, becoming hidden in the trees off in the distance. "Um, we should get walking before it gets any darker." Emily was somber as she spoke. Despite that, her growing unease was evident.

She couldn't disguise the feeling of dread at the approaching nightfall. Recent events had proven she hadn't had much luck during that time of day. Now it seemed as though Andre was figuring out that Emily knew something. Why else would he have targeted her in the computer lab? If he hadn't walked behind her, he would have never seen what she was looking up on the internet.

Tyler kept her hand as they walked. It didn't bother her at all though. It actually made her feel safer. She liked that he was the one she shared her information with. Fate must have brought him to her knowing she needed help.

"Tyler?" Emily asked. "I think Sebastian might be one of the good... vampires." It was so hard to even say the word. It caught in her throat and Emily had to force it out.

His hand gripped harder on hers for a second. "Don't worry Emily. He's not, I can assure you of that. I don't get that vibe from him." He was stone serious as he answered her. He appeared to have no doubt in his mind that his words were the truth.

Emily shot him an incredulous look. "Well if he's not a vampire what is he? He seems to have power of some kind. Remember that voice I told you about in my head? I can't explain it, but I am starting to think it's his voice."

Tyler gave her an earnest look. "Got me. I'm new to all this too ya know. I don't have a guide book to the supernatural. I just know it's real and somehow I'm wrapped up in the middle of the knot. It seriously sucks."

"Yeah, sucks isn't even the word for it."

Emily folded her arms around herself, but she wasn't cold. She needed some sense of security. Some sense that she... Emily Marie Jameson was still real. She was really trying to come to grips with the reality of the new normal that was settling over her life.

Before long, they were only a block away from her house. She led him the opposite route that Sam usually took. She dug her cell phone out of her pocket to check the time. Good, Sam wouldn't be home for quite a while. Tyler could walk her all the way to her door unnoticed.

Suddenly the night was even more menacing then she had ever thought it could be and she didn't want to be alone even if for only one block. It felt like there were creatures lurking in the shadows. The darkness seemed to be closing in on them with every step they took. It felt thick and heavy as though there was a heavy pressure building. It pressed on Emily making her lungs feel constricted. She considered hiding Tyler in her closet so she didn't ever have to be alone again. That was obviously crazy though.

Or was it? As they rounded the corner to Elm Street where she lived she wrestled with the idea. She hoped something like that wasn't necessary, but Tyler was the only one she knew of that was in on Lakeview's secret.

They were at the front walk to her door now. "Tyler…" Emily started, but she couldn't seem to bring herself to finish the question. She played with her fingers fidgeting nervously.

"Yeah?" Tyler seemed casual, but not fully present.

He must have been lost back in their earlier conversation too. Emily squared her shoulders, took a deep breath and prepared for looking like a total coward. "I, um, don't want to be alone." Emily said the words under her breath. It took a lot for her to admit vulnerability. Swallowing her pride she spoke again. "Will you come in for a while? You probably shouldn't walk out here alone anyway right?" Her concern was genuine, but definitely more self-serving than anything else. She hoped he didn't think she was a tramp looking for a reason to get him in her bed.

Tyler's expression though was relieved. "That's a good idea. I know it's not the guy thing to say, but I don't really want to be alone either." Tyler sort of bounced back on his heels.

Was he nervous too? That was kind of cute. "Okay except I have to warn you, if you are still here when my dad gets home, I'll have to hide you. He's difficult. Actually, he's kind of a belligerent drunk to be more exact." The last sentence burst out of Emily's mouth with embarrassment. Her cheeks grew hot and she was sure they were as red as an apple or pitcher of Kool-Aid. Sam was one of the prime reasons she never brought any one home, not even girls for crap's sake. She hated explaining to people what to expect once dear old dad got home.

Tyler sucked in his bottom lip for a second. "Or, we could go to my place. Before you say anything, I'm only suggesting it because we'd be able to talk more freely. It's not a line or anything, no funny business I swear." Tyler held up his hands in surrender like he had before.

Emily gave his suggestion honest consideration before answering. It would be nice to not have to talk in whispers and worry about Sam. She could write him a note and say she's sleeping over at a friend's. They were just having leftovers for dinner anyway so that was taken care of. It would be for educational purposes only. She wasn't a tramp, she reminded herself firmly. There really wasn't any need to feel like she was, that was just stupid. This wasn't about romance. It was about figuring out what was going on, and how to stop it.

She spoke slowly as if regretting her words. "Yeah. That's a… good idea." Emily realized what an idiot she must sound like and forced herself to get a grip. "Just let me write my dad a note." She turned away from him so she could unlock the door with the key she had fished out of her back pack while they were talking.

"Not to sound like a jerk or anything, but you might want to get clothes too."

Emily whirled around and gave him a quizzical look. She couldn't believe he had implied she would stay the night with him, so much for the "not a line" thing.

The shock on his face was obvious. "Wow. Simmer down, nothing like that I swore remember? It's just probably not a good idea to come back out once it gets late. That's all, I promise." He gave her an adorable crooked grin. His hands shot back up in their surrender position again.

Emily softened and smiled trying to assure Tyler that she believed him. "Sorry. It just seemed odd that's all." Realistically, it was kind of stupid to react like that. Hadn't she just thought she would write a note to Sam saying she was sleeping over at a friend's? Granted she figured she would still be coming home later. The note was just precautionary.

"Hey, don't say sorry. If I were a girl going through the same drama, I'd be skeptical too. Nothing surprises me anymore and I'm sure it's getting the same for you." Tyler dropped his hands. His eyes though seemed to be pleading with her.

It was almost as if he were trying to subliminally communicate to her, that he was one of the good guys. Emily knew that though. She could just tell. She could just trust him without doubt. Really, what other choice did she have anyway?

Everything was settled in the house in record time and they were out the door again. She hoped that Sam didn't go looking for her shot guns blazing or something. He would more than likely be late, she was sure. Hopefully he'd just come in and pass out.

Emily wished she had a car so she could do the driving for him. She did have a license, just no car. Sam was weird about his truck and wouldn't let her drive it. The truck was decent looking, surprisingly so considering the driver's condition most of the time these days. It wasn't brand new or anything by far, it just wasn't too battered.

She tried turning her father in once anonymously, but Sam was friends with all the cops in town and they let him off with just a warning. He was her father, of course she didn't want him to go to jail. He did deserve it though, by putting everyone in town's life in danger every time he got behind the wheel. It sickened Emily to the pit of her stomach that her own father might someday be responsible for harm inflicted on an innocent person. Thinking about cars and driving gave her a thought.

"Tyler? Why don't you drive?"

"I've got a license. I had to sell my car to pay for the move here. I'll get one though it'll be hot too." His voice grew immature by the second.

What is it with guys and cars? Emily envisioned Tyler's bachelor pad with hot rod magazines with half naked women scattered on his coffee table for decoration. With the thought, she gave a mental eye roll and laughed to herself. Maybe he would even have hubcaps hung on the walls as art.

The majority of the rest of their walk was done in silence. They made idle chit chat once and awhile, but both of them stayed alert ready for anything. After Emily's encounter with Andre in the computer lab, she was jumpy and more than a little paranoid.

All of the shadows looked like strangers were crawling through them. Stupidly she even squealed at the sound of bushes rustling beside them in the wind. The bush was only knee high, so the prospect of a dangerous predator waiting to spring was slightly insane. Sure enough, after she froze like a coward, Tyler bent down and discovered that it was just a cat trying to get comfy for the night.

"See," Emily said to Tyler after he stood back up. "I knew I was hanging out with you for a reason. My bodyguard." Her sarcasm was a weak attempt at recovering herself. It was fairly inevitable that she had seriously just lost like ten cool points.

"That's me, no feline to big or too small for these cannons." Tyler flexed his arm dramatically sighing with the effort. "It's hard to be this bad ass, but someone's gotta do it."

A car passed momentarily shedding light on them. Emily was able to see Tyler's flexed bicep more clearly. Outwardly he didn't look all that big. The contracted muscle that bulged under his shirt made him seem massive. The muscles wrapped around his upper arm like bands of steel. Emily found herself just leering like all those stupid girls she hated. They rippled as he moved promising strength. She'd be lying if she said it wasn't hot.

What was with her lately? First she drooled over Sebastian, and now Tyler? She really needed to get her hormones in check since apparently, they were raging.

The next turn brought them onto Main Street. Emily shuddered at the sudden pitch black sight in front of her. Not realizing what she was doing, she reached out for Tyler's hand. When everything was over she planned to write a letter to the Mayor. Main Street needed real street lights. There should have at least been real ones for when the lanterns got turned down for the night. Weren't town officials supposed to care about the safety and well-being of their residents?

Obviously sensing her discomfort, Tyler laced his fingers through hers and they just kept walking. Emily didn't look in any direction except straight ahead. She refused to look down the alley or anywhere else something might be hiding. There didn't appear to be anyone on the road, so that was comforting at least.

Tyler stood rigid and tense. His eyes darted from side to side and even behind them a few times. There seemed to be a bounce in his step as if springs were under his feet. Emily half expected him to break into a dead run and leave her behind. Not wanting to take any chances, she clutched his hand even tighter, just in case. The squeeze he gave hers back made her heart squeeze in return.

He nudged her across the street. "That's it, right over there." He led her across quickly even though no cars were approaching.

Emily eyed the narrow stairwell questioningly. It had a faint glow from a dim light overhead. It did no good though, seeing anything was next to impossible. Honestly, a night light probably gave off more illumination. Emily worried about the steep stairs. It would have been completely mortifying to do an amazing tumbling act back down onto the sidewalk. Sad but true, Emily was more than a little clumsy.

Absently, she wondered why there wasn't a door in the bottom entry way. Most of the other apartment entrances had them. They even locked for added security. It just figured that Tyler would live in one of the only places without added security measures.

Emily didn't ask about it. For one thing it wasn't the right time. For another, Tyler probably had no clue anyway. Luckily the stairwell was just wide enough for both of them to walk side by side. She didn't want to have to go first, but she didn't want to have to go last either. No door behind them would mean her back was exposed. When they got half way up the stairs they both froze at the exact same moment.

At the top of the stairs was a dark shadow. No, not just a shadow, it was a person. There was someone sitting at the top of the stairs, which of course led to Tyler's door. Before they even had a chance to react, the stranger stood and revealed his above average height.

Emily stopped breathing as Tyler pushed her down on the step below him, trying to shield her from the unexpected and unwanted guest. She thought for sure the sound of her rapidly increasing heart rate was echoing in the small space between them and Tyler's visitor. You could have heard a pin drop with no difficulty. The tension and fear in the air was palpable. Emily envisioned green eyes with glowing red borders. Whoever it was, she prayed they weren't hungry.

13

"Emily, go back down the stairs." Tyler spoke slow and quiet as if the person about to kill them couldn't hear.

Obediently Emily started backing down the steps carefully. Realizing the possible vampire wasn't going to lunge at Tyler to eat him, she began to turn so she could move quicker. Tyler apparently had the same idea. She could hear his shoes scuffing on the wooden steps. Emily thought her heart was going to leap out of her throat it was thudding so hard in her chest.

"WAIT!" a voice from the top of the stairs called. "You don't have anything to be afraid of. I'm here to help you." The voice was reassuring and cautious all at the same time.

Emily instantly recognized the voice and stopped. She would have known that voice anywhere. That voice kept her up at night. That fact wasn't by choice, she just couldn't help it.

"What are you doing? Move." Tyler sounded frantic behind Emily's back. Even still, she didn't move forward.

Instead, she started to turn back around. Tyler grabbed her arm stopping her. "It's okay. It's just Sebastian."

Tyler didn't let go of her arm. "What?" He asked incredulous. His body didn't relax at all with the news.

"It's Sebastian." Emily repeated.

"She's right Tyler remember? I met you the other day." Sebastian's voice sounded as if he were talking a small child off the top of a teetering ladder.

Emily thought for sure Tyler would turn all guy and get irate. It was the reaction a lot of guys displayed when they thought someone was talking down to them. Surprisingly, Tyler didn't. He took the comforting tone for what it was worth and released her arm. The two of them turned simultaneously to face Sebastian. Emily feeling small, rejoined Tyler on his step.

"What are you doing here," asked Tyler.

"I needed to talk to you. I've been meaning to, but I didn't think you were ready for it yet. What is she doing here?" Sebastian's words were full of distaste when he acknowledged Emily's presence.

Instantly crushed by Sebastian's rejection, she responded before Tyler had a chance to chime in. "Unlike you, I was invited." There was enough venom in Emily's voice to kill an elephant. Her eyes narrowed up at him full of reproach. It was possible that he probably didn't mean it like it sounded. Regardless, it was still rude. Especially since he talked about her like she wasn't even there.

"Emily I'm sorry I didn't mean it like that. Look, can we go inside and talk?" Sebastian took a few steps down the stairs getting closer to them and paused.

"Whatever, yeah. I guess." Tyler replied, sounding unsure. Besides the uneasiness Tyler was curious and that part of him one out over the other. He walked up the steps moving around Sebastian to unlock his door. Once it was open he turned and motioned Emily forward.

She barely saw the gesture. Thanks to the light that poured into the stairwell from Tyler's apartment, Emily was momentarily blinded. "You always leave the lights on." Emily didn't make it a question, just a fact. It was nice to see she wasn't the only one who had this habit. It made her feel safer. The two of them seemed to have a growing list of similarities. Emily moved easily around Sebastian and through the door.

"Well yeah. That way I feel like I'm not here alone," Tyler replied sheepishly. "Stupid right?" He sat down getting more comfortable on a plush red couch. There was a big ottoman that matched pushed off to the side against the wall. "Well I'd ask what your sign was, but I'd rather get to the point," Tyler said bluntly looking at Sebastian.

Sebastian chose to perch on the ottoman, so Emily opted for the other end of the couch. He had such a presence in the cozy living room. Without any effort he commanded it. Even the act of sitting down looked graceful when he did it. Every movement seemed controlled and precise like it had been planned. Emily imagined that even in a crowded room, it would be impossible not to take notice of Sebastian.

"I'm here about the strange feelings you have been getting. I know why you are here in Lakeview. You've pieced it together enough now that I can teach you the rest." Sebastian's hands rested casually on his knees.

Tyler started and looked at Sebastian with astonishment. Emily just sat there staring at him stupidly. She hadn't told Sebastian anything, she just found out about Tyler herself.

"How would you know what I have pieced together?" Tyler looked stunned and more than a little irritated.

"I went through the same process you are going through a time ago," said Sebastian.

"Process?" Tyler's face grew puzzled.

Emily couldn't move during the exchange. Something really weird was going to happen, she could feel it. She just sat with her hands folded in her lap, twisting them into different contorted positions. Her head moved back and forth between the two of them as though they were in the middle of a heated tennis match.

"Yes process. We all go through it in the beginning. I've told my mentor it seems cruel to allow our own to go through such confusion in the beginning. He says it's a necessary part of it all." Sebastian laughed to himself as if sharing a joke with them, only they didn't understand it at all.

"Could you get to the point?" Tyler was impatient now. His movements were like he had rubber bands around his limbs that were pulled tight ready to snap.

"Alright alright, don't be hasty we still have time." Sebastian leaned back casually resting his hands on the ottoman and continued. "I'm glad you have finally figured out the truth about the vampire situation in Lakeview. It didn't take you nearly as long to put it together as it has in the past with others. Part of the reason I couldn't come to you right away is because it helps build your instincts even if you don't realize they're building. Did you read the book?"

Tyler looked stunned. "You mean the one I got from the book store?" Tyler asked shooting a startled glance at Emily then back to Sebastian. "You mean Supernatural *Hunter*?"

"Yes, that's the one. I wanted you to read it. It's not up to date completely, but it still gives some information on hunting vampires."

Sebastian seemed pleased that Tyler read it, and not really all that surprised.

"Are you trying to tell me I'm a…" Tyler's voice trailed off. His right hand mimed a weird stabbing motion.

Sebastian sat back up putting his hands on his knees. "Yes Tyler, you are a vampire slayer. There are of course other names for it, though that is the most common." Sebastian waited a moment so Tyler could take it all in. "You will have to undergo training of course. Don't worry, you'll be surprised how much of it is instinctual, sort of like the feelings you've been getting. Like a vampire we live a very discrete life. We don't tell humans if we don't have to."

This grabbed onto Emily's attention and held it. She couldn't keep quiet anymore. "What do you mean humans? Aren't you a human? I don't believe-"

Sebastian cut her off with a hand he held up like a stop sign. "I know this is a lot to take in, but no we are not humans, at least not technically." Sebastian motioned to himself and Tyler. "It starts when we're babies and once the process truly takes form so does our abilities. Some might say we're immortal. That's not true, we can be killed. Granted it takes a lot to do one of us in and we heal very fast." His face took on a very serious expression.

Tyler sat for a long time not speaking, consternation clear in his posture. His elbows were on his knees his face buried in his hands. He wasn't crying but his hands were shaking. Emily was actually starting to worry he was in shock. It would be understandable if he was, she felt numb by this information. Even though Sebastian was only confirming their suspicions it didn't make it any less frightening.

It was Tyler who finally broke the silence surrounding them like a cage. "I don't get it, why me. I don't want to be a… vampire hunter. I don't even like to hunt." Tyler looked at nothing as he spoke.

Poor Tyler, Emily thought with sympathy for her new friend. This must be very confusing for him. It wasn't happening directly to her and she was baffled. Having a theory was one thing. What they had was a nightmare thrown right in their faces. The only problem was they couldn't just pinch themselves awake.

"I know you're confused. Remember like I said, I've been there." Sebastian put a hand on Tyler's shoulder briefly. "Look, I'm not going to bombard you with everything tonight. I will tell you that you were not picked at random. A lot goes into it. We don't choose you. We're more informed of your upcoming arrival beforehand so we can prepare for it. The selection process comes from somewhere else. A senior hunter was gifted with the power to find you and spark the process. Believe it or not it is something you are born with. There is a good possibility someone in your family was a hunter and you just don't know it." Sebastian rose to his feet, his eyes still on Tyler. "I will be back tomorrow to bring you to the compound. You have got to start your training immediately. There's no time to waste with all the recent activity happening in Lakeview." He gave Tyler a quick guy nod and started toward the door.

"Wait," Tyler called. "What if I said I didn't want any part in this?"

Sebastian spun back around to face Tyler. "Don't even talk like that. There isn't a choice and besides, it's your duty." He pointed a finger accusingly at Tyler as he spoke. "No matter what you say I will be back to retrieve you tomorrow. Don't try and bail even if you're not home I can find you. It's all part of the power you'll see."

"I don't wanna see," Tyler muttered to himself as Sebastian started for the door again.

Tyler's reaction was a little odd. He had said out on the road he felt he was destined for this. Now he acted as though it were a death sentence. Maybe it was. Unfortunately, only time would tell.

Sebastian didn't respond, but Emily did notice him shake his head slightly. He had to understand Tyler's dismay as he said he had been there once. It bothered Emily that Sebastian had hardly acknowledged her presence during his visit. She still had a lot of questions, more now than ever. It seemed like now was the perfect time to explain everything. Secrets apparently were surfacing so why not rescue all of them from his depths.

Emily jumped up and headed for the door behind Sebastian. Tyler only watched, he didn't have time to say anything before she was closing the door behind her. She had half expected Sebastian to already be gone like all those other times. Surprisingly, he was still there just standing on the stairs just a few steps down.

His back was to her. For a moment she just stood there watching him. He had to know she was there. Even if he did, he didn't make a move to face her. Finally she said, "what about me Sebastian?"

"What about you?" He didn't turn back to face her. Despite the obvious snub, he at least didn't advance down the stairs.

"Well, how do I fit into all this? I'm clearly involved somehow. I'm a human and you told me your secret, that has to mean something."

He slowly turned to face her. "Yes Emily, you do have a part in this. I'm not even sure exactly what that is. I can tell that even though you are one of us, you're different. You're not a full hunter. You have powers that we aren't even aware of yet. I don't know what that means and I'm sorry for that" He took one step backward down the stairs. When he stopped he stood there tapping his fingers casually on the banister looking bored.

Emily's eyes widened with fear. "What do you mean I'm one of you except I'm different? If Tyler can see better in the dark, sense the vamps and make things magically appear why can't I? I've never been in a fight in my life and have no instincts towards it at all."

Sebastian ignored most of her questions. "You have instincts. For some reason they are not within your reach as of yet. Neither I nor my mentor understand it because you are so clearly gifted." He sounded utterly confused.

"Thanks, but that really doesn't tell me anything." Her voice dripped with sarcasm. "Why is it one day you act like we are friends and another you can't wait to get away from me?" Emily glowered down at him.

"I've tried to tell you it's not safe for us to be friends. I lead a dangerous life and you don't need to be tangled up in it, especially when we don't clearly know your role in all of this." He continued walking down the stairs ending their conversation.

"Damn it Sebastian don't walk away from me. Didn't your mentor teach you manners?" Emily fumed with intense anger and disgust for the situation.

Sebastian didn't stop moving. He did slow down, just a little. "I don't mean to be rude, it's just that this conversation isn't going anywhere. I can't give you answers I don't have yet myself. I'm trying to get to the bottom of it, believe me. I have never seen anything like you in all my existence." Sebastian didn't wait for Emily's response before rounding the corner at the bottom of the stairs.

For a minute Emily just stood there staring after him. Then common sense rained in and she realized that she was out there alone and she went back inside locking the door behind her.

When she got in the house, Tyler had already turned down the couch. Hide-a-beds typically weren't very comfortable. Surprisingly, this one looked okay. The blanket he had waiting for her was a lighter brown than the couch. It looked very warm and soft. Emily couldn't help smiling at the effort.

"Oh you're back in. I figure you can take the bed and I'll take the couch." Tyler tossed a pillow onto the couch and sat down.

Emily watched him curiously, "bedroom?" She couldn't help the shock in her voice. "I thought this was a studio? Did you make a bed out of the tub or something?" She crossed her arms still watching him.

Tyler looked offended. "Give me some credit. This is not a small cramped studio. It's a very spacious one bedroom. So there," he said with a sharp nod and crossed his arms.

"Did you really just say, so there?" Emily giggled covering her hand over her mouth.

"So." Then he gave her a stubborn glare. Tyler's jaw was set, daring her to contradict him.

This of course made Emily giggle harder. "Just checking I guess. Are you gonna stomp your foot too?" Emily tried to stifle her laughter when she saw Tyler's expression. "I really don't feel right stealing your bed. I don't mind the couch it looks comfy." Emily eyed the couch thoughtfully. It honestly didn't look too bad.

"Guests get the bed. That's the rule."

"Whose rule," Emily asked.

"I don't know it's just the rule. I don't make'em I just follow'em," Tyler shrugged. "Well at least the good ones anyway." His smile was devilish and his eyes sparkled as if hiding a secret.

The thing of it was, Emily didn't really care where she slept. The biggest problem was sleeping alone. Learning that the world as she once knew it was a complete lie and goblins really did exist, had her feeling anxious. She didn't really know how to bring this up to Tyler without looking like she just wanted in his pants. He had very nice pants and even better back pockets actually. She just isn't one of those girls and never would be. She hardly knew Tyler and she didn't even think she liked him that way, at least she hoped not. That would only complicate things. There was a good possibility that with the new found knowledge of her quiet little town, they would be spending a lot more time together trying to figure out a solution.

Well here goes nothing, she thought. Emily squared her shoulders and let out a deep breath. Instantly her so called courage washed away and she bit her lip. She spoke in a rush. "Here's the thing. I um, well, I'm kind of afraid after hearing my suspicions are true and I don't want to be by myself." Emily bit down on her lip so hard she just knew she was going to draw blood if she wasn't careful.

Tyler's brows rose practically to his hairline as he considered this. "Well," he ventured slowly. "I'll be happy to keep you company between the sheets, if you need me." The devilish grin was back.

What a pig Emily thought. "No, no not like that never mind. Forget I said anything. Just show me the door to the bedroom and I'll be on my way." Emily had her best disgusted face on and she even crossed her arms for affect. She knew he was just screwing with her, but she wasn't going to let him get away with it.

"Hey, don't get your panties in a bunch," Tyler said laughing slightly at her. "No funny business I swear."

Emily's eyes narrowed. "You've had zero effect on my panties, thank you very much."

Tyler's wounded expression gave him a boy like quality. "Didn't I?" Tyler asked sarcastically. He clutched his hand to his heart like he'd been shot and fell back on the bed. "That was harsh Em".

Instead of giving him the satisfaction of continuing the little bicker fest, Emily just glared at him and sighed exasperated. She didn't want to let him know this was way more amusing then she was letting on. Stubbornly without saying anything, she turned as if she were going to head toward the bedroom.

Emily half expected him to throw his hands up in surrender as usual. What he actually did was well, nothing. She followed suit and didn't say anything either. When he didn't react to her move toward the room, she turned to look at him. They were both silent for a long moment just watching each other awkwardly.

"Alright look. How about this? So it's not so, you know weird we can both sleep out here. Living rooms are for friends, bedrooms are for scr-"

"Okay! I get it, I get it."   Emily cut him off, totally not wanting to hear from him what bedrooms were for.

"Sorry."

Emily smiled. "No big deal. So, how can we do this without... whatever." She gestured at nothing in particular.

"Well we are both full grown adults, at least you are. I'm sure we can handle sleeping in the same room and dare I say it, the same bed without uh..." He paused, thinking for a moment. "Physical relations getting in the way. I mean I don't know about you, but I can control myself." He gave her a crooked smile and winked at her.

"I can control myself just fine," shot back Emily, annoyed at the implication. Some guys have some nerve.

"Well alright then. I'll go in the door on the left and get changed. The one on the right is the bathroom. You can use that one if you want." Assuming she was fine with the arrangement he headed off for what she guessed was his bedroom. Before he did the sparkle in his eye caught the light. He was feeling very amused and pleased with himself.

Emily never responded, she didn't really see a point. She did let her eyes follow him as he disappeared through the door. After he was out of sight she plucked her backpack off the floor by the door where she left it and went into the bathroom.

It was of course a small room. She wasn't expecting something with a spa, but she wondered looking around how she would ever fit all of her stuff in a bathroom this small if she had a place like it. Immediately she scolded herself because that implied she might want to live with Tyler and that was not the case. She did find him attractive, but that didn't mean anything. Finding someone attractive was just human nature.

After she was dressed and her teeth were brushed, she switched off the light leaving her backpack in there for the evening. Using a scrunchie, she put her hair up in a messy bun while she walked to the couch. Immediately, she noticed Tyler was already back and was watching her with an expression she didn't recognize.

"What?" Emily asked.

"Nothing why?" Tyler spoke quickly like he had been caught doing something he shouldn't be.

She glared teasingly at him. "You were staring at me."

"Did anyone ever tell you that you really should loosen up? I just looked up because I heard you coming, that's all." This time his hands did go up in surrender.

Emily thought the mannerism was adorable. Of course she didn't show that to him though. She just shook her head at Tyler. It was obvious that it was more than that, but she was too tired to argue about it. Besides, they probably wouldn't get anywhere with the argument anyway. Tyler seemed to be just as stubborn as Emily was and she didn't know if she liked that or not. She sat down on the opposite side of the hide-a-bed from him not sure what to do. Sleeping in the same bed as a guy was a first. Were there rules about this sort of thing? Emily noticed there was a second blanket at the end of the bed now.

Tyler saw her looking at it and said, "Oh I figured this would make you more comfortable." He took the one on top. "See, now I have a blanket, and you have a blanket. Strictly platonic." He eyed her smugly daring her to disapprove.

Emily smiled her approval and slid her blanket toward her. She waited for him to lie down, so she could do the same. She was trying to act casual and not like a bumbling dork like she felt. Hopefully, it didn't show. It really wasn't that big of a deal. They were just friends. It would be the same as if she had one of her girlfriends sleep over. Except none of her girlfriends looked like Tyler, or smelled like him either. She noticed a scent like cologne in the air that wasn't there before. Did he put some on when he got changed? That definitely wouldn't be something just friends would do. Stop it! She scolded herself again. It didn't matter what his intentions were, she needed to get a handle on her hormones.

Emily felt her eyes droop. She was mentally and physically exhausted. She pondered whether or not to ask Tyler how he was doing with all he had learned. He had a lot to think about like who he was supposed to be. Emily decided against it. The silence was relaxing. It was nice to be there together and not have to talk. It didn't feel awkward anymore just, nice.

At around two thirty in the morning, Emily's eyes flew open with terror. The conclusion of the dream she had been having left her panting for breath. It was about a blood sucking monster breaking into her house to suck the life out of her and Sam. Judging by the light snoring coming from Tyler's resting form, he must have been sleeping okay. Selfishly she thought about pinching him or something. If this situation was going to give her nightmares and keep *her* up why should he get to sleep?

Any effort to keep the horrifying dream out of her mind was useless. Every time she closed her lids, all she could see was the glow of red. The one thing Emily was able to think clearly about, was the need to keep her loved ones safe. The first person that came to mind was her best friend.

It wasn't likely that Lucy was awake. Texting was always an option if nothing else. If she sent her friend a message than she would be able to get it whenever she woke up. Emily didn't know if she would have time to get in touch with her later. Slowly she slid off the hide-a-bed and went to the bathroom where she had left her cell tucked into the pocket of her backpack.

After scrolling through the contact list finding Lucy's name she hesitated. What was she supposed to say to her? Oh gee guess what, we were right. The pod people apparently have something to do with the blood sucking vampires that have taken up residence in Lakeview. So you might wanna be careful while you're in town, okay? So guess I'll talk to you later if we don't all die. Cool bye. Yeah, probably not the best idea.

She thought for a second and then began typing. *Hey can't talk 4 now our theories were right b careful will call when I can love u.* Without waiting for a response from Lucy, she put her phone on the floor next to her bed for the night.

14

The sound of someone knocking on the door woke them both up well, scared them up was more like it. They both sprang upright at the exact same moment gasping. Tyler recovered quicker than Emily and slid out of bed to see who it was. She glanced around trying to remember if she took her cell phone out of her backpack. She hated waking up and not knowing what time it was. A quick check at the walls proved to be useless. There wasn't a clock on any of them. Examining all the furniture she saw there didn't seem to be one perched anywhere either. She had never before encountered somebody who didn't have at least one clock somewhere.

Belatedly, she had a flash of memory and felt like a total moron. The cell phone was on the floor directly next to where she was sitting on the make shift bed. The night before, she had been text messaging Lucy before falling asleep. How could she have forgotten that? In her defense, the day before had been pretty overwhelming at best.

Tyler was still standing at the door. He was too big so Emily couldn't see who it was. Absently she recalled her father telling her she made a better door than a window when she was little and blocking the television. She wanted to throw a pillow at him and get him to get out of the way so she could be nosy.

She thought it would be sort of interesting to meet one of Tyler's friends. Then it occurred to her what might be perceived by the visitor as she looked down at herself and promptly discarded the thought. Obviously nothing had actually happened between the two of them. However, someone on the outside might not have seen it that way. It really didn't matter to Emily what people thought of her, but still.

Right about the time she had her mouth wide open in an unattractive yawn, Tyler turned ushering someone in the apartment. Feeling foolish, Emily laid back down covering herself with the blanket. It was too late to pretend to be sleeping. At least they wouldn't see her in her jammies.

It was Sebastian. Oh that's right, she thought. Emily sighed inwardly. Tyler was supposed to meet Sebastian's mentor and start training. From under the thick comforter she could tell they had moved closer to where she lay hidden like a skittish animal. They were talking in hushed whispers. Maybe they hadn't seen her sitting up after all. Maybe Tyler thought she went back to sleep. That was silly though, the door was practically in the living room. Slowly Emily moved the blanket so she could peek out just a little.

At one point Sebastian's head turned toward Emily. He looked as though he were in deep concentration and totally oblivious to the fact that he was staring right at her. Her face was mostly obscured, though she could just see him. Could he see her watching him? Before she hurriedly closed her eyes, she saw him turning back to Tyler.

Whatever they were talking about had Tyler looking very intent and serious. Sebastian almost seemed annoyed and then with a resigned shrug nodded before they both turned toward her.

Tyler moved over to her side of the bed and sat on the edge. "Hey, I've gotta go do that training thing now. I want you to come with me."

For a second she thought about stretching and making fake wake up noises. Figuring that was pointless she just pulled down the blanket. Emily didn't answer, but looked to Sebastian to hear his opinion.

"Tyler thinks you should meet my mentor." Sebastian sighed heavily. "I personally don't think it's a great idea, but I do agree there is more to you than most humans." Sebastian's tone was flat and his face looked bored by the end of his statement.

It shouldn't have mattered, but it really annoyed Emily. He acted as if it was a boy's only club, no girls allowed. Real mature she thought. Maybe his mentor resided in a tree house and that was where they conducted their super-secret meetings. "Well if you guys think I should. I don't really care either way." She was of course lying but they didn't need to know that. She was dying to know what kind of training was involved to be a vampire hunter. Emily added an indifferent shrug to further push that it didn't matter to her one way or the other.

Sebastian nodded. "Well that's settled then. I will wait down stairs for both of you to get ready." He turned smoothly to leave the same way he had come in. Before reaching the door he looked back over his shoulder. "Oh, and sorry if I interrupted anything." He said it as though it were merely an afterthought and then turned and left not giving either of them a chance to respond.

His mocking sarcastic tone was ridiculous. He hadn't interrupted anything except perfectly good sleep, the jerk. Just who did he think he was anyway? His Dr. Jekyll and Mr. Hide attitude was really starting to get on Emily's last nerve. One day he's sweet and maybe even a little flirty. The next thing she knew, he acted like it was an inconvenience that she was even hanging around. The fact that he seemed to be avoiding her the last two times he saw her, definitely wasn't helping Emily's opinion much either.

When they got downstairs Sebastian was waiting casually leaning on the side of the building with his arms crossed and his leg bent so his foot could rest on the wall. When he saw them he pushed off the wall with his foot and stood looking impatient. It was though they had kept him waiting for hours instead of the mere five minutes that had actually passed.

They walked most of the way in silence. Every now and then Tyler would ask Sebastian a question about vampires or the training process. For the most part Emily stayed out of it. It wasn't for lack of interest because she was practically chomping at the bit to get more information. It was just that her attention was only half on their sporadic conversation. What Sebastian had said back at the apartment intrigued and frightened her, making it nearly impossible to focus on much else. What did he mean by *there's more to you than most humans?* Of course she was a *human*. What else was she supposed to be? The last time Emily checked she hadn't developed a sudden craving for blood, so she obviously wasn't one of the vampires. What else was there? A picture of scary wolf men and little pixy fairies came into her mind making her shudder, so she forced her thoughts to drift elsewhere.

Emily wondered why someone like Sebastian wouldn't be driving something like the Batmobile or something. With his cool guy persona and cocky attitude, somehow walking didn't seem to fit his style in the least. Admittedly, he could probably make pink bunny slippers and flannel footy pajamas look cool. If Sebastian's mentor looked anything like him, Emily was in trouble.

The further they walked, the harder it was to imagine where in the world a training facility would be located for vampire hunters. If there was an actual building that housed such a thing, it surely didn't have a sign. She had pretty much lived in Lakeview her whole life and was fairly certain she would have noticed something that read *VAMPIRE HUNTERS INC.* Humorously, she passed the time picturing what a sign like that would look like. She imagined black Gothic font with deep crimson blood dripping off the edges of each boldly printed letter. For affect maybe it would have a large wooden stake going through the middle and eerie spider webs at the corners. That would look pretty awesome, but definitely too conspicuous.

Sebastian broke into the silence. "Where I'm about to take you can never be told to anyone, ever." He put great emphasis on the word ever. "If anyone knew about our operation we would be finished."

Emily had been so lost in her own thought that she hadn't even noticed where he had walked them. So her spilling the beans wouldn't be a problem. They still appeared to be downtown but in an alley with buildings on either side. The backs of the buildings didn't give any clues as to what street they were near. When they got about four buildings down Sebastian stopped.

Emily half expected a glowing door to materialize in front of him like in the movies. He didn't make a move at first in either direction to give any indication what they were looking for. Nothing changed about the surroundings as they waited. Maybe a goblin was supposed to jump out of nowhere and escort them to another dimension or something.

Finally he turned to the right. Tyler shot her a nervous look that she returned in triplicate. The building he was turning toward didn't have a door or even a window to climb through. Were they supposed to scale up the side like Spider Man?

Sebastian moved right up to the wall and placed a hand on it gingerly. Apparently pleased he gave a quick nod to himself and moved back a few steps before pulling something out of his pocket. At first glance, it wasn't visible what it was. When Emily was able to give it closer examination, it just looked like a rock.

Sebastian gave an almost imperceptible scan to his right and left and even upward. Still not speaking to them, he bent down and placed the rock on the ground. Time seemed to stand still while they waited.

Nothing happened. Now what, Emily thought quizzically, it really was kind of a letdown. Even as the thought passed through her mind though, things started to change. A pressure seemed to build in the air around them. She wouldn't have believed it in a million years if she hadn't seen it for herself. Out of nowhere, a section of the gravel started rattling. It was shaking with visible vibrations she couldn't feel under her own feet even though she was only about a foot from where Sebastian was standing. Then as if by magic, the trembling section dropped a few inches into the ground not disturbing any of the surrounding rocks. The dropped piece quietly slid under the building displaying nothing but darkness.

Emily gasped and stepped back. She looked over at Tyler, his mouth was hanging open and his eyes looked like they were going to bug out of his head at any second. That couldn't have happened. Before the ground started to shake Emily didn't notice anything that would have even hinted that there was a trap door there. Whoever was in charge of covering the hatch took their job very seriously.

"Cool huh?" Sebastian asked as if he had just shown them a neat card trick, instead of opening the earth with a rock. Cool didn't really seem to cover it. "I'm sure you have a lot of questions about this but we need to go before there are witnesses." Without another word, he stepped into thin air as he went down the hole. Seriously, it looked like he was floating downward.

Emily reached out and clutched Tyler's arm for dear life. She didn't know what was down the rabbit hole and that was fine by her. Home was looking a whole lot sweeter by the second. Even work sounded pretty good at that point. Any confidence she may have displayed earlier was nothing but vibrato.

Tyler nudged her forward, not unkindly. "Let's go. We don't really have a lot of choice right now."

All Emily could do in response was nod slowly. She was still in shock at the sight of Sebastian going down some mysterious hole in the ground like it was nothing. If they had to follow him at least she wasn't alone. Even though they had just met, Emily didn't think that Tyler would let anything bad happen to her.

Before she had a chance to protest, Tyler put a probing foot down the hole to test the waters so to speak. After his foot dropped to his ankle the sound of his foot tapping on something echoed slightly in the hole. "I think there's stairs," he said cautiously.

"Whatever, you go first." Emily put one tentative foot in front of the other. The death grip on Tyler's arm never relented. She didn't know what awaited them down there, and she wasn't going to take the chance that she was separated from Tyler. She assumed Sebastian could be trusted as well, seeing how there was no evidence to the contrary. Just in case, she didn't want to risk it.

Once they were down the stairs, the alley floor or underground ceiling thing shut without a sound. The only audible noise was a slight click once all the light from outside disappeared. They were only in the dark for a few seconds before dimly lit sconces illuminated their narrow path.

The extreme change in lighting made it difficult to see anything. Emily blinked hard trying to adjust her vision. A few feet in front of them she could just barely make out the shape of a big wooden door that had a rounded top. She had never seen such a thing except for in movies that were set in the old days that had exotic castles with elaborate turrets. The area they were in didn't really hold any significance or clues about their location. The walls were a dark gun metal grey that was almost black. The floor seemed to be the same color if not, the difference wasn't detectable.

When they reached the rounded door, Sebastian placed his hand above the large knob where a dead bolt would be located. After a short time, she heard another click and he opened the door. When Emily stepped through her mouth dropped open with a pop. She stopped walking abruptly, causing Tyler to stumble back a step. Her feet were locked in place at the sight before her.

It wasn't exactly the same as she remembered. Without a doubt though, Emily was staring down the hallway of her dream. The only difference was that the floor was green marble instead of red. She didn't understand how such a thing could be possible. Nothing like it had ever happened before. Alexander said it wasn't really a dream, but she hadn't completely believed him. It was a dream. Of course the soothing stranger would tell her it was real.

Hoping to find out more she asked, "Where is Alexander? Is he here too?"

"Um... yes we will be meeting with Alexander shortly," Sebastian stammered while clearing his throat. It was the first time Emily had seen him falter from his unshakable control. He watched her with utter astonishment. "We need to get moving. We'll have time for a full tour later."

Emily saw that Tyler shot her a quick but stunned look. His face looked as though he just realized the joke was on him and Sebastian and Emily were about to kill him. He swallowed hard and kept moving along the same path Emily had taken in her dream.

It was hard to see him look at her like that. She wanted to reassure him somehow, only she couldn't bring herself to say anything. As bad as it made her feel though, she couldn't focus much attention on his wounded expression. Her gaze was fixed on Sebastian's reaction to her question. It still seemed to be affecting him that she knew who Alexander was.

He watched her too, in small darting glances. The look on his face was almost comical. It was like he was worried and greatly surprised all at the same time. He apparently noticed her noticing him because he pivoted and headed down the corridor without another word.

When they completed the sharp turn to the left, Emily was amazed to see the scene of her dream in reality. At the end of the new hall she could see the wooden archways up ahead, elegant and beautiful. Soon they would be in what she assumed was Alexander's office. Shouldn't an office have doors? She thought the question to herself as they walked, but didn't dare ask out loud. It seemed like a really stupid thing to say.

Tyler's head was on a constant swivel, taking in all the doors. He was probably trying to get a look at the labels on the thick molding of the frames. Emily hadn't noticed labels in her dream. They were like small little plaques above the knobs. The light from the sconces danced off them giving them a gleaming shine that sparkled.

She noticed that Tyler was clenching and unclenching his fists stiffly at his sides. He looked as though he was preparing for a battle.

Well, a battle or the first chance he could find to bolt. The whole thing must be so scary to him. His life would surely be changed forever. Her mind tried to wrap around the fact that Tyler wasn't going to age. More importantly, his new main purpose was to kill blood sucking monsters before they killed his fellow man.

Trying to piece together how she fit into the puzzle was like walking a hundred miles in the desert without a single bottle of water. Was she supposed to hunt monsters too? The thought of herself wielding a wooden stake with a fanged creature in front of her made nausea creep up on her in a steady wave. The heaviness of it made her head hurt.

Just like before, when the hall opened up into the office the color of the floor turned to blue. It was illuminated more brightly than the hall but it was still just a soft light, easy on the eyes.

At the familiar crackle of a fire, Emily looked towards the impressive hearth. Alexander was sitting in the same overstuffed chair as he had occupied before. He was reading a book intently. His forehead was creased with concentration like deep lines on a wrinkled page. He rubbed his chin considering something. Then, as if pulled back to the present he slammed the volume closed with one hand gripping it by the spine.

"Ah Sebastian, I've been expecting you. And Tyler I'm very happy to finally meet you." Alexander stood to face them. His stance was that of a soldier. His smile was bright like a proud father's would be. The loving gaze stopped on Emily, but didn't lose an ounce of compassion. "Well dear Emily, we meet again." He gave her a modest tilt of his head in an old fashioned greeting. "I do hope the situation hasn't frightened you too terribly. I hope you understand more clearly now the imperative reasons for the… what did you call them? Oh yes riddles." A knowing smile tugged at the corners of Alexander's mouth. The only reason it was apparent that it was a smile was the sparkle in his eyes.

"Yes sir, I understand," Emily retorted sheepishly.

Alexander frowned, "my dear girl no need for formalities here. You are a part of our secret that makes you part of our family." He moved in front of her and raised her hand to kiss it. When his eyes met her again he had a gentle smile for her which made her feel better. "Well, or should I say, you are a part of this family, only we haven't quite figured out your position yet. Even though you're not like the other children, that doesn't mean you don't belong."

Tyler cleared his throat. "I don't mean to interrupt, but I have a million questions." He didn't wait for the go ahead before he started in on Alexander. "Mainly, what does this training entail?"

"No worries my son, I was just getting to that. It's gravely paramount that you're training start immediately. Things are progressing quicker than we had intended upon. I will show you to the training room you can change in there."

Emily suddenly noticed that Alexander wasn't wearing a tailored suit like before. He was dressed like a ninja all in black. The clothes made him look even more fierce. Instead of the businessman she had met before, she stood before a man that was a force to be reckon with.

Before leaving the room with a bewildered Tyler, Alexander turned to Sebastian. "Why don't you show Emily to her room and maybe take her on a brief tour."

Sebastian nodded sharply. He didn't respond to the older man, but looked as though he had gotten a mission from his commanding officer that was of the utmost importance. The only thing he didn't do was salute. It was obvious that Sebastian held a lot of respect for his mentor.

Emily completely puzzled asked, "my room?" She looked from Alexander to Sebastian for a response. When one didn't come, she continued. "I think there must be some mistake. I don't need a place to stay. I can't stay here. My father-"

"Don't you worry about Sam. He will be taken care of," said Alexander looking unconcerned by the objection.

"Take care of him?" What was this the God Father? Were they going to kill Sam? "I'm sorry but what does that mean?" Emily stared at Alexander incredulously. It should have surprised her that he knew Sam's name but at this point nothing surprised her anymore.

"We can adapt his memory so he will not worry about the fact that you are not home. He will think you are simply with friends. He won't even know how long you are gone. Each day will seem like the first, even though he carries out his daily living unscathed." His voice softened considerably. "The vampires are suspicious of you. I'm truly sorry dear, but it's no longer safe for you on your own."

"What? You're gonna screw with my dad's memory?" Emily was absolutely shocked with that revelation.

"I assure you no harm will come to your father." Alexander stepped smoothly to Emily and placed a hand on her arm. "You have my word on that Emily. He will also have protection in the event that someone goes poking their fangs where they don't belong." Alexander mimed fangs in the neck making her shudder.

Emily just stood there with her mouth dropped open practically to the floor. She suddenly felt scared and very alone. It was all so confusingly mind boggling. The rabbit hole, vampires, memory tampering, all of it, it was just too much.

Alexander said something to Tyler, though she didn't catch it. Their voices seemed to echo in her mind, bouncing back and forth never quite making sense. She continued to watch as Alexander ushered Tyler to a door at the far side of the room near the leather couch. That wasn't there in her dream either, she thought absently.

For a moment after the door closed Emily just stared at it blankly. She couldn't do anything else. Her mind had shut down with a puff of smoke on overload. Hopefully a backup generator kicked on before she fell into a coma or something.

Sebastian cleared his throat, drawing her eyes to his. He gave her a wistful smile and then bowed over dramatically as if she were a queen. "Shall I show you to your chamber my lady?" He used a horrible British accent.

Waking up from the daze, Emily giggled. It was split seconds like those that made her want to like him. The only problem was, those seconds tended not to last long. "What? Now you're gonna be charming and friendly again?" Emily raised a perfectly plucked brow at him. "To what do I owe this pleasure?" The accent she attempted was just as silly as his was, which made her giggle harder.

For a moment, Sebastian's carefully groomed control was broken and he actually looked offended. "Look, I know I have been disgraceful to you. I'm sure you're confused. You've had a lot of information thrown at you and it's gotta be hard to cope. I was just trying to be nice." He raked a hand through his hair. "It's still not safe for us to be friends. This life is too complicated and obviously dangerous."

"I get the danger and maybe even the complicated." Emily glared at him indignantly. "None of that is a good reason to send me mixed signals. Nor is it a good reason for you to avoid my questions, especially when I deserve answers. I get the secret thing, but guess what? The hunter's out of the bag now, so you don't have to worry about me I can handle myself." She knew her tone was far more cutting than it really needed to be. He really deserved it though.

Emily was tired of all the secrets. Why tell one and then think the rest should be kept quiet? If she has a part in this mess somehow, then she needed to know everything. He was just so infuriating. Only Sebastian could leave her feeling good one minute, and stung the next.

"You're right." He may have agreed with her, but his somber expression didn't transform. He gave away nothing as always.

Emily couldn't help feeling taken aback. Now it was her turn for the dramatics. She threw a hand up clutching at her heart. "What? Just like that?" More seriously she said, "Okay, I might be right. That doesn't mean you're gonna explain things to me does it?"

"No it does not mean that. I will answer anything you want to know as long as I can. Let's get you settled first."

"I don't really have stuff to get settled." Emily muttered. "My bag is back at Tyler's but I don't have clean clothes in it anyway." Emily was still annoyed by the sleepover prospect but she was starting to soften just a little. She understood that it was probably the best and safest for her and even for Sam.

"Don't worry about anything. We can acquire anything you need from your house or by other means if you are willing to use new things. The second is the safest option. It's less exposure and less contact with Sam." Right then was probably the softest Emily had ever seen Sebastian's face.

"I don't think I ever told you my dad's name. How did you know that? You can read my mind." The words came out in a rush but she didn't care. Emily knew the answer to the last one before he even said it. It was something she had been trying to figure out a way to bring up for a while.

Sebastian looked surprised but quickly put his stone mask back on. "I told you we have plenty of time for questions later. I told Alexander I would show you your room and that's what we are going to do," he said evading her question. Sebastian turned and left the room without giving her a chance to argue.

Which for the record, she totally would have argued. First of all, she wanted, no needed answers. She had been pretty patient and understanding about all the Sci-Fi mysteries taking place. Second of all, his vanishing and storming off in the middle of a conversation was getting really old. When the going got tough, Sebastian got going and that just wasn't going to cut it. The only thing worse would have been if they were on the phone and he randomly hung up on her. Emily hated that with a bright purple passion. Why couldn't he be nice and sweet like the day he visited her in the book store? Sure he was still evasive, but at least he was friendly. Never once was he condescending.

Suddenly all Emily desired was a moment alone. Since the library she hasn't had even one minute of solitude. There was so much going on and she just needed to get her head on straight. It felt like everything was drastically spiraling out of control. Nothing seemed sacred anymore and everything she thought was just make believe was now physical, solid and very much real.

Her mind was so conflicted that she truly thought it would explode, or at the very least, stop working all together making her fall away into the darkness. Without Emily's permission, her breath began to come quicker and her chest felt constricted. Was she having a heart attack? That was ridiculous, she knew she wasn't. Panic attacks were something she had become very familiar with when her mom had died but she hadn't had one for just about three years. There was no doubt about it. She had to get out of there. Sebastian nor anyone else could never under any circumstance see her breaking down. "Hey, is there a bathroom in this place?"

15

Okay so it wasn't all together truthful that Emily had to go to the bathroom. It was stupid to lie, but she didn't really want Sebastian to know what she was really up to. If she had been honest about the fact that she had been about to lose it there, he would have thought her weak and that wasn't the case. Her mind had just reached its full capacity of drama and the paranormal.

The instant that she had been behind the safety of the closed bathroom door, she willed herself to relax. What she wanted more than anything else was to call her best friend. Lucy would understand all the crazy. Even if she didn't understand, she would fake it well for Emily's benefit and just then, that sounded like perfection.

It put her body in tremendous turmoil that releasing the information that was plaguing her wasn't prohibited. None of the others would have got it. It didn't matter that Emily trusted Lucy implicitly. It didn't matter that Lucy would agree to take the secret to the grave, and it didn't matter that it would help Emily regain some of her sanity.

Emily wondered what they would do if she did tell. Sebastian alone would more than likely go into tantrum high and mighty King mode if she had told him what she wanted. He had made it pretty clear that telling anyone about what was going on was forbidden.

Did that mean she had to listen? Realistically there wasn't any proof that she was a slayer. If she wasn't a slayer then did the same rules apply? There was actually no real proof she belonged in this world at all. Sure, Sebastian could do some weird mind speak with her, but did that mean she belonged?

How could she not call Lucy? And was it possible that Sam really wouldn't know she was gone because of some mind zap thing? It all just seemed so... well for lack of a better word, not real. This was like a horrible waking nightmare that never went away.

Murders, rapists and robbers, those sorts of monsters Emily understood. Those sorts of crimes were always on the News and in the daily paper every day. It seemed completely unimaginable that someday on the News, the Anker would report about a murder in which the person was drained completely of blood and the lead suspect was an undead vampire that was thousands of years old.

Emily walked over to the small bathroom and turned on the cold water. She cupped her hands and splashed a healthy amount of the liquid on her face. It helped a little but didn't take the feeling of melancholy away.

The bathroom was bright and it allowed her to get a good look at herself in the mirror. There were deep bruise like circles under her eyes, just above her high cheek bones. Where her cheeks were usually flushed there was no color. Her electric blue eyes looked wild and frightened.

She supposed the fear couldn't really be avoided. Any person would be a little freaked after finding everything out that she had. It would have been strange if she didn't feel a little overwhelmed. Who was she kidding? She felt like someone had knocked all the wind out of her and then twisted her mind into a pretzel.

After wiping her wet hands off on her jeans, she contemplated digging her phone out of her pocket. Just when she thought she had herself convinced that calling Lucy was the way to go, she squelched the idea. Something deep within Emily told her that divulging the secrets she had learned was a bad thing. It would make her feel better but at what cost?

Telling her friend would keep her safe, but it would also scare her. Emily really didn't want to be responsible for that. Lucy rarely was out after dark anyway, so she was probably fine. Giving her exhausted reflection one last surreptitious glance, she shrugged inwardly and turned to head out of the small bathroom.

Sebastian was waiting out in the hall for her. He didn't really look impatient, as much as concerned. The second he saw her the look evaporated like a passing wave. "Are you ready?"

147

He stood there so firm and tall that Emily wanted to look around for a commanding officer. She thought about telling him to drop and give her twenty and thought better of it. "Ready," she responded sounding way more confident than she felt.

Emily's room was absolutely perfect. It was totally surreal how well the room fit its new occupant's personality. If she had a choice of how she could decorate her room at home, this would more than likely be the way she would do it.

It was larger than her room at home. It wasn't big enough to seem scary, or echo or anything. The walls were soft brown, almost tan. The carpet was deep blue and probably the thickest and plushest she had ever walked on in her life. She imagined forgetting the bed and just curling up on the comfy floor.

The bed looked just as inviting. It was a queen size with a dark cherry wood frame that looked like a sleigh. The quilt was a pattern of black, white and different shades of blue. Her favorite colors were blue and orange. Between the two though, blue was higher up on the list. Any shade, it didn't matter. There was a mountain of pillows that looked as fluffy as clouds. They were all different sizes but arranged meticulously.

The closet was medium sized with mirrored doors. Off to the side of that, was another door. Emily appraised it considering if maybe it was a bathroom. She made a quick mental note to find out how in the heck they got plumbing down there. In fact, how they got everything down there. Maybe they had a Genie in a bottle or something. In a world where vampires and their rival hunters could actually be real, magic must not be that far off.

The pictures on the wall were framed to match the wood of the bed. All the prints were done in varying stages of night time. There were cityscapes mostly but also a few sunsets on the beach type pictures. They were the types of photos she always wanted to own.

Lucy would seriously have freaked if she knew about this place. It was underground, but couldn't be described as anything other than lavish. The cryptic nature of this world would have kept her friend guessing for a lifetime. This was exactly the type of puzzle that she would love a chance to piece together.

"Is this room okay? It seemed like something you would like. Plus I thought you would like to be close to Tyler. He will be next door." His voice was thick with implication. Before she could comment, he continued. "I will also be a few doors down the hall, in case you need anything." Sebastian's gaze was piercing. Whenever he looked at Emily the look was always piercing.

Sebastian had a way of looking deep within her soul in a way she had never experienced before. Without a single word he could send her pulse racing a marathon. That unfamiliar feeling in her stomach was back too. Only this time, it didn't hurt. It felt like butterflies were taking flight in her belly. She had heard that expression a thousand times. Emily never got it, until she met Sebastian. It almost made it difficult to even answer him. She knew his comment about Tyler should have bothered her. It was just so hard to stay angry when he was looking at her like that.

"This room is just right. It's bigger than I thought it would be. The doors in the hall didn't seem to be that far apart." Emily was locked in a staring contest with Sebastian that she couldn't win. Unwillingly thanks to her awkwardness she shied away from his intense blue eyes. She instead focused all of her attention on picking an invisible piece of lint off the sleeve of her hoodie.

"I'm sure you've heard the expression. Things aren't always what they seem?" He waited obviously looking for a response before continuing.

Emily nodded. As she did her eyes widened and she made a circle motion with her hand, encouraging him to get on with it...

"Well, you will find that is a phrase very well understood in our world. Reality isn't at all what humans think it is. If they saw for one minute what we see they would be institutionalized." The left corner of his mouth tugged a little.

Emily imagined his crooked smile. Tyler's was cuter though. It had a boyish charm that you couldn't help but find adorable. "Do you always sound like a riddle wrapped up in a fortune cookie?"

It wasn't that she wanted to be rude to him exactly. It was more like she just refused to let her guard down completely no matter how friendly it seemed like he was being. The niceties didn't seem to ever last long with him. Getting hurt or rejected was not an option.

"Don't you like to figure things out for yourself?" Sebastian shot back mirroring her sarcastic tone.

"Yes, but some things are impossible to figure out on your own." The intensity of her stare should have burnt a hole right through him. He was a quick study. There was no way he didn't realize she was talking about more than his earlier riddle.

The expression on his face turned blank, exposing nothing. "There is no such thing as impossible." Sebastian turned his gaze to a picture on the wall. "Some things are just better left buried." The words were under his breath but still audible.

Enough was enough. Emily decided to cut through the chit chat. There was way too much supernatural junk going on to waste time with small talk and it was clear that this dodge ball style conversation was going nowhere. "Sebastian, why can I hear you in my mind?" Nervous for his answer, she moved to a small arm chair by a table. She fidgeted with her fingers as if she could remove them one at a time and replace them in different positions like a Mr. Potato Head doll.

Silence. Sebastian wasn't even looking at her for once. His eyes moved to a different picture on the wall and he shifted his weight uncomfortably. His body was rigid and his jaw clenched and unclenched reflexively.

"There's no point in keeping it from me. I already know everything now. What's one more detail?" Emily didn't take her eyes away from her fingers even though she was attempting to sound strong and firm.

It was important that she tried to get the answers that she so very much craved. The difficulty was in whether or not Sebastian would comply with her curiosities. It wasn't likely and she knew it. He wouldn't tell her anything he didn't want to. Pushing him to far would just make her new life miserable. It was a definite possibility that she would have to depend on Alexander for the endless amount of conundrums that had been presented. Not knowing the older man very well, it was difficult to know if he would be any more informative.

There was no sound, but Sebastian was suddenly kneeling in front of her on one knee. His hand untangled one of hers and clasped it gently. "I'm not really sure. It's, normal for hunters to be able to communicate in certain situations. Normally though it's only true with hunters. Vampires can communicate like this also with their victims." He stared intently up at her jump starting the contest again.

Emily's body tensed with a little bit of confusion mixed in with irritation. "Well I'm neither a vampire hunter nor their victim. So what am I a freak or something?" Self-doubt was like a knife into her heart and tears pricked at her eyes.

"I assure you Emily you are far from a freak. You are so much more than that. You're... special. You might not be a hunter fully but you are somehow connected through blood line or through some other fashion. I think that's why I'm drawn to you so much. Hunters are drawn to other hunters so that we can better locate each other especially when we haven't met yet." His thumb softly rubbed the center of her palm as he spoke.

It felt good to let him do the comfort thing even in such a small way. Giving up on figuring out what she was, she moved to a new question. "So are there other hunters here right now?" Stupidly Emily looked around the room as if one would materialize suddenly through a magical puff of smoke or something.

"Yes there are other hunters here but not as many as there should be. The coven of Vampires in Lakeview seems to be growing. Before you even ask, there are no good vampires here. And we don't know there purpose here. The leader of this coven is smart. They know we are here or they aren't taking any chances. They cover their tracks better than I've ever seen and I've been at this a long time."

Emily couldn't help a small chuckle at the sound of that. "Sebastian you couldn't be that much older than I am."

"I'm ninety years old, for your information." His hand pulled away from hers and he stood abruptly with indignation.

"What? Really?"

"Yes," said Sebastian bitterly.

"Really?" Her look was one of utter shock. "Wow." This had to be his idea of a joke. Yeah that's it, a joke. Why did he have to ruin such a nice moment?

"Wow what?"

"Um, it's just, you look good for being an old man and all." Now she really couldn't help the laughter that escaped from her lips. It was a full-fledged laugh that she tried uselessly to contain.

The look on Sebastian's face was priceless. She waited for him to get angry at her for laughing at him but it never happened. Instead she watched as his eyes twinkled and his lips twitched fighting back a smile. Huh, looks like there's a sense of humor in there after all. Of course though, it was quickly erased and the mask put back on. At least he didn't look like a rock anymore.

"It's not that funny." Even as he said it she could tell he was amused. "Once I retire I will regain the aging process. A real ninety year old wouldn't be much in a fight."

The idea that aging could be temporarily halted made Emily's brain work in overdrive. It was almost as unbelievable as the reality that vampires existed. As she thought about Sebastian's age, another thought moved to the forefront of her mind. "How old is Alexander?" As she asked her face scrunched up in confusion.

"That is a conversation you should talk to him about." Sebastian smiled slightly. "Alex loves to tell his story."

"Why can't you at least tell me his age?"

Sebastian gave her a sardonic look. "You're a girl. You know it's rude to ask someone's age."

If that was his attempt at making a joke, Emily didn't notice. "I'm not asking him. I'm asking you." She crossed her arms defiantly.

"Alright fine, he is almost three hundred years old."

Emily didn't even have words for that information. Sebastian had rendered her speechless. Sure, it seemed logical that an immortal could live that long, but a slayer wasn't quite immortal. Emily couldn't even fathom how many battles Alexander must have been in and clearly won judging by the fact that he was still alive. She wondered how long he had been retired from the fighting part of this life.

Abruptly he changed the subject. "Tyler should be getting ready to break soon. Alexander will want to see us then. Shall I take you to the training room?"

"Lead the way I'm all yours." Emily gave him a flirty smile and in turn mentally scolded herself. What was she thinking? She never flirted with guys. Well, at least not intentionally and she never initiated the flirting. Sebastian was simply asking her a normal question. No flirting was required. This mandatory hostage sleep over wasn't an excuse for her hormones to grab control of her and run. She's been in co-ed situations before, she could handle this. At least that's what she kept telling herself.

16

The training room reminded Emily of a dance studio. The only thing it lacked was a bar stretching across the mirrored walls all the way around. There were mats on the floor and what looked like punching bags hung in various points on the ceiling. It wasn't very well lit. Thanks to the time that had passed by then, her eyes had completely adjusted to the dimness. You would think they would want good lighting so they could see what they were doing.

As they watched, Tyler went through motions of instruction from Alexander. Tyler weaved around the punching bags like a car around Drivers Ed cones. Amazingly though, before passing one he would make a move of attack on it quickly before moving to the next. Even though his actions were violent, it was unbelievably graceful. Emily wondered how much prior fighting if any Tyler had before falling into the slayer life. He looked like an expert out there. Judging by the look on Alexander's face, he agreed.

Behind them the door opened with an audible click. Someone was coming in. Emily knew it wouldn't be a vampire. They supposedly couldn't get down there. She couldn't help but be a little scared at the thought of the newcomer. Sebastian said there were other hunters living there. That's probably all it was. She hoped anyway.

"Hey Bass, is this the fresh meat?" Emily looked toward the new male voice just in time to see him nod toward Tyler.

"Yeah, that's Tyler." Sebastian gestured towards Alexander and Tyler before returning his gaze to Emily. "And this is Emily. She will be staying with us for a while. She will be in Max's old room."

The guy shot Sebastian a deeply reproachful look. "How could you put her in there? There were other rooms."

"Kyle, don't be unreasonable. I thought she would be more comfortable in the room next to Tyler's. Casey is on the other side so Max's vacated room was the next logical option." Sebastian sounded like he was explaining something difficult to a small child.

"Damn it Bass! Don't get all high and mighty on me. You could have a little soul. He was one of your brothers. Or are we that easy for you to forget and replace like baseball cards?"

"Chill out Kyle. I don't want to get into this with you right now. You know how I felt about Max." Sebastian seemed weary of Kyle for some reason. His fists were clenched tightly at his sides, like he was trying not to come unglued.

Sebastian's tone only made the other guy more annoyed. He looked like he was chomping at the bit. "Don't patronize me I'm not a kid." Kyle's jaw tightened and he was starting to speak through his teeth almost in a growl. "Where did you put his stuff?"

"I put it where we store all the hunters' stuff that no longer lives here. It's boxed and in the storage room," said Sebastian coldly.

"Look, if it's a problem I don't mind switching rooms. I didn't pick that one." Emily tried to interject, hoping to diffuse the situation that was becoming more and more heated.

"No." Sebastian responded firmly. "That's not necessary. You're fine where you are." He made a noticeable attempt at softening his tone, but his icy stare never left Kyle's. "Kyle needs to let go of his sentimentalities."

This seemed to infuriate Kyle, though he didn't say anything else. His face grew red and his jaw kept twitching as he repeatedly clenched and unclenched his teeth. Apparently giving up the argument Kyle just stalked off slamming the door to the training room behind him. The noise echoed off the mirrored walls like a fire cracker. Emily jumped.

"I'm sorry about that, Kyle's overly sensitive sometimes."

Emily swallowed before saying, "I really don't mind switching. Did something happen to Max?"

"Yeah, he died. Kyle needs to learn to let go of the past. No you're not switching," Sebastian replied with a tone of such finality Emily gave up.

"Hey Em," Tyler called from across the room. "What do you think?" Tyler was beaming.

Emily wasn't completely sure how to respond. Did he mean about her room. Maybe he was talking about the little exchange between Sebastian and Kyle. If so, she really didn't know what to think about that. Finally she decided that was stupid because he wouldn't have been able to hear them talking. "You look great out there," she called back hoping it was the answer he was looking for.

It must have been what he was looking for because his eyes practically disappeared with the approving smile that grew as she watched. "Alex is a good teacher I've already learned a lot." He wiped sweat off his forehead then turned back to the punching bags. Tyler pummeled it to the point of no return and seemed to love every minute of it. It should have deflated under the assault and battery he was putting it through.

"Hand to hand won't kill the leeches," Sebastian explained. "Even if it won't take them out, it's needed to weaken their strength. They are unfortunately gifted with brute strength, probably the equivalent of at least ten men. Plus, it's fun," Sebastian admitted with a cocky grin. "They look like they're about done in here for now. If you want I'll take you to get something to eat and then we can meet them back in the office. Alexander wants to further explain exactly what you guys are up against. He doesn't like surprises and so he needs you to be prepared. This isn't a tea party you know."

Emily copied Kyle and clenched her jaw. I'm not a little girl asshole is what she thought. What she actually said was, "fine whatever." He made her so unbelievably crazy she could just scream. How someone could make you feel so warm and good one second and so very ticked off the next was beyond Emily.

The room Sebastian took her too was bigger than her kitchen at home. The center had two large round tables with chairs. The entire outer perimeter of the room was counters, refrigerators and freezers. There were four fridges all together and four freezers. There were five microwaves in various spots along the counters. Emily was a little shocked. She had never seen this many of the same appliances in the same room before. Well, unless you count Sears or something like that.

"What's with all the fridges?" Emily asked motioning vaguely around the space. When she did she discovered they were not alone in the room.

A girl stood with her back to them in the corner under a burnt out light. Her medium blonde hair was short. It didn't even touch the back of her neck. She was dressed in dark washed Capri's and a black tank top with flip flops. She looked like she was doing something, but Emily couldn't tell what that was.

"Oh that's just Ivy.

The girl apparently called Ivy spun around at the sound of his voice. "And you're just a dick," she shot back. She was holding a sandwich and some kind of soda. It looked like a coke. The can was red anyway.

Emily hoped they had Pepsi she has never really been a Coke fan. It's too syrupy. Ivy walked over and plunked the load onto one of the tables. She had one of the most self-assured confident walks Emily had ever seen. Immediately Emily was jealous, which she hated but couldn't help. She had always wanted to be able to carry herself like that. Emily was a confident person most of the time. It would be nice if she could at least send that vibe out into the Universe. No matter how hard she tried to exude self-assurance, it tended to just appear clumsy and awkward.

"Who's the girl?" Ivy asked sounding indifferent either way.

"Ivy this is Emily. Emily, meet Ivy." Sebastian motioned back and forth as if to make sure they didn't get confused.

Come on we're the only ones in the stinking room. Give us some credit, Emily thought giving Sebastian a smug look. "Hey Ivy nice to meet you." Emily stretched out a hand to the other girl.

Instead of returning the gesture, her face turned to one of disbelief and distaste. "Yeah um, like wise I'm sure." She turned her head to Sebastian. "She a slayer?"

"No not exactly," replied Sebastian.

Feeling hurt at Ivy's obvious snub, Emily decided to elaborate. "Actually, they don't know for sure if I'm supposed to be a hunter but I seem to have gifts like one." Emily smiled satisfied for reasons she wasn't really sure of.

Ivy looked utterly disgusted at the idea of having something in common with Emily. "Well isn't that just peachy," she said with mock excitement and clapped her hands together. A fake grin was plastered across her face.

What a beach, Emily thought scornfully. Beach is the word Emily liked to say instead of the curse word it sounded like. It might seem silly but she really tried to not cuss very much, even if the situation called for it.

She really wasn't going to like Ivy. Not even a little bit, she could tell that right away. It was crystal clear that she was one of "those girls". The ones who thought they were better than everyone and that other girls were the scum beneath their feet.

Sebastian sighed and rolled his eyes. "Ivy lay off her alright. We're just here to get something to eat before we have to meet with Alexander." Sebastian moved over to one of the fridges and pulled it open.

"What does Alex want with her if she's not even a true hunter? And you know it's not safe to share our secrets with, humans." Ivy spoke with enough acid to melt the entire room down to nothing.

Emily clenched her teeth, other than that though, avoided saying anything. It was really difficult. That girl wasn't worth the energy. If any energy was expended, it would have been to jump over that table and smack that rude look right off her too cute face. Yeah that would feel way too good. Girls like Ivy drove her so nuts. Ivy didn't even know her. Who did she think she was making snap judgments on her like that? Emily crammed her hands in her pockets to hide her fidgeting. This trait wasn't something she was proud of. Unfortunately, it manifested whenever she was nervous or angry. Ivy would probably have seen it as a sign of weakness and pounce for sure.

"She very well might be a hunter. It's just that she wasn't summoned, and doesn't seem to be showing the other telltale signs. Either way Ivy just lay off. Just eat your sandwich and we'll be out of here in a minute. Emily what do you want?" Sebastian said turning his attention back to Emily.

Emily attempted to sound undisturbed by Ivy's repulsion towards her. "I'm not really hungry, but I will take a Pepsi if you've got it."

"Coming right up." When he stood upright again he was holding two bottles with blue labels.

Yay for Pepsi! Emily's mouth was starting to water. Everything seems better after a little caffeine rush. She could almost taste the carbonated goodness. Sebastian handed her the bottle and they left Ivy sitting by herself. Emily risked a glance back over her shoulder at the other girl. She was slightly surprised that Ivy was glowering at her while she chewed her food. Emily turned back hoping Ivy's room was nowhere near her own. The less she had to see this girl the better. This situation was bad enough without adding a newly found enemy in the mix.

When they returned to the office Tyler and Alexander were already there. Tyler was making himself right at home stretched out across the entire length of the leather sofa. He looked totally exhausted. The vision of him lying there with his shoes kicked off was kind of cute. One of his socks was starting to come off. She could see the flopped over material folded over on his big toe.

Alexander was sitting at his desk writing something. He was completely transfixed in whatever he was doing. Tyler was the first one to notice their arrival.

"Hey where's mine?" Tyler asked eyeing their sodas enviously.

"Sorry," Emily replied sheepishly.

"I figured you would have gotten something in the training room," Sebastian said apologetically.

Tyler smiled, "I did." He held up a Gatorade like he was going to make a toast. "Just thought I'd make you feel bad."

"Well it didn't work," Emily retorted teasingly.

Tyler gave her a cheesy smile and promptly stuck his tongue out at her.

Emily giggled but quickly squelched it when she saw Alexander's unhappy expression. She cleared her throat and shifted uncomfortably as though she had been caught stealing.

Alexander sighed and pushed aside his pen. Casey just reported in. There might be some activity tonight."

Sebastian looked taken aback. "Already, they never feed this close together. How many?"

"Three," Alexander answered. "It might be nothing. Casey said they are just acting suspicious. They tried to get someone in the house. Thankfully she started to scream. They didn't want a scene so they let her run."

"Good if that's all then me, Kyle and Casey should be able to handle it," Sebastian said relieved.

Alexander shook his head. No, that won't work. Casey is on surveillance and Kyle is combing the woods. Ivy is going to be meeting him after she eats."

Sebastian's brow furrowed as he crossed his arms. "Why isn't she with Casey?"

"They got in a fight," replied Alexander shaking his head. "You know how Ivy can be with him." He gave Sebastian a knowing look.

Sebastian nodded tightly and moved on. "Alexander, I don't know if I can take them all by myself, but I will do my best." He puffed out his chest as if to show his power. His eyes seemed to burn at the possibility of the fight.

"No son that isn't possible. I can't afford to risk you in that way. You will have to take Tyler as well."

At the sound of his name Tyler's head snapped up and his eyes bulged from their sockets. "Take Tyler? Tyler isn't ready," he blurted. All the color had drained from his face.

Alexander gave him a reassuring look. He looked like a concerned dad. "Tyler, you are a natural. I have never seen any other hunter retain and utilize our strategies as you have displayed today." Alexander stood and went to a small rectangular table against the wall. "They're definitely on the move. Casey says they appear to be careful in their selection process. If they're not choosing at random than they must be after more than just feeding."

"Tyler's right," Sebastian pleaded. "Even if he has grasped the strategies, he hasn't been trained in what to expect from the leeches. Fighting them is a bit different from fighting an unresponsive punching bag."

The fear was suddenly washed off Tyler's face and was replaced with indignation. "I kicked that bags ass thanks. And besides, I'm all you've got *Superman*. Maybe it's true that I'm not ready. That doesn't seem to really make a difference. I'm going to have to get ready right? There's no other choice."

The two stared it out for a very long minute. Sebastian was the first to break the silence. "Fine. It's your funeral. Just don't get in my way and we do this my way, or you stay.

"Sure Princess, but what about Emily?" Tyler looked smug now.

It just figured. One second Tyler's all afraid and then the next he bristled at the first sign that his manhood might be questioned. Just like guys to turn a life threatening fight into a chance to toss around their machoness like a bunch of immature idiots.

"What about Emily? She stays," Sebastian replied firmly.

Since when does Sebastian get to be her parent? She already had a dad and she didn't like him making decisions for her without her consent either. "No… Emily goes too. I can take care of myself."

Sebastian laughed humorlessly. "Sure you can, have you ever even been in a fight with a regular person?" He swiped at his eye removing a fake tear. "That would be great. I got little miss naive on one side and Robin Hood's fairy man on the other. What a great team I have to work with. Thank you Alexander."

Emily squared her shoulders and her eyes blazed at him. "Look, I'm an adult. I make my own decisions and I'm going whether you like it or not. I won't get in the way I don't even have to fight. I'm going." She crossed her arms over her chest and glared at him defiantly daring him to contradict her. For an instant she thought about stomping her foot, but figured that would have been counterproductive.

"You can't force her to stay behind Sebastian. We don't take away ones free will you know that." Alexander spoke in a regretful tone, but Emily was still glad for the support, even if only halfhearted.

"Fine," Sebastian thundered.

"Hmm," Emily said smugly. She knew it wasn't very mature but she couldn't help herself.

She was getting tired of him trying to treat her like a fragile baby. He had no idea what she was capable of and it wasn't fair for him to make assumptions. For all he knew she had a black belt and could kill someone using only her pinky. Of course she wasn't a black belt. Obviously her pinky wasn't a death tool but none of that was the point. She was glad Sebastian got shot down on his daddy trip he deserves to be knocked down a peg once in a while. It's good for him.

Sebastian left the room laughing. "Fine. Come on little baby ducks…" His words trailed off with his departure.

Coming to life again Tyler spoke to no one in particular. "And I'm not a fairy," he sulked. When he pouted he looked like a little boy.

Emily didn't say anything to Tyler as they followed several feet behind Sebastian. She felt like a rubber band pulled taut, ready to snap any minute. The indignation she felt toward Sebastian tasted bitter in her mouth and she couldn't shake it. A competitive nature had always been inside Emily and he knew just how to make it rear its ugly head. Tyler didn't talk either, apparently still pouting from the fairy comment.

The weapon's room was terrifying. There was every kind of knife, sword, and crossbow you could think of. Gleaming silver caught the light from every corner of the room. There were even guns with boxes labeled silver bullets on one of the shelves. Emily saw weird canisters that looked like they held glitter. Sebastian explained those weren't glitter. They were pure silver powder. They burn a vampire's skin on contact. He gave one of the salt shaker sized containers to Emily. He warned her that they could also cut hunters so she would need to be careful where she aimed. He armed Tyler and himself with crossbows. He handed Tyler two blades that had severely jagged teeth. He grabbed two for himself and slid them into his belt. Tyler carefully slid one of his knives out of the black leather sheath for examination. The light bounced a reflection of the blade and onto Tyler's wicked smile. His eyes caught Emily's and she saw they were all lit up like a child on Christmas morning. Sebastian tried handing Emily a knife, but she shook her head. She figured she would just end up stabbing herself or a tree. Both options would be counterproductive

17

Lakeview was dark with little to no activity, anywhere in site. There really wasn't anything out of the ordinary going on, except that in the past, there still would have been kids out playing under the street lights in the warm summer air. Now, there was no sound of children playing. There was no smell of a late night barbeque blazing. There was only the dull hum of the street light bulbs as they passed them. Off in the distance Emily could faintly hear the sound of sporadic cars driving to their destinations. It really wasn't that late. If nothing else, there should have been more traffic. There should have been people driving home from work doing last minute errands, or teenagers driving to the next party spot honking the whole time to signal more party goers to the direction of the fun.

As the three of them passed the vacant looking residential streets, Emily scanned the houses for signs of life. It seemed necessary to prove that her hometown wasn't turning into the town of the dreaded sundown. Through tightly pulled curtains she could make out the faint hint of light peeking through the cracks. There were no sounds, nothing indicating anyone was home at all. No blaring TV's or stereos as they passed. It just didn't feel right.

Emily's stomach cramped with a mild pulse, making her more alert. In turn, her heart rate began to race. That couldn't be a good sign. The pain in her midsection seemed to be a built in alarm system that let her know her life was about to be in jeopardy. Every time she felt it, she had been attacked by a vampire not long after.

They heard a noise coming out of an alley and Sebastian was the first to take a careful look around the corner. He turned his head back to them with a manly nod. Emily saw that Tyler nodded back, though she had no idea what the exchange meant. Just in case, she gripped the silver shaker in her pocket. Tyler moved around her and motioned for her to stay put. He moved so stealthily Emily didn't hear his feet or even his clothing make a sound. Sebastian moved out of his way equally as quiet so Tyler could have a look.

Tyler spun back quickly and leaned on the fence they were hiding by. He tipped his head back on the boards. His expression was more than a little wary. Emily had wanted to take a look for herself. Judging by Tyler's reaction, she wasn't so sure she wanted to know what was going on in that alley. She gulped, bit her lip and started for the edge of the fence.

Sebastian snatched a hold of her arm and yanked her to him. Her small body banged into his hard one with a jolt. She could feel the lines of his peck muscles flexed hard to take the blunt of the impact. The feel of his well-defined body made her dizzy. It only took a second to recover and then she was furious.

Emily glowered up at Sebastian. She couldn't see into his eyes, but she knew he could see into hers. "What? I just wanted to see what-"

Sebastian put a large hand over her mouth. She had a sudden memory of the first night they met, which was also in a dark alley.

"Do you want him to hear you?" Sebastian hissed the words into her ear. "Tyler I'm going to take care of this clown, stay here and watch Emily."

Tyler nodded nervously with one hand on the butt of his knife. His body seemed to tremble with the anticipation of what was about to happen. He was scared, that much was obvious.

Emily started to protest and Sebastian put his hand back over her mouth. He shook his head fiercely, silently warning her to be a good little girl and stay quiet. Sebastian took out his knife and peered back around the fence. Before Emily could blink, he was gone, melting into the shadows of the alley.

Emily held her breath waiting. She grabbed a hold of Tyler's hand that was not gripping a knife and held it as tight as she could. She didn't want him to leave her. He was her friend and that meant a lot to her. She didn't let many people in.

The sound of a snarl ripping into the summer night air made Emily and Tyler jump. Tyler's hand tightened on Emily's for a second and then he let go, pushing her protectively behind him. The answering growl was evident to be a warning that wasn't just a threat. It was a promise. Emily couldn't tell who the aggressor was. Obviously it was a vampire, what else would it be? She just wished she could see something, anything.

A whimper broke through her concentration. Someone else was back there. For whatever reason, it had never occurred to Emily that the vampires might be using the alley as a feeding ground. The whimper came again, but this time its owner was clearer. The voice sounded like a child, a teenager at the very oldest. It was a girl. Emily could hear a set of feet scrambling to gain purchase on the gravel on the alley floor. Once they had traction they were headed towards Tyler and Emily. Emily's mind flashed back to her experience in an alley similar to this one.

Pushing back the memory, she tugged at Tyler's arm. "Ty someone's coming," Emily whispered franticly.

Tyler tensed and Emily heard the sound of him removing a blade from its sheath. "Take this just in case."

Emily felt the offering of the knife's shaft on her fingers. Without thinking she grabbed a hold of it expertly as if she had been doing it for years. "Get ready," she said, hearing the footsteps get closer. Whoever it was coming to meet them was running now.

Emily took a deep breath and held it, wishing she were invisible. Strangely though, she wasn't as afraid as she should have been. Suddenly there was a figure bolting out of the alley and heading in their direction. The shadowed figure stopped and seemed to be taking in the observers. It clearly wasn't Sebastian. It was much to slight to be him. Emily took a small flash light out of her jacket pocket and pointed it over Tyler's shoulder at the stranger.

At the sight of the small, bright beam of light the figure recoiled back and almost fell on the rocks. It didn't look like a vampire. Everything she had learned so far, taught her that vampires and apparently their hunters, could shroud themselves in total silence. Whoever this was seemed petrified at the sight of them. Emily had a feeling that a crazed vampire wouldn't have even batted an eye lash at them, let alone be afraid. The person looked ruffled like they had been in a hurricane or something.

Without hesitation, Emily moved around Tyler and shown the light in her own face. Maybe the person thought she and Tyler were vampires. After being in the dark for so long the brightness was a shock. Emily had to blink a few times to adjust to the change.

"What are you doing?" Tyler tried to pull her back behind him, with no luck.

Emily knew she was right about this one. This was the owner of the whimper they had heard. Every fiber of her being was telling her she needed to help this girl. Emily locked her feet in place and somehow steadied herself so that even Tyler couldn't budge her.

The sound of violent fighting broke her attention and she turned to see down the mouth of the alley. Sebastian was in full on combat with one of the vampires. He was expertly dodging and weaving around blows. He countered and connected with several of his own. Emily didn't think he had his knife though. Had he lost it during the scuffle? He couldn't kill the vampire without a blade. The fighters were too close to each other for Sebastian to pull out his crossbow.

"Tyler go help Sebastian," Emily demanded firmly like a drill sergeant. "I can take care of the girl, just go."

A struggle seemed to be going on inside of Tyler. It was his will and desire to protect Emily verses the need and instinct to aid in the fight. After a moment he turned and took out his bow. This was apparently his compromise. This way he was able to stay close to Emily. If necessary, he was in a position where he hopefully could take out the vamp. Within seconds he had a silver tipped arrow trained on the two figures.

Emily left him to his business and moved to check on the other girl. As Emily got closer, the girl stepped back in preparation to run. Emily held a hand up in front of her urging her to stop. She didn't know if the girl could see her. Emily tried to communicate with her eyes that she would be safe, at least she hoped that were true.

"It's okay," Emily pleaded. "We are the good guys I promise. Was there only one that attacked you?"

The other girl stopped moving. Even though she didn't answer, the poor girl at least didn't seem to be on the verge of running away anymore.

Emily sighed with relief. No confirmation of more vampires was good enough for Emily, even if she hadn't technically gotten an answer. "Okay that's good. Are you hurt?" Emily tried to give her a once over with the flash light but couldn't see much. That is until the beam of light reached the girls neck. "Oh my Gosh! Are you okay?" Emily moved toward her in a rush.

Streaming down the girl's throat and drenching her dark T-shirt, was a steady flow of blood. As if she hadn't noticed, the other girls hand flew up to examine what Emily was talking about. "Oh God," she breathed sounding totally panicked. "Oh God it hurts."

It reminded Emily of a small child. The girl didn't seem to notice the pain, until she noticed the wound. From the look of all the blood, she should have been in agony. The poor girl's breath was coming in small heavy pants now. If she didn't calm down, she was going to hyperventilate.

Emily tore off her coat and wrapped it in a ball. It wasn't an ideal bandage, but it would have to do. She applied the coat to the girl's neck and pressed as hard as she could, without knocking the poor thing over. She looked as though she was going into shock. The longer Emily was with her, the better her eyes seemed to adjust to the darkness. "I need you to come over by the fence. There are a few bushes you can hide behind until I come back for you. I have to help my friends okay?" She put her arm around the other girls shoulder to guide her to their hiding place.

"I want to go home," the girl sobbed. "Please don't leave me." She dug into Emily's arm so hard Emily could feel the sting of broken skin where her nails had dug in.

"I know you do," Emily soothed. "We'll get you home soon. I need you to just sit here for now okay?" Emily sat the other girl down so she was concealed behind the bushes. "I'm Emily by the way. Who are you?" Emily was whispering now since they were closer to the chaos.

"Beth," the other girl said her voice wobbling.

"Hey, I know you, don't I?" Recognition snapped into place within Emily. "Beth Thomas, right?"

Beth nodded weakly.

Emily went to high school with her. Beth was in one of Emily's English classes. "Alright Beth, you stay here. I'll be back for you as soon as I can, I promise."

She didn't give Beth a chance to protest again. She stood and hurriedly moved to the alley. Before she got very far, Emily was stopped short because a cold hand grabbed her around her neck. Emily gasped and tried to struggle free. It was no use. Whoever had a hold of her had a grip of steel. The more she struggled the tighter the hold on her throat became, as though she were stuck in a body sized Chinese finger trap. It was becoming harder and harder to take in a breath.

"Don't move and I'll loosen up," a menacing voice breathed in her ear. His breath had a recognizable scent.

It was almost intoxicating to Emily's senses. A dizzy feeling began to wash over her with a growing intensity that made her knees shake. Unlike before though, something clicked in her brain and the wooziness fell away as quick as it had come. "What do you want?" Emily struggled to speak around the force of his hand around her throat.

"Why leverage of course. Your friends are killing my friend. This angers me. I believe they will stop if they see what I have to barter with." He sounded carefree like this was just another day in the life of a psycho. It probably was for a vampire.

"Let me go," Emily pleaded. When he didn't she tried to get a hold of the blade she had shoved into the waste of her jeans.

He got to it first and dropped it to the ground, just out of the reach of her foot. "You really didn't think I'd let you get to that, did you?" The vampire made a tisk-tisk noise and shook his head at her disapprovingly. "Silly girl, silver blades are for hunters and you I'm afraid, are no hunter. You know nothing of this life. I wonder though… Do your chums even realize what a true treasure you are to them? Well, I guess we'll soon find out won't we?"

Emily wanted to scream to get Tyler and Sebastian's attention. She could see them now. They were really letting the vampire have it. They were so engrossed in the fight they hadn't even noticed that Emily was now captured not more than ten feet away from them. Just as Tyler raised his blade to the vamps throat, Emily's captor spoke.

"Oh boys, I wouldn't do that if I were you." There was a taunting edge to his voice. "I believe I have something you might want to trade for my friend."

Tyler froze and looked up, saying nothing.

It was Sebastian who responded. Andre let the girl go, or your leech friend here dies."

Andre? It was the vampire creep from the computer lab. Emily was gripped with fear now. Both of the vamps that she had encountered besides him were terrifying. There was just something different about Andre. The look of fury and what she now assumed to be hunger, flashed in her memory like an unshakeable nightmare. As if sensing her realization, the hand around her neck clenched even harder and she choked for air.

"I really don't think you are in any position to bargain young Sebastian. All I have to do is tighten my hand a little more and her sweet little neck will be snapped like a twig. You kill him and she dies before you have time to blink." Andre ran his nose along Emily's jaw line lovingly, breathing in deeply as he did. "That would be a shame too. It's positively sinful how decadent she smells."

Emily winced at the thought of his teeth breaking the skin at the hollow of her throat. "Sebastian kill him. Don't worry about me." Her words came out in a hoarse whisper from Andre's pressure but Sebastian still seemed to understand.

Tyler's blade was still trained on the fallen vampire's throat. It wouldn't take much for him to finish the job. Emily's eyes darted back and forth from Tyler to Sebastian and finally to the practically dead *thing* on the ground. She had to do something. What could she do? There was no way that she could over power Andre. At most, all she could have hoped for was that he did snap her neck. At least if he did, there wouldn't be any lingering pain.

The three of them were still exchanging words, but Emily blocked them out. They became almost like a blur of sound, like a distant hum. Their voices swam together like nonsensical gibberish. Every passing second brought her closer to the devastating realization that her life was about to end before the night was up. There were so many things she still hadn't done. She had never told Lucy what was going on with the vampires. She had never had a real boyfriend. Would George cut her a break if she didn't show up to work because Andre cut out her throat? Who would take care of Sam? Andre's voice was the hardest to block out because he insisted on keeping his lips near the corner of her jaw when he spoke. His words although broken, kept penetrating the walls she had put up in her mind. One of her mother's famous mantras pierced her thoughts like a warm blanket. Quitters never win…

Suddenly the solution was there. *The silver powder*. If she could just get the lid off without Andre noticing. Her hand moved almost in perceptively into her pocket. Andre was so engaged in the duel with the other two he didn't seem to think twice about her movements. She made a purposeful point to continue to struggle a little. If he thought she was trying to break free, he might not think that she was trying anything underhanded. He clearly underestimated her.

The lid was off the plastic container. She was almost there, just a little more. She wasn't really sure how to use the powder but she dug her fingers inside trying to get a hold of some. Remembering what Sebastian had said about the powder needing to be activated she tried to figure out a way to throw the powder somehow.

"Struggling will do you no good my dear girl," Andre whispered almost seductively into her ear breaking her concentration for a moment. He still hadn't noticed what she was doing. Or if he did he was waiting for the last possible minute to catch her in the act. Then he would kill her for sure.

Emily couldn't think about that. She had to try. What other choice was there? Besides, her life depended on it. Either way he could kill her, she didn't have anything to lose. She hoped anyway, dying really didn't seem like an appealing option.

When her hand came out of her pocket it was fisted around a mound of the silver powder. Almost there. Through her struggling she managed to cock her head to the side so she would have a clear shot at Andre's face. Her eyes remained in front of her. She could tell that Tyler could see what she was doing. He was trying not to give her away with long glances but she knew that he knew.

Time was running out, she couldn't afford to wait any longer. Soon, Andre would resort to inflicting pain on Emily to get his point across. Right now he was just a cobra preparing to strike. Once he was in full action mode, it would be harder to fight back. With one small but quick motion she thrust her arm upward releasing the powder into Andre's face at point blank range.

18

Andre howled as the silver crystals took effect, eating into his flesh. It burned him instantly on contact. Each flake burst into a small pocket of flame that tore into his skin, melting like acid. Andre lost his grip on Emily's neck.

As she watched, he clawed at his face trying to put out the burn and scrape off the powder. It was no use, the powder wasn't powder anymore. For a second Emily couldn't move. The sight in front of her paralyzed her where she stood. A part of her, a very small part wanted to help him. She battled with herself as she watched the vampire's agony. Then she remembered he wasn't on her team. Just moments before, he had threatened to drain her like a bottle of Propel on a hot day. With that in mind, she raced across to where Sebastian and Tyler still held the other vampire.

"You okay," asked Tyler. He was breathing hard and his eyes kept darting to the panicked Andre, who was trying to make his way out of the alley in retreat.

"Yeah, I think so," Emily replied breathlessly.

Sebastian knelt down next to Tyler. "We can do status checks later. We've got to finish this before Andre comes back with the others. They can't follow us out."

Tyler just looked at him confused. "Why don't we just go kill Andre?"

It was a logical question. Emily wondered that herself but didn't want to ask. She was in no mood for Sebastian to turn all high and mighty and switch into lecturing teacher mode.

"No time." Sebastian shook his head. "He might be hurt but he's old. He will heal quickly and he will have run away even quicker." Sebastian glanced back toward the mouth of the alley where Andre had been. "That one will take more planning." He spoke regretfully and with no wiggle room for opposition.

"Okay," Tyler said hesitantly but clearly relenting. He brought his attention back to the monster at his feet. "Is there anything I should know before doing this?" As he spoke he lowered the blade back down to the passed out vamps throat.

"No. Just give it everything you've got with one clean swipe, the quicker the better and there are no other instructions. It's not like you need to be careful of injuring it or anything. That's the whole point." Sebastian stood now probably trying to give Tyler some room. He grabbed a hold of Emily and pulled her back a few steps. "Just get it done man. If you can't then move aside and I'll show you how it's done."

Tyler's gaze moved from Sebastian, to Emily and finally to the pale white figure lying before him. It was obvious to see Sebastian's implication that Tyler wasn't man enough to handle it. Tyler bristled slightly at that but still looked unsure. He shook his head fast. "I can do it just give me a second."

Sebastian looked over his shoulder as if his name was called. "We don't have a second damn it! Just do it," Sebastian demanded.

Emily could hear the girl in the alley whimpering again. Something was coming. Emily wanted to go and help her. However, she knew she wouldn't do much good against a vampire army with no real fighting skills whatsoever. She looked back to Tyler hoping his job was done and they could leave. His arm was frozen, poised in position to slash the undead throat, which was still pressed firmly against the knife. Sebastian was right. There was no time to lose soon it would be snack time featuring them as the main course.

Without knowing exactly what she was doing, she rushed to Tyler's side. Swiftly removing the knife from his grip, Emily held it in the ready position. Wielding razor sharp daggers was never something she was taught but somehow she knew what to do. Holding the shaft of the blade felt like second nature as if she had been doing it her entire life instead of just the last few seconds. With a gulp she raised the blade. A voice inside her spoke firm telling her to lift the blade, hold it steady and bring it back down with everything she had. Oddly the voice didn't surprise her. It wasn't Sebastian's this time. It was her own, confident and true. Closing her eyes she brought it down and slashed across the vamps throat effortlessly.

When her eyes reopened, she was instantly shocked at what she had done. She had killed him. Not just killed him, she had decapitated him. She, Emily Jameson who had never even punched someone, let alone cut their head off had given an undead creature their final death. All she could do was stare down mutely at the two separate parts. There was a body and there was a head. There wasn't even a lot of blood. The officially dead, thanks to Emily, vampire was wearing the same expression as before she cut him. He just looked as though he was sleeping. Well, sleeping with his eyes open and zero color in his face, but still. Even though it was the right thing to do, she couldn't get over the fact that she, not Tyler or Sebastian, had been the one to do it.

Right before her eyes the vampire vanished. He just fell away into dust on the ground. She scrubbed at her eyes trying to clear them. That had to be a trick of her mind. Maybe she had just blocked out the traumatic scene that had played out in front of her. Only she hadn't. She remembered everything perfectly. The only trace that the vampire had even been there was a gold chain that fell with a clank onto the rocks. Emily picked up the chain and looked around. She knew it wasn't possible, but she thought maybe he somehow came back to life and was just gone. Instead, of the reality that he had vanished into thin air, without a trace left behind except a piece of jewelry.

Sebastian snatched up her arm and hauled her up to her feet. "Good, it's done. Let's get out of here." Without another word, he scooped her up into his arms cradling her like a fragile baby.

The world around her became a blur after that. Sebastian's face was still clear and so was Tyler's next to him. Everything else seemed to wiz by as if she were looking out a car window, but much faster. They were running? The sensation made her dizzy and more than a little nauseous. She felt as though she would throw up at any minute. All she could think was please God give her enough notice to at least turn her head. This wasn't exactly the most optimal position for getting sick.

Wait a minute, what about that girl? They couldn't just leave her there. Emily fought against the gravity pulling her head back down to her chest to speak to Sebastian. "That girl! We can't leave her there. The other vamps will get her if they come back looking for us."

"They'll find her either way. She has a blood tie with one of their brothers. It will weaken since you killed him but they can still track her for a time after." Sebastian's expression never changed. It looked as though he were talking about going shopping, instead of a girl being left for dead.

"Sebastian," Emily demanded. "Isn't it our job to protect humans from the vamps? Or do you get to pick and choose which ones are worthy of saving? Let me down!" Emily was struggling against his hold, trying to break free. "I'll help her myself. I don't need you."

"I'm going to go back, but we have to circle around. So calm down." He shot her a sardonic look. "I'm assuming you heard our plasma craving friends back there headed right for us? What were we supposed to do? Excuse me crazy undead mob. Could you please pause in your quest to seek vengeance for hurting one of your brothers and killing the other? It will only take a second and we'll be on our way. Just let us get this girl who is wounded and dripping delicious blood. And I'm sure you won't mind if she comes with us. You can just make other arrangements for your dinner thanks." Even at a dead run Sebastian's sarcastic tone came through loud and clear. "Somehow I think my way is the better alternative, if you don't mind that is."

Emily felt guilty for her tirade, he did have a point. "Yeah, your way is fine," she allowed meekly. "I guess I didn't think you cared about her, that's all. And besides, it's not like I have a very good view point from my position. How was I supposed to know where we were going? No wonder babies cry all the time."

Tyler laughed, "Never really thought about it like that."

"Just remember, I'm not the monster," Sebastian said dryly not looking at her.

The guys started to slow their pace. Emily attempted to crane her head up so she could see something, anything. As she did this she envisioned a baby bird poking its puny little bald head out of the nest for the first time. Her eyes widened at the sights around her. It was weird how well her eyes had adjusted to the darkness. It still looked dark out but more like twilight. It should have been pitch black. It was like the night's events kicked her senses into hyper overdrive.

Off in the distance there was the scent of a burn barrel permeating in the air. Someone had their house speakers blasting at full volume. Emily wondered absently if maybe there was a party going on or something. It was kind of hard to imagine regular life carrying on around them. Life goes on she supposed. Why couldn't she have been part of the lucky oblivious bunch Lakeview still had left?

Sebastian slowed, walking like a prowling cat on the hunt. Without any warning he put her back on her feet. The speed of the gesture gave her a head rush and made her a little dizzy. Emily put her hands out to her sides trying to maintain her balance. Soon the spinning sensation was over and she was able to see where they had stopped.

They were only about two houses away from the alley. Tyler and Sebastian looked like they were on red alert with their hands poised and ready near their weapons. Emily strained to hear anything that might resemble even a hint of danger.

Unconsciously she moved her hand to where her knife was kept on her newly acquired belt. It wasn't there. She had almost forgotten that Andre had thrown it in the alley earlier. Hopefully there were still remnants of silver powder in her pocket. If nothing else she could rub it in one of their eyes or something. A blind vampire probably wouldn't be very productive. All she would have had to do was run out of their reach after that. The thought of playing Marco Polo with a blind vampire almost made her laugh out loud despite the situation.

Sebastian motioned for them to stay put. He moved OO7 style along the sides of the houses and behind shrubbery. No matter how hard she tried, Emily couldn't hear anything over there. Well, she could vaguely hear the light steps that she hoped belonged to Sebastian and not a freaky nightmare come to life. This was weird considering up until that point she remembered thinking about how silent he and Tyler moved. Now, she could even hear the sound of Tyler's shallow breathing and his thudding heart. She'd never been able to hear anyone's heart before. Huh. It must be adrenalin. She had never been attacked by a vampire then turn all warrior and kill one either. Yeah, the night was just stocked full of surprises.

Get over here. I need you guys now! It was Sebastian's voice but it wasn't coming from where it should. She was hearing it in her head. The sound of it made her jump slightly. She hadn't heard it since she had been with him. The command and desperation in his voice came through loud and clear.

Something's wrong, Emily whispered to Tyler. At least she thought she had.

Tyler faltered slightly. "Did you hear something?" Then, as though something had just occurred to him, he gave her a second look. "Did you just...? How did you do that?" Despite his hushed voice, he sounded utterly bewildered.

Emily had apparently spoken to him in her mind. "I have no idea." That wasn't supposed to happen. She got messages from Sebastian, but she didn't send them.

Flirt later! Help now! Sebastian broke into their confusion like scissors through paper.

The sardonic nature of his words didn't even register. The emotion behind the words however, came through and processed just fine. "Sebastian needs us now. We gotta go, now." It was hard to whisper when Sebastian was screaming in her head.

Tyler cleared his throat and began to scramble. "Sorry," he said sheepishly.

Emily felt like the worst person on earth. She shoved her confusion to the back burner and got her head back in the game. She and Tyler would have to figure everything out later. Safety first, she reminded herself.

The two of them followed the same path Sebastian had taken. They weren't certain what they were coming up against. Just about anything could be happening. Caution was the best measure, at least until they were sure it was clear. The wind had a chilly bite to it that almost burnt her cheeks. Why did they have to be in a town where it was colder more than warm every year? Emily knew the thought was trivial in comparison to the drama facing them, but it somehow made her feel better to think normal thoughts.

As they eased their way as fast as possible against the wall of a house, Emily heard a TV on in one of the windows. It sounded like a horror movie, equipped with screams and everything. The music coming from inside was dark and building. It was like it was about to reach the climactic ending, where they catch and fry the killer or something. Even though it creeped her out, she found it ironically funny. If it weren't for the fact that she had her mouth clamped shut, she probably wouldn't have been able to stop a giggle from coming out betraying her careful silence. Emily couldn't help but think how oddly fitting the muffled instrumental music was to their current situation.

They were crouching expertly behind the bushes surprisingly, making little to no noise. Emily concentrated on not allowing her shoes to shift the river rock beneath her careful footsteps. The longer they were in the silence, the more uneasy Emily felt. She willed her heart to slow down and relax. Then she noticed that Tyler's was beating in double-time too and somehow that made her feel better.

They reached Sebastian at the mouth of the alley where they had been before. There was no sign of danger. As far as Emily could tell, there was no sign of vampires at all. She gave a quick scan down the alley. None of the shadows moved or looked out of place. There was nothing further down the street either. When they got closer to Sebastian, they found that he was kneeling down at the corner of the fence. When they saw what he had been so urgent about, Emily and Tyler gasped at the same time.

There was someone lying on the ground motionless. It was the girl from earlier. It was Beth Thomas. She was drenched in even more blood than before. At least, it looked like blood. Her light colored top had a large black stain covering most of the material. Emily thought she could even smell a faint coppery scent.

How weird, she thought somewhat absently to herself. Even though they weren't that far from Beth, the distance still should have been too great for Emily to smell the blood. As they stepped closer, Tyler made a quick scan in all directions looking for any sign of the enemy.

The closer they got, the heavier the blood smell became. It was so strong, that it made Emily's nose wrinkle in response. She didn't even like the smell of her own blood when she got a paper cut. Sure there was a lot of the pooling liquid, but she had never been able to become grossed out simply by smell alone. The sight wasn't even an issue for her which really grossed her out. Emily had always hated the sight of any wound no matter how small. This was probably the most horrific wound she had ever seen up close in real life.

"Ah hell," stammered Tyler. "Is she…" The end of Tyler's question hung in the air between them like ice beneath their feet, threatening to crack. Tyler's vision was transfixed on the girl lying in front of him. His eyes looked petrified. His facial features hid it well behind a stoic expression.

"No," said Sebastian. "She's hardly breathing and I can barely make out a heartbeat, but she's not dead. We've got to get her to Alexander." As he spoke he carefully picked up Beth cradling her like he had Emily before. She looked like a limp rag doll in his arms. Her head was flopped back over Sebastian's arm, looking as though it were about to fall off. "Tyler, carry Emily so we can move quicker."

"Check," responded Tyler obediently. He didn't snatch her up like Sebastian had. Instead, he held out his arms as if silently asking her for permission.

Emily didn't give him a response out loud. She just moved closer to him, allowing him to sweep her off her feet in a smooth graceful motion. Dang, she finally got swept off her feet and she didn't even get to wear the Cinderella dress. Also, it wasn't exactly a honeymoon threshold she was being carried over. Even in the midst extreme crisis moment, she couldn't help but notice her heart rate increase as he held her close. It was ridiculous she knew, but he was adorable even if she didn't like him like that. Did she?

Before she had time to ponder the idea, they were off and moving again. Like before, everything became a blur as they sped down the deserted streets. If people in their houses looked out and saw them, they probably wouldn't even notice. They were moving too fast. If they did see anything, they wouldn't know what. By the time they came up with a guess, the four of them would be long gone.

As they ran, Emily wondered if the vampires that had found Beth were looking for them now too. Surely Andre had told them about the encounter and that's why they were coming in the first place. Would they look for their friend, or just assume Tyler had finished the job? Emily cringed at the thought of them discovering it was her and not Tyler. They would probably laugh and take pride in the lack of effort required to kill her. She couldn't think about that. The right thing had been done and in the long run, that was all that mattered. At least that's what she kept telling herself anyway. Plus, what about the blood tie Sebastian spoke of earlier between Beth and the vamp? Wouldn't that just lead the bad guy's right to them?

The changes in Emily that had developed during the struggle, kept creeping to the front of her mind. It felt selfish and wrong to think about herself. Beth was dying not more than a foot from her. Although, if she continued to think about that, she might go into melt down mode, which wouldn't help anyone.

Her increased night vision was cool, but not really that big of a deal. The instinct to behead that vampire was what plagued her. It came out of nowhere. Maybe living with Sam taught her a few things. Except, it wasn't like she just punched him, or threw him against a wall. Sam's temper seemed mild compared with what she did. What Emily had done, she hadn't even seen in a movie. Something so morbidly grotesque had never been so up close and personal before. Did it mean she was a vampire hunter too? She couldn't be, could she? Sebastian should have some kind of insider information about her. He could get into her head after all.

She and Tyler seem to have some kind of mind mojo going on with each other too. She spoke to him in her mind, without even realizing she could. He didn't answer her in the same way. Nevertheless, his verbal answer was clue enough that he heard her. What did that mean?

They kept telling her that she played some role in all of it. If that were true, it would sure be nice for someone to figure out what that meant. Nothing seemed to make sense anymore. Emily put her hand to her forehead. Man she was getting a killer headache.

19

Back at the compound, Sebastian laid Beth across a cot in a room that was labeled as the infirmary. The large room hadn't been part of the mini tour Emily had been on before. The lighting was much more extreme than the rest of the underground hidey hole safe haven thing. She supposed it would have to be, considering what it was used for.

As Sebastian slid his arm out from under Beth's head, she let out a tiny groan. It was the first sound that the listless girl had made since they found her. That must be a good sign. At least Emily hoped it was a good sign. Beth really didn't look so good. Her skin was completely void of any color. It was as stark white as the vampires that had tried to make a meal out of her. Luckily for Beth, they had just succeeded in making her a snack instead of the feast they had probably hoped for. Even so, there wasn't much of her that wasn't covered in blood. Beth's face held no expression. Her lids were closed making her appear as though she were merely sleeping. This made her look younger somehow, more innocent. Then Emily's eyes drifted back down to the gory display that engulfed the rest of her. Maybe not.

Alexander was ready and waiting when Sebastian retreated back to give him room. There was a roll cart next to the cot at Alexander's side. It had lots of shiny instruments that Emily didn't recognize. Alexander opened a drawer and pulled out a syringe. Next, he pulled out several long tubes. Emily was completely bewildered. What was he going to do to her?

Her expression must have matched her thoughts, because Sebastian said, "he's going to give her a transfusion. She's had way too much blood drained out of her tonight." Emily nodded weakly but said nothing.

"It's her only chance of survival at this point. There is nothing else we can do but wait for this to take effect. It's a good thing you found her when you did." Alexander's words were meant for all of them. He didn't look up from his work as he spoke. He expertly injected Beth with the needle and then immediately sent a steady stream of blood to her through the tubes.

Within minutes, he pulled off his gloves with a snap that made Emily jump. "Sorry," Alexander apologized softly. The senior hunter had never even looked up. Apparently his position gave him stronger senses of motion. Or, he had eyes on the back of his head like moms and teachers. He slid over two machines. They looked like a heart monitor and she thought the other one might be oxygen.

In no time at all, Beth was hooked up to the machines. Emily had been right on what they were. Alexander informed them all that a ventilator wouldn't be necessary since she was breathing on her own. Her breath was shallow and sporadic enough though, that he thought putting an oxygen mask on her was important to keep her stable. The heart monitor bleeped in time with her heart. It was slow. Too slow in Emily's opinion, not that her opinion meant anything of course. She wasn't a doctor after all. To be perfectly honest, she barely knew how to check her own heart rate. It was either fast, or it was slow. She just knew that Beth's heart rhythm was going much slower than her own and hers seemed to be normal.

"What now?" Tyler asked breaking the silence.

"We wait," replied Alexander. "I will stay with her for now so the three of you can get some sleep. We will need to take shifts in the morning." As if the conversation was over, he moved to a table on the other side of the room and grabbed a book. He brought it back to the chair that he had placed beside Beth's bed.

"Sounds good Alex," Sebastian agreed. His hero worship of Alexander was obvious.

They walked back to their rooms in silence. The sight of Beth lying on the ground back in the alley traveled slowly through Emily's mind. The memory of her blood stained body was inescapable. They seemed to imbed themselves into every nook and cranny of Emily's brain. She counted how many steps it would take to get to her room to keep her brain occupied. It didn't work, she kept losing count.

Pictures of her mom lying in a too bright hospital room stained the forefront of her awareness. The situation with Beth brought all the memories out of the locked vault that she had buried deep in the back of her head. She felt tears prick her eyes, and didn't allow them to spill over. Beth wasn't Melissa. The two were in no way connected and in no way alike. Even still, the blinding light of the infirmary and the tubes attached to Beth's arms begged to differ. Her mind could distinguish between the two but her heart ached in protest.

This day was just too exhausting and not just physically. Emily yearned for a switch that could be flipped that would transfer her passed this portion of her life. Truth be told, she wanted a time machine that could take her back to five years ago. There are so many things that she would have done differently. There were so many things left unsaid that left gaping holes of regret deep within her soul. Maybe things could have been different with Sam too, everything could have been different. The past had come back to torment Emily and she wanted desperately to have the power to push it all back into the vault where it belonged. Once it was tucked safely away she would be sure to wrap impenetrable chains and a cement barrier around it. She couldn't afford to fall apart now.

"Here we are," said Sebastian breaking into her thoughts.

They were standing in front of Emily's room. Tyler nodded and went off next door to his room without a word. He looked exhausted. She watched as the door closed behind him with a light click.

When Emily turned back Sebastian was still standing there watching her. He looked as though he were waiting for her to say something. Emily wasn't really sure what that was. Man, he sure looked hot standing there under the sconce lighting in the hallway. The light reflected in his eyes making them sparkle. Emily wished he didn't have to be such a jerk sometimes. It made her angry that she had to like him. She just couldn't help it. He was completely gorgeous. They had been through a lot together, and that day spent in the book store was awesome. They talked about anything and everything. He was witty and charming. Ever since then though he had been flipping a switch and turning into a guy that thought she were an inconvenience. It was so confusing and it sure didn't help her headache that seemed to have a pulse all of its own.

How ridiculous, she finally was attracted to a guy and he had to be the wrong one. He was a bad boy by nature, who is completely arrogant and self-assured. Emily imagined that if Sebastian walked passed a mirror, he would probably gaze at himself lovingly, blowing himself kisses as he admired his reflection.

"What?" Emily asked him accusingly. "Why are you staring at me?"

Sebastian's cocky grin was back. "Paranoid?" He leaned casually against the wall next to her door. "Someone can't just look at you for the sake of doing so? So touchy aren't you?"

Emily took a deep breath and fought back the fury that threatened to explode all over him. It was somewhat irrational but she couldn't help it. Enough was enough. "Um yeah, let's see, pretty sure I have the right to be touchy. Don't you? I have been ripped out of a world that already wasn't all that normal and thrown into freaking Masterpiece Theatre. All things considered I'm doing pretty well I think." It was true too. She had survived horrifying attacks multiple times, all of which she later found out were by vampires. She had been brought down to some underground mystery location. She beheaded someone. Granted, that someone just happened to be one of the undead monsters that would have killed her, as well as Tyler and Sebastian if given the chance. Oh, and some poor girl she went to school with was fighting for her life. She couldn't fight in a hospital because a vampire *drain and run,* was pretty hard to explain to Emergency Room staff. Well yeah, just another day in the life of Emily Jameson.

"Okay okay, you're right. I'm sorry. You didn't exactly have time to get used to all this like me. You are doing quite well all things considered." His eyes pleaded down at her.

Dramatically, Emily put her hands on her hips like all those girls she hated. "Damn right I'm right. And another thing," she paused waiting for him to jump in and cut her off. Surprisingly, though, he didn't. "Why do you act like we're friends one second and I have leprosy the next? Do you have split personalities or something? While we're at it, I'm not a baby or a little girl. So, you don't need to treat me like one is that clear? I can run by myself and apparently I can take care of myself too. I've survived three attacks, not to mention during one of them I killed one of those monsters. If this is some kind of sexist thing…"

"You're right." His eyes looked her up and down appraisingly. "Definitely not a little girl." His words might have been a compliment but his look was something else. In one motion he moved off the wall and was inches away from her. They were so close Emily could feel the heat from his body.

His lips came crushing down on hers before she had a chance to put up any sort of fight. In reality, she didn't want to. Her body tingled all the way down to her toes. Sebastian's lips were strong, aggressive and soft all at the same time. He moved both of his hands up to cup both sides of her face. It was Emily's first real kiss and she felt like she could do it forever. A small moan escaped his lips against hers. Her body responded sending white hot desire flooding all over her to places that had never before been awakened. Just as she felt herself melting into his chest where she so longed to be he pulled away from her abruptly.

He shook his head as if trying to erase the last few minutes. "This is wrong." Sebastian turned and walked down the hall to his door. Before he stepped in he glanced back at her for just a second. His expression was carefully blank. The door closed leaving her in the hall alone.

Emily took a deep breath and let it out loudly, totally exasperated. "Well, goodnight to you too." She grumbled the words to the empty air where Sebastian had been standing. "It's been fun." Then Emily too turned and went into her own room. She was suddenly void of any fatigue. She was completely amped in fact thanks to that little episode in the hall, she didn't think she would be able to close her eyes even if she wanted to.

When she flipped on the light and flung off her shoes she was stopped in her tracks by an over dramatic sigh. She wasn't alone in the room. That couldn't be, they said all were safe down here, hadn't they? Vampires supposedly had no way of getting in here. She was so tired of these surprises.

For a single heart stopping second she just stood with her back toward whoever was in her room. Her annoyance was immediately followed by an even bigger feeling of being petrified. What if it was Andre coming for revenge? Quickly she recovered herself and jammed her hand into her pocket. *Crap!* There wasn't enough powder in her pocket to even pinch out. Looking slightly too either side of her for anything she could use brought her up short. Of course there was nothing that would stand up to the strength of an undead super killer. She eyed the door wondering if she would be able to get out of it and to Tyler's room before the intruder caught up to her. There was no use. Vampires had the ability of super speed. That was why the slayers had been gifted accordingly. She unwillingly gave up and slowly turned to meet her fate.

20

"Isn't love grand?" The female voice was light and airy speaking through another sigh. It was Ivy. She was lying across Emily's bed with her hands folded behind her head looking utterly relaxed. A wicked sneer stretched across her cherub face. Her right leg was casually crossed over her left. She wore thick soled black boots that Emily thought for sure were steel toe. Those were ass kicking boots no doubt about that. Ivy's foot danced rhythmically to music that wasn't playing.

Emily envisioned some sort of Goth Satan worshiper music playing through Ivy's mind while she lay across the bed looking as though she belonged there. "What are you doing here?" Emily's whole body grew tense with anger. She could feel her muscles contracting, readying themselves to spring on the awaiting enemy. Wasn't Ivy supposed to be one of the good guys? Ivy was a hunter or slayer or whatever. That was supposed to mean she was one of the good guys. Emily didn't know why but she really didn't like Ivy and it verged on hate. She hadn't even known the girl that long but it was one of those unavoidable feelings that conjured up on its own.

"Girl talk of course," Ivy said with obvious fakeness dripping off her lips like acidic syrup. "Maybe we can even do each other's hair and nails." Suddenly all the false cheer vanished from her face. Her beautiful sapphire blue eyes turned to wicked flames before narrowing into slits. "And then, I can let you in on a little secret. Sebastian, yeah he's mine. That means keep your little newbie hands off of my man. You got me?" Even with her cat like stare the false smile never left her lips, making her tone sound sugary sweet and not overtly threatening like the words suggested.

"Not that I saw your name printed on his forehead or anything, but we are just friends. If that status were to ever change, it still wouldn't be any of your business," Emily spit at Ivy full of venom. Her face though modeled Ivy's fakeness with a similar smile. "You got me?"

"Is that so?" Ivy stood and glared at Emily fiercely. "Then why is it that our little hottie was in my room last night? Hmm... maybe he was helping me balance my check book. Oh wait. I don't even have a checkbook." Ivy's hand flew to her chest in mock horror with a gasp. "That must mean... he's mine." Ivy walked purposefully toward Emily until she was only a foot away if that. "He and I have always had a thing for each other. I'm not going to let you waltz in here and ruin that for me. Just back the hell off, or you're gonna get hurt, understand? There's only room for one woman slayer around here, and that's me. Don't think because you suddenly have been let in on the little secret, and supposedly have a few meaningless powers, that you mean shit around here to Alexander or the other guys." Her tirade was long enough that when she finally stopped, she was panting slightly.

Emily didn't understand Ivy's crap about being a woman slayer and all that. She figured she would have to figure out that part later. For the moment she just focused on the possessive boy drama Ivy was trying to conjure out of nowhere. So bad she wanted to shoot back, *HE KISSED ME YOU BEACH!* That probably wouldn't have done anything but push Ivy over the edge. Plus, she wouldn't understand Emily's word and just make fun of her for that too. Ivy was the kind of girl that would have made it all Emily's fault, no matter what she said.

Emily fantasized about punching Ivy right in her pretty blue eyes. That would have felt so good. Too good, unfortunately though, it couldn't happen. Ivy seemed just crazy enough to manipulate the situation to her favor. She would probably tell Alexander and Sebastian that Emily attacked her for no reason and that somehow she was a traitor to their whole operation. Like it or not, the slayers were all she had to count on. It was obvious the vampires wanted her and she couldn't stay with Sam. He might be a jerk, but he didn't deserve any of the undead drama.

Ivy interrupted her mind babble making Emily jump a little. Ivy smiled at that. "Are you even listening to me loser?" She looked furious at the thought of being ignored.

"No, not really. Truth is, you're kind of boring." It was true. Emily had been so absorbed in her fantasies that she hadn't even realized Ivy was still speaking. Oh darn, she must have tuned her out. What a pity.

"Whatever, I don't have time for you to try and be cute. Just lay off Sebastian and we'll be straight." Ivy didn't wait for a response from Emily. Instead she stalked passed her pushing into Emily's shoulder hard on the way out. "Oops," she said innocently before exiting.

"Stupid beach," Emily muttered to herself as she turned to close the door. Well, slam it rather, a little too hard actually. She heard the bang echo down the hallway probably following Ivy on her evil way. Good, Emily thought. At least she sort of got the last word she figured smugly. It was stupid she knew. All it probably achieved was that it gave Ivy the satisfaction that she so didn't deserve.

An hour later, Emily was still sulking about the argument and what she should have said or done differently. Ivy wasn't worth the time it took to say her stupid name but that didn't seem to matter. There Emily sat on the end of her new bed, wiping hot furious tears from her eyes. That always happened when she got to mad. It wasn't that she was sad or anything. There was just too much pent up emotion coursing through her that needed to be released.

It made her angrier that she was allowing herself to get so worked up over the whole thing. It really wasn't worth it.

Emily had never wanted to hit another human so badly in her whole life. That wasn't like her at all. Normally, if someone made her mad, she just shrugged it off, no big deal. Ivy however, had the art of getting under someone's skin, down to a science. The day had been too much. Ivy coming in her room all crazy Beach-like, was just the last straw.

Was it totally wrong that Emily couldn't help but wish that someday a vampire would eat Ivy? Okay, so maybe she didn't want anything to eat her. It would be nice if someone could at least wipe that snooty look off her face. Ivy acted like she owned this place and that had to change.

Sebastian seemed to have more authority than Ivy that's for sure. Emily wasn't sure about Kyle though. They seemed to be on the same level. He too was angry the last time she had seen him but at least he didn't lash out at her directly. Instead, he just lashed out about her to someone right in front of her, as if she weren't really there. Is that the same thing?

Either way, she wasn't real keen on the idea that half the people in the compound didn't want to jump on her welcome wagon. They were so crazy. It wasn't like she chose to be there. In fact, she didn't want to be there anymore than they wanted her there. There had to be another option.

Going through the motions, Emily pulled off her clothes and moved to the dresser. It was an unconscious action that she was used to doing at home. Before realization could dawn on her, she pulled open the bottom drawer. It wasn't until she saw the neatly folded pajama sets that she reflected on the weirdness of that. She carefully picked up a light blue pair of sleep pants that had a camisole to match. The pants had cute little blue and green stars on them. Sure enough, they were her size. How was that possible? They weren't her pajamas from her house. When had anyone had time to get them from the store? Shrugging off the mysterious appearance of perfectly fitting clothes she just put them on and crawled into the big comfy bed.

Even more time passed, and Emily pretty much gave up on the prospect of getting any sleep at all that night. Every time she closed her eyes, pictures of the decapitated vampire stained her lids. Even though it was absurd to feel guilty, she sort of did. She was responsible for the death of another person. They technically weren't human, did that count? It was so hard to wrap her head around that, whether it was deserved or not. Involuntary tears welled up in her eyes. They weren't like the anger induced tears directly after the Ivy episode. The wetness made them sting. It was the tears way of threatening to overflow at any second if she didn't chill out.

Finally, she threw back the covers in defeat. She wanted to talk to Lucy so bad she could taste it. Unfortunately, at least for now, that wasn't an option. The closest thing to Lucy she had right then was Tyler. So far, he's always had Emily's back and could probably help Emily sort this entire fiasco out. The only problem was that Tyler was more than likely asleep. The day had taken a toll on him too that much was plain when she watched him go into his own room for the night. It felt wrong to begrudge him of his much deserved rest.

She had to get out of that room that's all there was to it. Maybe she could just go for a walk around the halls and wind herself down like one of those pull string toys. Her curious nature would probably just drive her anyway. She loved to explore new places and find out how they ticked. The compound seemed like a goldmine for that sort of thing.

As she exited the room she wondered if Ivy had gone to her own room. Emily hoped so. She really didn't have the patience for another encounter with Beachy the Vampire Slayer. Who knows, maybe she ran to Sebastian's room to make up lies about Emily. Whatever, if Sebastian or anyone chose to believe that psycho Goth Barbie doll then that was their problem. Sternly, she willed herself to stop thinking of Ivy. There were way more important things to worry about.

Emily's walk didn't last long. She found herself stopping at Tyler's door. After pressing her ear against the wood and hearing nothing, she figured he was more than likely sleeping. Of course he was all sane rational people would be passed out after the day they had. So what was her problem?

Without thinking she reached up and knocked softly on the door. Immediately she regretted it. It wasn't fair of her to force Tyler away from sleep just because she couldn't crash. Within minutes though, she heard him shuffling out of bed and trudging to the door with heavy steps.

When he opened the door his mouth was open wide in the middle of a huge yawn. "What's up," Tyler asked sleepily after he opened the door and saw her standing there. He used the back of his hand to rub the sleep out of his eyes to get a better look at her. "Are you okay?"

He probably thought she looked like a mess. Her eyes were probably blood shot from crying and lack of sleep. "Yeah I guess so. Can I come in?" She tried to offer him a smile, but she was sure the gesture didn't cut it. It didn't feel like her lips curled up, not even a little.

Tyler's room was nothing like Emily's. It had a totally different theme. The floor was rustic looking hardwood that looked very old, almost ancient. It didn't look worn out or anything. It was the kind that was supposed to look like that. Actually, the whole room had a rustic feel to it. It was definitely a guy's room.

"Cool room," she said still looking around.

Tyler looked at her as though he might fall back asleep standing there. "Thanks. Go ahead and sit anywhere."

Immaturely she thought about popping a squat right there where she stood. Thankfully, Emily decided against it. Tyler probably wouldn't get the joke. Or if he did he wouldn't notice since he wasn't even fully awake yet. "Thanks," Emily replied moving to one of the chairs to sit down.

Tyler followed her and sat in the chair opposite her. "Sorry, I'm just tired. It's been a day you know?" He wiped a big hand across his eyes probably still trying to get the sleep out.

"Yeah, a day."

"So... why are you here? Were you lonely in that big room all by yourself?" Even through exhaustion Tyler managed his crooked grin. "I'd be happy to keep you company..." Tyler trailed off his voice thick with implication as he stifled an escaping yawn ruining his sarcastic smoothness.

"Ha ha," Emily retorted mockingly. "No it's not that. Duh. I just couldn't sleep. I guess it's just everything that happened today. I keep seeing that guys face in my head and can't get it out. I killed him Tyler."

"Hold on a second," Tyler put a hand on hers. "That guy was a blood sucking leech that wanted to drain that Beth girl. It wasn't a human. You shouldn't feel bad. I should."

"You? Why?" Emily asked disconcerted. "You're not the one that cut the guy's head off like a crazed savage."

"Exactly," said Tyler firmly. He sounded full of regret. "I'm supposed to be a slayer and kill the bad guys like a savage. Instead you come in on a white horse and save the day after I choke." His shoulders slumped and his face was full of pain.

"Tyler..."

"No Em it's true. I choked and you kicked ass. You burned the hell out of that other one and took over chopping the head off mine," Tyler replied envious.

"Yeah I get it, enough with the graphic replay okay? I was there, remember?" She ran a hand through her hair. "Sorry I just don't think my stomach can take it again." Emily's belly rolled and sloshed like a tiny boat on a big ocean. She actually could almost feel her face turning green. "The messed up thing is, at the time I didn't even know what I was doing. It needed to be done, no offense, so I did it. I don't even know where it came from. It was like all the fear was washed away and replaced with courage and know how. Only I don't know how and don't think I want to."

It wasn't apparent if Tyler was even conscious anymore, until his eyes reopened and he sat back up. "I don't know Em, but you have something inside of you that makes you belong in this world, whether you like it or not. You know, maybe we're supposed to be a team. Like one of those famous duo's in the movies like…" His voice broke off and his face scrunched up while he thought of an example.

"Buffy and Willow?" Emily offered helpfully.

"Exactly," Tyler shot back sarcastically. "I get to be Buffy, she's more bad ass." Tyler waggled his eyebrows suggestively at her.

Emily laughed. "Does that mean you think Angel is hot too?"

"Aw, you got me. I can't help it. I just love me some Angel. Except he's way cooler as Angelus, when he joins the dark side." Tyler laughed too now.

Emily snorted. "Seeing how you're a guy, I'm surprised you didn't say Willow. She's got that whole girl thing going on." She giggled.

Tyler's laughter stopped abruptly. "Oh, good call. Good lookin' out Em."

A hard laugh burst from Emily's lips. Tyler looked adorable. Sure he was a pig, but she started it.

Despite the devilish grin across his face, the fatigue was settling in again. "See, you just got to make light of the situation and it's not so bad." Tyler yawned again. His mouth opened so big in fact, a train could have probably used his mouth as a tunnel. "Man, sorry. Just can't seem to wake up." He apologized through another yawn, this time covering his tunnel politely. "I'm glad you're here Em. I think we were brought together for a reason I really do. You want to stay in here tonight?"

Emily pulled her head back and her eyebrows shot up, "what?"

His hands flew up in his famous surrender. "No no nothing like that I swear. I'll be a good boy. Stay on my side of the bed and everything. God, I'll even take the floor if you want. I just thought it might make you feel better that's all I promise."

Accepting his explanation, Emily sat back more comfortably in her chair relaxing her tensed face. "Definitely tempting, but I think I might just go see if Alexander needs some help with Beth. Thanks though, I really appreciate it Tyler. Rain check?"

"You got it. Now get out of here. I got dreams of Willow and Buffy to look forward to now." As an afterthought he added, "Thanks for that by the way.""

"No problem dork, glad I could help." Emily stood saying her goodbyes and goodnights to Tyler before leaving. She found herself giving him a great big bear hug too. It felt good. Tyler was a good friend to her. He made her feel safe and comfortable. She wished she could have known him when she was younger. He seemed like he would know how to have a good time under different circumstances.

He wasn't a lot taller than her but his frame was much wider. His arms around her made her feel small and protected. The fact that she technically saved his butt didn't matter. Emily felt the tensed muscles in her body relax as he gave her one last squeeze before releasing her. It was stupid but when he backed away from her Emily felt cold and stressed again. These people in her "new life" were getting in past herself made wall more than she wanted to admit. She did have to admit that it was nice.

When Emily turned to leave, Tyler gently grabbed her arm. "And hey, you really need to lighten up. You don't have to assume that every time I ask you to stay the night it's a ploy to get in your pants." He released her arm and ruffled her hair playfully. "Not that you don't have nice pants, I'm just not a total douche that's all."

Hating when people played with her hair, Emily dodged out of his reach. She made sure to smile while she did, so he wouldn't get offended. He was right. She needed to stop being such a prude. "I'll try and remember that." She promised as she turned again to leave.

Before Emily even closed Tyler's door she glanced back to see that he had already crawled back into bed. He would probably be asleep before the door clicked shut. Emily smiled at that. At least one of them was getting some rest. He deserved a little *Tyler* time.

Once Emily was in the hall again she looked around to make sure she was actually alone. Part of her half expected Ivy to jump out and scare her. It was a relief to see that she was nowhere in sight.

She hurried back to her room and snuck a peek inside. It looked empty anyway. Good. She didn't want to, but she was going to have to talk to Alexander about getting a lock for her door. She didn't want any more surprise visits from Ivy, or Kyle for that matter. Ivy may recruit him over to the *I Hate Emily* Fan Club. Honestly, he didn't really seem like he had to be persuaded very far. She flipped the light off and closed her door back up tight. Emily wished with everything she had that Ivy wouldn't come back and rummage around, or worse, destroy her stuff. Even though she didn't really have stuff of her own at the compound yet, that wasn't the point. Her space was still hers and no one had the right to invade it. Emily padded off in the direction of the infirmary, hoping Beth was still okay when she got there.

21

Alexander had a cot slid over next to Beth's in the dim room. The bright fluorescent lights were no longer burning overhead. Instead, there was just one lamp on over by the desk. The different lighting made the room look less scary and sterile. Ever since her mother died Emily had loathed hospital settings. The infirmary room had proven no aversions had been concurred within her.

Both of them looked to be asleep. Across Alexander's chest, was a novel laying open. He must have been reading when he fell asleep. Emily crept over to his cot and slowly slid the book from his still form. Not thinking, she closed the volume before even looking for a book mark.

Oh perfect, that's really rude Emily, she scolded herself. Oh well, there was nothing that could be done about it now. Out of curiosity, she flipped the book over to examine the cover. Emily half expected it to be something on combat strategies, or what to do in case of a vampire bite. She was shocked at the normalcy that depicted the cover. Alexander, the head vampire slayer himself, was reading a first edition copy of *Little Women*. What was it with the slayer men? Did they all enjoy reading what was stereo-typically considered to be chick lit?

Without a chance of stopping it, a giggle escaped Emily's lips. Quickly she clamped her hand tightly over her mouth. Unfortunately, the deed was already done. Alexander's eyes popped open and Emily froze. Ah great, now she had done it. Waking up Tyler was one thing, waking up Alexander, was entirely different. She bit her lip waiting for him to say something. For her part, Emily couldn't speak. She could have at least said she was sorry for disturbing him, but she couldn't even manage that. Her hand was still pressed over her mouth like an idiot. Quickly she dropped it to her side and put the book down on the nearby table. The action made her look as though she just got caught with her hand in the cookie jar.

The corners of Alexander's lips twitched. "You find something funny about *Little Women* young lady?" He sat up in one fluid graceful movement, with seemingly no effort at all.

"Um... No sir, I mean uh... It's a very good book," Emily replied awkwardly stuttering like a moron.

His eyes looked amused by her shame. "Emily, I've told you to refer to me as Alexander. I may be your elder and superior in command, but we attempt to avoid formalities here where ever possible."

She shifted uneasily. "Right. Sorry, I'll try and remember, Alexander." Emily said softly, her face turning a bright hot red.

Alexander stood and moved away from the cot, to move toward Beth. The wounded girl didn't look as though she had moved a muscle since the last time Emily had seen her. She was however, wearing what looked to be hospital scrubs and all the blood was wiped off her skin. The color seemed to be returning to her face as well. At least she didn't look like she was already dead anymore. Despite her still unmoving form, Beth looked much better. If it wasn't for the bandage over the bite mark and IV tube sticking out of her arm, she would look as though she were merely sleeping.

Then as if hearing her thoughts, Alexander broke the silence making Emily jump. "The girl is resting well. I expect she will make a full recovery. Her heart is strong and she's responding to the transfusion very well." Alexander gingerly placed two fingers on her wrist checking her pulse. When he was done he nodded once to himself in satisfaction with the mental calculation.

"When will she wake up?" Emily asked in a whisper, not wanting to disturb Beth.

Alexander moved to stand closer to Emily before answering. "Her body has gone through a great trauma and has shocked itself into a deep slumber to protect itself. Young Beth will wake up when she is ready to return to life."

Alexander sounded so wise. Sometimes his words made him sound as though he was from another time and place, far from this little town. Honestly, he could very well be just that. Emily was sort of afraid to ask him how old he was. A small part of her hadn't believed Sebastian, when he had said that Alexander was nearly three hundred years old. It just didn't sound plausible. Despite Emily's disbelief, she really wasn't sure of the protocol and didn't want to do anything to prove even further that she didn't belong there.

"You conflicted with young Ivy this evening, did you not?" Alexander asked breaking into Emily's thoughts.

Emily's mouth dropped open with shock. How could he possibly know that? "Uh, I guess you could say that. She doesn't seem to like me much." Emily said, working hard to keep the annoyance out of her voice. Ivy had obviously tattled on her like a little kindergartner. Figures, Ivy would probably do anything to get Emily as far away from the slayers as possible, especially Sebastian. Emily sighed, completely exasperated.

"Ivy is merely intimidated by you. She more than likely feels that you may steal some of her thunder around here." Alexander reassured soothingly.

Emily looked at him incredulous. "Steal some of her thunder? I don't even know what I'm doing here. I don't want this. I'd give this up and go home in a minute if I could."

Alexander rested a hand comfortingly on her arm. "Dear girl, you have been through much trauma yourself in the past few days. It's important to relax and find your center. Don't let Ivy or any of the others affect your comfort level. You belong here. I have a feeling your stay will be a long one in our world." If possible, his voice softened even more and he smiled warmly at Emily. "Even if that fate is not an appealing one to you at this time."

"I just don't get why she doesn't like me." Emily couldn't help the mild pouting tone that came through her inflection. "I didn't do anything to her. She thinks I'm after Sebastian. That's just crazy. I have no intentions on-"

Alexander cut her off, not unkindly. "Emily, as I have said she is intimidated by your presence here. She is an alpha personality, especially being the only female in our compound right now. Miss Ivy does have admiration for Sebastian. While he is fond of her, it isn't at the same level of admiration that she holds for him. Also, you seem to be gaining abilities that she did not gain so quickly, or in which she hasn't gained at all."

Emily's incredulity returned. "How would she even know about my…" She stumbled over the word, "powers. I'm barely starting to discover things that may or may not even be powers? That's part of why I came to talk to you. I really need some answers."

Alexander went back to his desk in the corner of the room. "You will find that slayers have ways of tapping into an instinctual intuition, which regular humans do not. For instance, Tyler's ability to think of something he needs as a weapon can appear to him at his will. Not all slayers have that ability. Kyle has premonitions about future attacks, injuries and other future events. Sebastian can teleport from one location to another at his will." Alexander stopped speaking and gave Emily a moment to take everything in that he had just explained.

The extra moment for absorption didn't make a difference. "What? Sebastian can teleport like on Star Trek?" Emily was completely dumbfounded. Although, that would explain how Sebastian could somehow disappear after he walked her home.

Alexander's lips twitched, just a little. "Not exactly like Star Trek, but yes I suppose in a sense it's something like that."

"That's incredible. Do the vampires have stuff like that about them too?"

"They do appear to have special abilities that make them stronger. Though they seem to be gifted to the species as a whole, not by individual." He rifled through papers on his meticulously organized desk. "You will find that this world isn't what you are brought up to believe. The term supernatural, isn't just for books, legends and myths." He raised a thick brow at her. "In fact, there are even humans that are gifted with certain abilities that most aren't even aware of. Some of those gifts would tremendously aid in our efforts. Unfortunately, we are strictly forbidden from revealing our true identities to humans. I suppose it's a sort of conundrum."

Alexander seemed to be trying to convey a message to Emily. The trouble was, she had no idea what he was trying to say. It made sense to her that the whole under world couldn't be revealed. It would omit panic and chaos amongst the humans. That would definitely not be a good thing.

It did put her in quite the predicament though. Not telling humans meant not telling Sam, or even Lucy. How could she possibly keep such a big secret to herself? Wouldn't they notice something was off about her? Well, if she was ever able to return, that is. And if she couldn't return, what would that be like? Emily couldn't imagine a life without Lucy in it. There had to be a loophole to the rule, and she would find it. She *had* to find it. "I understand Alexander. That does make sense." The Lucy problem would have to be solved later.

Apparently satisfied with her answer, he moved on to another topic. "I have already sensed some of your gifts. Can you tell me what you have been noticing? I don't mean to be intrusive. It's just that it's necessary information. I hope you understand."

Emily took a deep breath to dive in and was cut off short. Something vibrated in Alexander's pocket, instantly grabbing his attention. "Is everything okay?"

Alexander gave her an apologetic smile and reached for the interruption in his pocket. It looked like a pager of some kind. It had more buttons though, and continued to vibrate until he pushed something on its side. "I'm very sorry, but I need to check this. It's the…" His explanation was lost as he looked at a display screen. He blanched and his face went very pale. Suddenly, his fingers were in motion jabbing at several buttons at once.

Alexander?" Emily asked perplexed by his shift in mood.

His head shot up as though he had forgotten she was even there. "Emily… I'm terribly sorry. I'm going to have to cut our conversation short." He looked regretful but only for a moment. After that he was all business. "Will you please go to my office? I'm calling the others there as well." He turned his body in dismissal.

That was bad. Something big was happening. Whatever it was, had been so bad that Alexander wanted everyone in the office at the same time. She didn't argue with Alexander, instead she just set off towards the direction of the meeting place.

22

Of course, Sebastian was already waiting when she got there. He probably had done that weird teleport thing. That was going to take some getting used to, that was for sure. If it wasn't for the situation going on, she would have loved to give him crap about it. She would say something like... *beam me up Scotty.* That was childish Emily knew, yet she still got a secret thrill out of what his face would have looked like when she said it. Her dorkness helped ease her tension over whatever was about to happen.

As her mind wandered, others started entering the room. Kyle stalked meaningfully toward Sebastian. Oh goody, Emily thought dryly. Ivy trailed in after Kyle, even better. Her piercing blue eyes instantly found Emily's, and narrowed.

"Isn't it past her bedtime?" Ivy asked her voice dripping with acid as per usual.

"What's going on Bass?" Kyle spoke as though he hadn't heard Ivy's remark at all.

Ivy glowered at him, but otherwise said nothing. Clearly being ignored wasn't something the other girl was used to. She just marched over to one of the arm chairs by the fire place and flopped down. Her face quickly transformed to a slow languid smile as she gazed up at Sebastian.

Was that supposed to be seductive? Emily thought she just looked like a cat ready to pounce. Maybe that was the point though. Sickeningly, it was true that some guys went for that sort of thing, even though it was disgusting.

"Kyle, I got the same message you did," Sebastian replied frustrated. "I know as much as you do."

Kyle matched Sebastian's tone easily. "Well it must be big if he summoned all of us in the middle of the night."

"Just wait and see. I'm sure Alexander will be here soon to explain." Sebastian's eyes fell back on the flames in the fire place.

Ivy licked her lips considering. "Where's the new guy? I haven't met him *yet*." There was a heavy emphasis on the word yet. When Ivy said it, she gave Emily a meaningful look.

"I'm not sure." Emily replied noncommittally. "When I left his room earlier he was pretty tired…" Emily trailed off letting her words hang in the air. She only said it because she knew the image it would conjure for the other girl. She and Tyler had only in fact been talking, but her enemy didn't need to know that information. The satisfaction in watching Ivy's expression falter was too good to resist.

Sebastian's head snapped up and his eyes locked on her. His expression was hard and made Emily uneasy. Why was he looking at her like that? He clearly didn't think of her in that way anyway, so what did it matter? If looks could kill though, Emily would have been six feet under. Sebastian swiftly hid his reaction, but not before Emily had a chance to catalogue it for later reference.

Tyler burst into the room like his butt was on fire. He was still putting his head through his shirt as he entered. Emily got a peak at his wash board stomach and definitely liked the view. They may have been just friends, but that didn't mean she couldn't appreciate the merchandise. She snuck a glance at ivy and saw the other girl was equally appreciative. Stupid Cow.

"So nice of you to grace us with your presence." Sebastian's words were clipped, and his face was like stone. "Maybe if you weren't so exhausted from your bedroom acrobatics, you would have been here sooner." His implication was thick and he darted a glance at Emily, before returning his flame eyed gaze on Tyler.

Emily gasped. Even for Sebastian, that was too far. She couldn't believe he had said such a thing.

Ivy and Kyle chortled.

"Huh?" Tyler was confused, and rightfully so. He looked as though he had walked in late to class, only to find there was a quiz on the menu that he hadn't studied for.

Emily was saved the embarrassment of having her lie discovered, by Alexander strolling into the room. He headed straight for his desk where he promptly took a seat. The entire room silenced like a classroom full of students, who just realized their teacher had eyes in the back of her head.

"I'm glad you are all here." He said it as though he hadn't just summoned them all.

"What's up Alex?" Kyle said.

"We don't have a lot of time, so your attention is imperative. Casey has reported in. There's been an incident."

Ivy uncrossed her legs and leaned forward. "What now?"

"Casey overheard one of their conversations. They are displeased with the earlier events of this evening. They've decided to take action sooner than expected." Alexander looked weary. His forehead was lined with stress.

Emily couldn't hold herself back any longer. "What does that mean?" She began playing with her fingers, as she always did when she was nervous.

"This doesn't involve you little girl!" Ivy exploded. "Just sit there and look not pretty."

"Ivy," Alexander said reproachfully. "This is neither the time nor place for your menial vendettas."

Ivy actually looked stunned by that. She probably didn't get corrected much.

Serves her right, Emily thought smugly.

Alexander continued. "They've taken several humans into their lair. Casey heard them speak of turning the humans, and using them against us."

Turning the humans? What did that mean? As soon as the question formed its thought bubble, she understood. The vampires were planning to make more vampires. This really was bad.

The room immediately erupted into a bustle of activity. Everyone was talking at the same time, making preparations for the coming battle. Tyler looked over at her with an odd expression. It was fear, mixed with determination.

Alexander spoke halting all plans. "I'll of course need all of you for this. There will be too many vampires and humans to just send the usual. I must stay here and tend to Miss Thomas." He looked sorry for this, but resigned.

"No problem. We can handle it," replied Sebastian firmly.

It seemed strange to Emily that Alexander would even consider going along. He was a retired slayer, who had begun aging again. Didn't that mean he couldn't fight? She made a mental note to ask questions about that, when it was a more appropriate time and place. Either way though, if he had thought about going for even a second, then whatever was going on must have been epic.

Alexander nodded gravely. "Well children, you better head out. Casey will be needing assistance." The older man seemed to be battling within himself as everyone left the room.

Emily waited until they were all gone and said, "Alexander?" She raised a hand to place on his shoulder but dropped it. He wasn't an intimidating person at all. Just then however, he didn't look like he was in a touchy feely sort of mood.

Alexander smiled weakly at her. "I'm alright child. I'm just worried about you all. I regret having to stay behind. I just have a bad feeling about this. Do you understand?"

She thought she did actually. "Do you mean like a cramp, or gas bubble?" Oh my God! Gas bubble? She did not just say that, did she? Her face grew hot with instant mortification.

Alexander's smile grew, but it didn't touch his eyes. "Yes Miss Emily, exactly like that." He shook his head. "I guess I never really thought about it like that."

"Sorry," Emily mumbled, still embarrassed. At that moment, she would have liked nothing more than to crawl in a hole.

He waved a hand at her in dismissal. "No need I assure you. As I was saying, my feeling tells me something bad is going to happen. It makes the prospect of staying at the compound much less appealing. We should have planned better. Casey should have never been left there alone. I should have known they'd be out for vengeance after one of their own was killed and another severely wounded."

Emily sucked in a breath, but was brought up short.

"No no child, it's not your fault. It had to be done," Alexander soothed. "Go now. Your brothers and sister will be departing soon."

"Yes sir... I mean Alexander," Emily corrected. Without another word, she left to find the others.

The prospect that Alexander shared in her ridiculous stomach alarm system problem, was kind of a comfort. It was nice to know she wasn't the only strange one. If they had that in common, did they have anything else? If so, what did that mean?

23

Sebastian explained that he could take people with him on his Star Trek adventures. All he has to do is simply touch them at the time he moves from one place to another. Apparently the teleport thing worked for more than one person. Before Emily caught up with them, Tyler was quizzing Sebastian all about the mechanics of it. Somehow or another through that, they discovered that Ty could do it as well.

It really was an amazing and cool gift. Emily just liked to make fun of it because it was kind of fun to tease Sebastian. It wasn't every day you met someone who could disappear and then reappear in an entirely different location. The whole thing fascinated Emily and she wanted desperately to know how it worked.

Tyler being able to teleport was a big deal. It meant they wouldn't have to use their van. Yep, they had a van… an actual vehicle. Emily wondered why Sebastian had never used it for any of their travels. Also, now that she was thinking about it, why hadn't he teleported them out of the alley earlier? That definitely would have made things easier. She was *so* going to have to ask him about that.

For the latest expedition, Sebastian could transport Emily as well as Kyle and Tyler could transport Ivy. Yuck. Emily really didn't like that idea. She didn't want Ivy to touch a single hair on Ty's head. Whatever, she wasn't going to whine about it. If she did, it would just prove to Ivy that she was immature.

The guys transported them a block away from the vamp's house in an alley. Really? Emily was really starting to despise alleys. Couldn't they have dropped them in a bush or something? Nothing good has ever happened in an alley, and she doubted that would be changing anytime soon.

It was still dark outside. Well, pitch black to be exact. Emily's new heightened night vision senses were working in full affect already. That was something at least. She scanned every nook and cranny of the alley just in case. There were garbage cans and some old discarded appliances, but that seemed to be it.

The whole group seemed to be on high alert while they walked. Dressed all in black, they appeared like just a Goth gang of kids planning to terrorize the neighborhood. Thanks to the darkness, their gear and weapons were pretty well hidden, which was good. If there did happen to be anyone outside, they wouldn't get freaked by the sight of the arsenal they were carrying. A frantic call to the police by a skittish neighborhood watch dog, would be the last thing they needed.

The temperature was chilly, which added to the malevolence of the evening. Emily felt like an extra in a bad horror flick. Was there a rule somewhere that scary situations had to take place in the cold? Didn't anything ever go wrong in the desert? If not, she planned to add Arizona to her list of places she wanted to move, as soon as this was all over.

Emily had been given another knife and her silver powder had been replenished. Kyle thought she might be good with a crossbow. He tried to give her a brief rundown on the proper use of the awkward contraption. That *so* wasn't going to happen, Emily passed on that one. Sure, she evidently had some kind of a gift with the dagger, and the silver powder was easy enough. A crossbow on her first day, seemed like pushing it just a little too far.

Just like earlier, there wasn't anyone out on the streets. Curtains were closed and even most of the porch lights were off. In the distance, Emily could still hear the thudding base from that party. Huh, they were really going for it tonight. After all, it was two thirty in the morning and they were still going strong. They must not have gotten the memo that the undead were in town for a visit. The thought of a hungry vampire crashing the party made Emily's whole body shudder. That would be a blood bath none of the party goers would have a chance to escape.

The group slowed as they neared the dark house at the center of the cul-de-sac. All looked quiet to Emily. The curtains were drawn so tightly, you couldn't see a sliver of light from the inside. Of course, Emily's opinion didn't count for a whole lot, since she had no idea what she was doing, or what she was looking for.

Even with her insecurities, Emily felt like a live wire. Her body seemed more alive than it ever had before in her entire life. Some part of her knew that if she tried, she could jump higher and move faster and quieter than she ever imagined. That didn't mean much though since the fear and paranoia still ran cold in her veins. Despite her apparent instinctual talents, she had no official training whatsoever. Hopefully whatever happened wouldn't be that bad because otherwise her inadequacies would be discovered.

"Look," said Sebastian as he pointed to the house next door to the vamps.

Immediately when Emily trained her vision to the spot he had indicated, she saw that the windows were boarded up with wood that had been tagged by graffiti. Surprisingly, the vandalism was kind of pretty, in a creepy sort of way. The window on the left side had what looked like blue flames licking up the side of the board. Coming out of the flames, was a multi-colored dragon. The window on the right also had the blue fire. Instead of a dragon though, this one had brightly colored flowers. The two different designs were a startling contrast with one another. It was like it represented the struggle between what was evil, and what was pure.

The door of the house was left wide open. That couldn't be good. Note to self… don't enter the old abandoned house… ever. Maybe the vamps were using it for something. It seemed logical. Plus, they wouldn't care if the door was left hanging open. They were the boogie men after all.

Sebastian motioned for them to move toward the empty house. Kyle and Ivy headed around back wordlessly. Even without training, Emily knew what they were doing. If they blocked both openings, it would make it harder for any monsters to escape and get the drop on them.

Tyler appeared to be ready, even through his definite apprehension. Emily couldn't blame him one bit. Her fight or flight mechanism was screaming for her to run and hide. Another part of her seemed to be hungry for the action. She would be lying if she said she didn't want to kill those vampires. They were hurting people and they had tried to hurt her. That wasn't okay and they had to be stopped.

Sebastian came closer to them and whispered. "We'll take the front. I'll go first." He paused to give Tyler a meaningful look. "I want you at the rear. Emily needs to be in the middle until we can assess the situation in the house."

Tyler nodded solemnly.

Sebastian continued, "Casey is more than likely standing watch over the vamps house. Until we know what's going on in this one, I want both of you with me." He didn't give either of them a chance to say anything. Within a second, he was gliding towards the house in a crouch, ready to spring at any given moment.

Tyler put an encouraging hand on Emily's shoulder. He nudged her slightly, coaxing her to move forward. She silently obeyed and willed herself to be brave as she moved. She couldn't see Tyler, but she felt him ghosting behind her guarding her back.

As she passed through the threshold of the house, her senses were overtaken with a rancid smell that made her nose wrinkle. It wasn't easy to place though. It smelled like copper, trash and mold all rolled into one. It was absolutely terrible and she had to swallow back the vomit that threatened to surface. Aside from the smell, there was no noise or anyone in sight in the vacant home's small living room. It was evident that the homeless had turned this into their stomping ground. There was no visible sign that they had been there recently, which made Emily nervous. Did the nasty vampires eat them? Emily hoped not, no one deserved that.

Their search party moved stealthily down the hall to the next room. As soon as Sebastian entered the kitchen, he leapt into action. He wasn't striking against any attacker that Emily could see. There didn't appear to be anyone in the room at all. Emily gasped and let out a little squeak, as her eyes focused on where Sebastian was kneeling on the floor. His movements were so fast, it was like a blur. The sight in the kitchen was so horrific that she couldn't even enter. When she froze, it caused Tyler to run into her back.

"What the...?" Tyler asked confused.

Lying on the floor at Sebastian's feet, was a body that definitely wasn't alive. It was male and almost completely covered in blood. Emily's heart pounded as she took in the sight. His throat was ripped out and he had other wounds matching that one, all over his body. It was the most horrific thing Emily had ever seen. Judging by the look on Tyler's face when she glanced at him, he had come to the same conclusion.

Sebastian looked up at them and gestured to the back door. "Tyler. Get Kyle and Ivy, now. Tell them we need to do a sweep of the rest of the house." Despite the control of his voice, the urgency was obvious. He lifted Casey's arm to check for a pulse at his wrist. Not liking what he found, he moved to the slayer's neck shaking his head wearily.

"You got it." Tyler didn't even hesitate as he made his way around the dead person lying partially in his path.

Emily gulped and bit her lip. "Vampires did this, didn't they?"

"Yes. I knew we shouldn't have left him alone after what had happened earlier." Sebastian stared down at the body in complete anguish. His whole body was tense with pent up emotion that clearly wanted to escape.

Emily's eyebrows shot up with confusion. "What? You know him?"

Before he could answer, the others returned into the house. Ivy took one look at the scene and rushed to Sebastian's side. "CASEY!" Ivy bellowed. "No, Casey no, this isn't right!" She reached out and uselessly felt for a pulse.

"Ivy, he's gone," Sebastian said not unkindly. He looked up at Kyle. The only emotion on his face was in his eyes. "I need you to sweep the rest of the house. I didn't get a chance to before we found Casey."

"Sure Bass," Kyle gulped hard. He maneuvered past them and down the hall without another word.

At the mention of Casey's name, Ivy sobbed. Sebastian put a comforting hand on her shoulder. She stared into his eyes intently, as if pleading for him to tell her it was all a dream. He must have realized that and he shook his head slightly. Her sobs commenced again.

Emily couldn't blame Ivy. This was just terrible. She could feel a huge lump in her throat and she swallowed hard. The boy lying on the retro tiled floor, was a slayer. He was Casey, the one she hadn't got to meet yet. He looked younger than she was. He could have been older though, she guessed. The slayers didn't age the same as regular people.

Kyle came back into the room, breaking into her thoughts. "Clear Bass," he reported. "There's some blood in one of the bedrooms. It was still wet." His eyes looked haunted. It was obvious he was trying to look anywhere, but at Casey's still form.

Sebastian nodded. "Casey's wounds are still fresh. And it hasn't been that long since he reported to Alex."

"I knew I should have been here!" Ivy wailed desperately. "This is… my fault. Maybe if we wouldn't have fought. Maybe…" Ivy dropped her head and just stared at Casey.

Sebastian put his attention back on her. "You couldn't have known. Besides, by the looks of these injuries, there was more than just one vamp here. You could have been killed too."

"I don't care!" Her voice was thick, but it still echoed in the empty room. "He would have had a better chance."

"It's not your fault," Emily soothed.

Ivy shot her a venomous glare. "You don't know anything about this newbie! Don't attempt to act like you do!" Her eyes pierced right through Emily's.

Emily took an involuntary step back. Something in Ivy's eyes wasn't rational and it was easy to see, that she was barely holding onto her sanity. She was looking for anyone to lash out on and just then Emily was the perfect target. Honestly, Emily didn't begrudge her of that. She was grieving for a fellow slayer that had fallen. The anger she displayed was completely understandable.

"Ivy," Sebastian intervened. "Don't take it out on her." He stood and wiped his hands on his pants. Even though they were black the blood on them that was left behind was still visible.

Ivy didn't respond to either of them. Instead, she stared down at Casey looking totally defeated. Tears ran down her face, leaving tracks of eyeliner behind. Her body was slumped and she held onto Casey's hand for dear life.

It really didn't bother Emily that the girl had freaked out on her. It could have been a lot worse. When her mom died, she lashed out at everyone. It was extremely obvious that Ivy cared for Casey. It was the most human emotion that she had seen from Ivy, since they had met. Despite the awful circumstances, it was slightly comforting to see she had feelings, besides hatred. Ivy reached out and gently closed Casey's eyes. He wouldn't be seeing anything anymore.

The death in the air suddenly became too much. This was a lot different than seeing Beth's injuries. The emotion in the room was a heavy weight that was palpable. It was bringing back feelings that Emily didn't want to resurface, ever. She had to get out of there. She tried to get passed Tyler to go into the living room, but he stopped her.

He gave her a sympathetic look. "It's going to be okay." He wrapped an arm around her waist, pulling her towards him.

Emily welcomed the comfort and melted into his chest. Traitor tears escaped her eyes, making his shirt wet. She fought them back and they came anyway. With Tyler it was different. Vulnerability was an easy emotion to slip into when he was around. She hadn't known him for long and that didn't seem to matter. He made her feel safe. She was so thankful that he was going through all of it with her. Going through it alone would have been unbearable.

Sebastian cleared his throat uncomfortably. "We need to get next door before anyone else needlessly dies tonight. Kyle and Ivy, I want you guys to wait until we get to the back of the house. Once we get closer to the door, I want you to move in at the front." His voice was void of any trace of emotion now. He was all business. "We will have to come back for Casey." I'll lock the front door so no one stumbles across him and calls the police."

Ivy sobbed again. "I can't leave him Bass." The emotion that poured out of her was raw and gut wrenching.

"You don't have a choice." He answered firmly, but not without kindness.

I can't do it." Ivy was pleading with him now. Tears streamed down her cheeks like a down fall of rain.

"I know you love him, but he would want us to get this done." Sebastian stared down at her, willing her to see reason.

"He's my brother Sebastian!" Ivy screamed the words at him.

Her brother? Emily was stunned. This was the first mention she had heard of any of them being siblings. It made sense. Of course there would be siblings. This was a family business wasn't it? Emily wondered absently, what that meant for her own family. She immediately pushed those thoughts to the back of her mind. It wasn't the time for questioning her own lineage.

Sebastian's eyes softened. "I'm well aware he's your brother and I'm sorry. I know it hurts to leave him, but it's what he would want. You know that Ivy." He reached out a hand to her in offering.

Ivy wiped the tears from her face and swallowed hard. "I don't want to," she said weakly. Ignoring her own words, she slowly grabbed his hand and allowed him to pull her to her feet. "Let's get this over with. I wanna kill those bastards and go home." She straightened her spine and squared her shoulders. Her eyes scanned the room, as if daring the rest of them to comment further.

Sebastian gave her a nod and half-hearted smile that didn't reach his eyes. "Alright then. Let's get this done." He led his group to the back door of the kitchen and the second party followed behind. Emily couldn't help but imagine the terror that awaited them next door.

24

Sebastian listened intently at the back door of the vampire's… lair? It seemed weird to Emily to think of it as a home. Tyler was checking the back windows, for any sign of the undead lurking inside. Emily really wasn't very far behind Sebastian, probably only a couple feet. Even still, she felt exposed and vulnerable out in the open.

The wind blew ruffling her pony tail and she shivered. Every little noise made her shift uneasily with the potential fear, that they might not be the only ones lurking in the shadows behind the old house. Her night vision might have increased tremendously, but somehow that didn't make her feel any better. It just made her want to keep her head on a constant pivot, peering in every nook and cranny for any hidden monsters.

Suddenly Sebastian's voice in her mind put a halt to her fears. *The coast appears to be clear. I'm going to get Tyler's attention so we can move in.*

No need, she mind spoke back. Then not really knowing how she did it, she switched gears and tuned into Tyler. *Ty, it's time to go.*

Shortly his answering, *alright*, broke through her mind and he was headed towards them.

Emily snuck a glance at Sebastian and was pleased to see he was shocked. "Did you do that?" He said to her quizzically with his eyebrows raised practically to his hair line. The shock over rode him for a minute, and he forgot they were supposed to be using the mind link to stay inconspicuous.

She smiled smugly at the ability to catch him off guard. Instead of responding Emily focused on sliding her knife out of its holster at her hip. After that, she double checked that the canister was loose on her silver powder supply. The time it took to get the lid off during their last battle, was ridiculous. At the thought of the last encounter, her hand unconsciously raised to her neck. She lightly probed the spot, where the filthy blood sucker had choked her.

Once they were all three in attendance, Sebastian motioned towards the door. He conferred with them in the lightest of whispers so not to be overheard by the enemy. "This is your first mission. Don't get split up. Emily you stay with me."

She couldn't help feeling indignant at his command. Sure she hadn't had much training. Okay, well she hadn't had any training. In all fairness, Tyler had only had one official training session with Alexander. Why was he deemed to be more superior? Either way, she had been the one to kill the vamp in the alley, not Tyler. She schooled her features to look threatening. No one even seemed to notice, so she doubted it worked.

The room they entered was some sort of coat and shoe room. Two walls were lined with racks. There were enough coats and shoes displayed there to clothe a small town easily. Emily eyed the jackets skeptically. Some of them were long trench style garments that reached all the way to the floor. A hungry blood sucking monster could have been positioned behind one waiting to strike pretty easily.

Still feeling the sting of Sebastian's insinuations, she marched over and quickly moved aside the coats. She hoped the guys didn't see her hands shaking. Despite the fact there wasn't a blood sucking monster waiting to eat her, she jumped back just in case. Sure it was silly, although it wouldn't have been, had there actually been a vampire hiding there.

Sebastian moved toward the door that would take them further into the house. "If you're done scamming for clothes, I think we should get on with this."

Emily's eyes narrowed at Sebastian strongly enough, that laser beams should have shot out and bit into his flesh. Not having much choice, she followed them. She glared at Tyler until he went after Sebastian. It wasn't necessary to sandwich her in the middle. Knowing how to handle herself had been her job ever since her mom died. Fury radiated off of her and if it wasn't for the need to be stealthy, she would have let Sebastian know exactly what she thought of his righteousness.

It was easy to see that Tyler didn't want to go before her. He was just trying to do what he was told. The reluctance that warred on his face softened her just a little bit. The need to keep her safe was out of compassion. With Sebastian, it was more about a primal need to exude dominance and that just wasn't going to fly.

So far the back of the house was unlit. They made it through the spotlessly unused kitchen without any incidences. You could seriously hear a pin drop in this place. Emily was afraid to breathe. Her heart was hammering in her chest. It would surely give away her presence to the vampires. Come to think of it, there really was no point to sneaking up on the bad guys. They were probably well aware of the intruders coming to get them.

Emily froze when the front door opened as they were making their way through the living room. Luckily it was just Kyle. Where was Ivy? Had something gotten her? They couldn't have, Kyle wouldn't be so calm. Ivy might not be the most agreeable person, but Emily was sure no one would be okay with her destruction.

Emily looked to Sebastian concentrating hard. *Where's Ivy?*

She's coming around back. He never stopped walking as he sent her the message. He glided smoothly up a wide staircase without making a sound.

As Emily ascended the stairs after them, she couldn't help but notice how beautiful the feature was. The path up the stairs narrowed like a funnel. At the top, a hallway branched off on both sides. There were several doors and expensive paintings along the wall. She hadn't noticed it right away, but the wall that was on the side of the stairs wasn't there. Instead an intricately carved railing stretched the length of the entire hall.

Sebastian seemed to be listening intently with his head cocked to one side. He motioned to the right with his hand holding a sparkling dagger. They made their way across the floor where he had indicated. Emily thought it would have been better to split up but could see why Sebastian didn't.

Splitting up would cause one of them to make their sweep alone. Not knowing what they were walking into, didn't make that a very good idea. Wasn't the whole reason they were here because the vampires had taken a group of humans in here? Where were they?

You would think if nothing else, they would be able to hear noise from the humans.

After about the third door Emily and Tyler exchanged a weary glance. Clearly they were mice walking straight into a trap. Emily shifted uneasy as she waited for Sebastian and Kyle to come out of the room. Once they returned empty handed, they moved to the next door in their path.

The guys were still ahead of her. She had peaked into the room they had just come out of. It looked like a bedroom, a normal bedroom at that. It seemed stupid but Emily expected to see coffins instead of actual beds.

When she realized they weren't waiting for her she tried to follow. She was stopped by a cool hand sliding across her throat. There wasn't even time to react. She tried to suck in a breath to scream at the others but the hand squeezed cutting off her air supply.

"Hello Emily," a voice breathed in her ear. "I didn't expect to see you here."

Emily's blood ran cold. She knew that voice. "Hello... Mrs. Cleary." She had to force the words out of her mouth before she choked on them. The same woman that was holding her hostage was the same scared woman she labeled a pod person after running into her on the way to work the other day. "We're here to help you."

Mrs. Cleary laughed. "No, you're here to kill me. I should probably warn you, I'm a little harder to kill these days sweetie." As she spoke her lips brushed over Emily's neck.

There was no way this could be happening! At least that's what her mind tried to think. It was just a defense mechanism though. No matter how bad her mind wanted to reject the truth, there it was threatening to strangle her. Those monsters had turned sweet Mrs. Cleary into one of them. She had known the woman since she was a kid and now it appeared likely she would die by her hands.

The reality of that was staggering. Emily tested her captor's grip by trying to move. She didn't get very far when Mrs. Cleary's other arm wrapped around her waist and tightened like a vice. Emily shrieked.

The guys raced back to her with Tyler in the lead this time. "Emily!" He called panting. "Bitch you better let her go!" Tyler stopped and trained his crossbow on them. It was shaking slightly with his apprehension. Emily was strategically positioned in front of

Mrs. Cleary. The best Tyler could hope for when he let off his shot was to not kill Emily. The chance that he would hit his mark was unlikely.

"Watch your mouth young man." Mrs. Cleary said reproachfully. Apparently her mothering instincts were only intact when it came to curse words. Putting Emily in a choke hold didn't reach her mama bear side at all.

"Where's your leader?" Sebastian asked seeming to ignore Emily at the heart of the fray. He wouldn't even look directly at her.

"He's around. Don't worry. You'll be seeing him sooner than you think." The female vampire's voice was nonchalant. She wasn't worried in the least that she stood there out numbered.

Just then Emily noticed a shadow moving up behind Sebastian. She screamed. "Behind you!" The grip on her throat got tighter cutting off her air and any other chance at speech.

"No no Emily." Mrs. Cleary scolded mildly as though she were talking to a toddler. "We don't want to give away the ending before it's time."

Kyle and Sebastian spun around to see the new threat. It was Mr. Johnson. Emily recognized him from the bank. He looked different. His skin was flawless and his eyes were that awful green that looked like they were glowing. His stance was predatory and full of menace.

"Nice work Sara," Mr. Johnson soothed.

Emily realized belatedly that Sara was Mrs. Cleary. She had only known the older woman by her last name. Now she could only be known as leech. As if hearing her thoughts the grip around her throat got even tighter still. Emily gasped and coughed trying to catch her breath. "Just let me go!"

"Now where would the fun be in that?" Mr. Johnson asked seeming genuinely curious.

"Enough! Where is Andre?" Sebastian barked. His dagger was poised and ready and he stepped closer to the male vampire.

The slow smile Mr. Johnson gave him in return was sickening. It revealed that he was definitely one of the bad guys. His K9's were fully lengthened to a sharp point like thick needles. Emily wasn't sure but she thought she saw blood on one of them.

"He's busy right now but if you'd like to leave a message…" his voice trailed off. The sarcasm in his little impersonation was thick. "He's making more…"

"Shut up Michael!" Mrs. Cleary instructed. "Remember what Master said."

Mr. Johnson, or Michael closed his mouth and gave her a tight nod. He took two purposeful steps towards Sebastian. He didn't get any further though because a crossbow bolt struck him in the chest. Blood pooled around the arrow and Michael fell to his knees. He grabbed at the arrow but couldn't gain proper purchase. With a gasp his upper body pitched forward and hit the floor with a thud.

Sebastian turned to Tyler with a half of a smile tugging the corner of his lips. "Thank you." Sebastian didn't offer up any further praise. That would mean he would have to admit he was just saved by a newbie.

Tyler didn't answer. Instead he turned and regained his focus on Emily. Repositioning the crossbow, he threatened "Want some?" The malevolence in his voice made it barely recognizable.

Mrs. Cleary however, was not impressed. She simply laughed. "Go ahead and shoot. Who do you think you'll hit? Me? It's more likely you'll get dear sweet innocent Emily here." She crooned the part about Emily as though she were talking to a baby.

"Kyle go check out the rest of the rooms down there." Sebastian motioned in the direction they were headed before Emily had been grabbed.

Kyle swallowed. "Sure thing Bass." He didn't seem very enthused about heading off alone.

Emily couldn't blame him. They had no idea how many newly made vampires were waiting to attack. One man walking into a nest alone didn't sound that appealing to her either.

This had gone on long enough! She had just about had her fill of *almost* dying. Without giving herself time to think, she reached for the knife sheathed at her hip. Using all her strength she jerked her body to the side and thrust her knife back and up. Mrs. Cleary instantly let go of Emily and fell to the ground. She lay there flat on her back. Her body was in an unnatural position with Emily's knife sticking out of her chest. Emily had killed another vampire. Not just any vampire but a vampire who she had known and loved her whole life.

Sebastian didn't give her much time to regret what she had done. Without a word he strode to the body at her feet and made a smooth downward arc with his dagger. When Emily looked down she saw that Mrs. Cleary's head was no longer attached to her body. There would be no coming back for Mrs. Cleary that was for sure. Turning to Tyler she saw that he was giving Michael the same fate.

Tyler winced at the sight at his feet. "Yuck. How do you people get used to this?" He bent down and wiped the blade of his knife on Michael's pants.

Sebastian raised a sardonic eyebrow at him. "You people? You are one of us, or have you forgotten?" As if he had just remembered Emily's presence he turned to her. "Are you alright?" He put a hand under her chin and lifted it up for inspection. "You've got a nasty welt but that will be gone soon. Our kind heals fast."

Before she could respond to that information three vampires burst out of a door from down the hall, no, two vampires and Kyle who was flying into the banister with a sickening crack. He recovered quick and positioned himself to spring at a linebacker sized vamp in front of him. One of the rings to the banister had splintered with the force of his landing.

Emily's first reaction was to hide. Standing in a hallway didn't leave many options, so she moved against the wall. Sebastian and Tyler jumped into the action without hesitation. Part of Emily wanted to join them but she couldn't seem to make her feet move.

The smaller vampire wasn't nearly as big as the linebacker, though his ruthlessness was still just as menacing. He threw a punch at Sebastian's face that should have sent him sailing. Just as fast as the punch was swung, Sebastian dodged, masterfully avoiding rearrangement of his face. The fist did manage to connect to his shoulder and push Sebastian back a few feet. Tyler and Kyle were teaming up against the burly one. Emily noticed while he was big, his accuracy left something to be desired. His moves seemed clumsy. He had the brute force, but no skill to back it up.

She was clenching her fists at her sides so tightly it made her knuckles turn white. She kept expecting another door to open and more monsters to get in on the fight. Her eyes darted to the other end of the hall. It seemed clear for the moment, so Emily trained her eyes back on the rumble happening not more than six feet away from her.

The linebacker got a good hit on Kyle sending him into the wall about a foot from Emily. She immediately went to him checking to see if he was okay. His arm was dangling at an unnatural angle. He had blood streaming down his mouth and from the back of his head where he had impacted the wall.

Before Emily could properly assess his injuries, she heard Tyler cry out in pain. Without thinking, she shot up to find the source. The stupid linebacker had his hands around his neck and had him backed up against the banister. Tyler's body was bowed back so far that if the vampire let go, Tyler would fall over the rail. Emily looked to the other slayers in the hall for help.

Unfortunately, Sebastian was in nowhere near the right place to be of any assistance. All of his focus was on the vampire he had managed to throw into a door. The wood had snapped and broke off the hinges. She looked down at Kyle. *CRAP!* He was definitely still out of commission. It was up to her. What was *she* going to do? That thing was ungodly huge in epic proportions.

To her advantage, his back was to her. She could get the drop on him if she could just move fast enough. The knife she had used against Mrs. Cleary lay discarded on the floor of the hallway. For one ridiculously scary second Emily thought maybe she hadn't really killed her. Then she remembered that vampires turned to dust once they were dead. That fate seemed oddly fitting. They were unnatural creatures that deserved to turn into dirt. Ignoring the thick blood that coated the blade, she picked up her dagger. When the light caught the blood, it glistened. Her stomach twisted.

Before she could give herself a chance to think about it, she charged. As she neared the monsters, her abdomen felt as though it would explode from the pulsating cramps that tore through her insides. There wasn't a choice, she had to keep going. Tyler was in serious trouble, and that really pissed her off. Once she was in closer proximity, Emily plunged the knife into the linebackers back with all her strength. She felt the blade hesitate on his ribs and she pushed harder still. When it was all the way to the hilt, she twisted.

For a heart pounding second she thought she had done something wrong. The vamp's hands were still pressing down on her friend. Time seemed to have stopped moving all together. Finally, his arms relaxed and he pitched forward against Tyler.

The limp weight of his body would send them both over for sure. Emily got a hold of Tyler's arm and pulled with everything she had. Tyler used his other hand to push against the dead linebacker's chest. He grunted with the strain but managed to push him to the side. Now free, he fell into Emily toppling them both to the floor. Emily looked up just in time to see the vampire fall. His weight broke through the banister hurling him to his final resting place.

Emily gasped. This was really happening. She had killed another one. There really wasn't time to examine the growing number of notches on her belt. If the two of them stayed put, they were like sitting ducks. Moving didn't really seem like a good option either. Emily's muscles screamed and burned just under her skin.

She and Tyler were both panting hard from all the exertion. She willed her breath to steady and her heart to calm down to at least two hundred beats a minute. If it kept up at the rate it was, it would probably beat right out of her chest. She tried to inspect Tyler's injuries but he shrugged her off assuring her he would be okay.

They were so engrossed in their own melodrama that it wasn't until just then that they both turned their attention toward Sebastian was doing with his efforts. Not surprisingly, he had made his kill and had just finished with the decapitation. Emily winced. This might be her life now, but that didn't mean she had to like it. With a heavy sigh Sebastian turned to them.

When he saw them on the floor he hurried over. "Are you alright?" His eyes were on Emily. "You're not hurt are you?" He reached out a hand to her to help her up.

Once he had lifted her up she brushed the hair out of her face that had escaped the pony tail. "I'm fine. Tyler and Kyle got the brunt of it." She waved a hand toward Kyle indicating his form that still lay on the floor against the wall.

"I'm fine Bass." Kyle said hoarsely. "My shoulder's out of the socket though. It hurts, but I'll live."

Sebastian moved to his side and assisted him up. Without a word he grabbed a hold of Kyle's arm and reefed it back into place. Kyle grimaced but otherwise had no visible reaction. Emily's mouth dropped open brilliantly with a pop. She would have been screaming like a banshee if she were him.

Apparently unfazed, Kyle continued. "Those two were the only ones I found when I did the sweep on that end. We still need to check the other side." He took the bow from his back and inspected it for damage. It must have been broken in some way because he cursed to himself and threw it to the floor. He reached to his belt and pulled out a dagger matching Sebastian's.

"Let's get it done," Sebastian replied firmly. He looked to Emily and Tyler. "Watch yourselves. Andre's been having fun tonight and who knows how many more newborns we're going to find." He started to turn to head down the hall, but Emily stopped him.

"Where's Ivy?"

Sebastian's face went cold but his eyes were sad. "She's probably standing guard outside. Casey's death got to her." With that he turned and started down the hall again. That subject was not one of his priorities. He didn't hide his true emotion on the subject. Whether he wanted to admit it or not, he was worried about Ivy.

The rest of the upper floor of the big house was clear. Emily was surprised. She kept expecting boogie men to jump out of every closet, or grab her ankle from under every bed. She followed Sebastian and Tyler down the stairs. Sebastian stationed Kyle at the rear of their group. He evidently didn't think Emily could handle it after what had happened with Mrs. Cleary.

When they had first come in the house the lights downstairs were all off. The first thing Emily noticed when they turned the corner from the stairs was that the light from the office was now on and the door was cracked. She could have sworn they left it all the way open. Every fiber of Emily's being told her to run. She had enough of the fighting and of the supernatural for a life time.

Tyler and Kyle posted themselves on either side of the door. Kyle looked to Sebastian and nodded.

Taking the cue, Sebastian threw open the door and rushed in like the swat team with Kyle and Tyler in tow. Emily not wanting to be alone followed behind. She was not prepared for what they were walking into. Andre stood at one end of the room beside Ivy who was tied and gagged in a chair.

25

Tyler held his crossbow steady and aimed at Andre's chest. Kyle and Sebastian were bent into a defensive crouch ready to spring at the first sign of danger.

Andre had been the one to take Emily hostage earlier. The second she entered the room, she saw him. She could still feel the way his hand had felt around her throat, as though it was still there. Part of her tried to look threatening, but he intimidated the heck out of her.

There was absolutely no visible sign of any injury from the burn she had inflicted on him with the silver powder. Aside from a little redness, the wounds were completely nonexistent. Even with the red, his skin looked like marble. He stood so still that he could have passed for a statue.

When she had first come into the room, fear pounded through her at the sight of Andre. He carried the air of an alpha that demanded attention. Everything else in the space melted away leaving nothing except Andre, Emily, and her own terror. Thanks to that she hadn't noticed that he wasn't alone in the room. There was a female with him and she didn't look happy.

"So nice of you to finally join us." Andre's voice crooned. "Miss Ivy and I were just having a little chat. We wondered how long it would take you to find us." He put a hand on Ivy's shoulder, probably to fake camaraderie. Ivy flinched but couldn't move away from his touch. His melodic voice took on a more confidential tone. "Truth be told, the dear girl isn't much of a conversationalist." He said it as though Ivy were simply ignoring him, which wasn't the truth. He must have forgotten about the small little detail, that he gagged her.

Emily couldn't help herself. "Let her go!" She didn't much like Ivy but no person deserved to be a vampire's play thing.

Andre focused on her for the first time and smiled revealing way to many teeth for comfort. "Emily my sweet you've returned to me. I was so hoping you would."

Emily raised an eyebrow. "Yeah, not by choice. Let Ivy go and we'll be on our way." Her inner core shook wildly but she couldn't let that creep see how much he got to her.

The vampire laughed… actually laughed. "Now now, no need to be hasty. We will get to Ivy soon enough. You and I have so much to discuss first." Even through the unnatural green of his eyes, the glint of excitement that passed through them was plain to see.

It was more than a little likely that Andre had no intentions of talking to Emily at all. It was more feasible that he wanted revenge for the fact that she had burned him. He probably had plans to tear out her throat and eat it for a snack. Ugh, she thought completely and utterly disgusted. Emily threw up in her mind just a little bit.

Sebastian moved forward. "Andre this is over. We've already killed four of your people. One I might add was one of your valued henchmen. I know you've been busy tonight. Tell us where the other newborns are."

Andre's eyes turned shocked at the sound of his henchmen being killed. Despite the moment he was taken off guard, his expression and posture didn't waiver. "I'm not surprised about the three newborns but you've destroyed Charles?"

A cocky grin stretched across Sebastian's face. "I did. It wasn't difficult." He took another slow but purposeful step toward Andre. "I took great pleasure in making it as painful as possible too."

"No matter. My second in command can be replaced." Andre crossed his arms casually just for show. He tried to act like Sebastian's closeness was no threat at all. "I gather you intend to destroy me as well." It wasn't a question. He spoke casually about his death like someone else might discuss the weather.

"That's the plan," Sebastian answered dryly.

"I can respect that boy, but there are matters we need to discuss first. Then you may be free to unleash your attack." He turned to Emily. His eyes bore into hers as if searching for something.

"Unless you're picking how you want to die we have nothing to talk about." Tyler retorted sarcastically. He was gripping the crossbow so tightly it should have snapped under the pressure. The expression on his face and the way he held his position was so determined and completely focused. The boy who was afraid to behead a vampire back in the alley was gone. In his place, stood a brave and gallant warrior itching for the chance to take down the enemy.

It had to be said, Andre wasn't ignorant that was for sure. He was always careful not to fully expose his chest to Tyler. Thanks to the vampire's age and speed, they couldn't just jump him. He would dish out a counter assault faster than they could even blink.

"Oh, but we do young man. You're a cute puppy, seriously adorable. Unfortunately, you really don't have enough bite for my taste." although his words were for Tyler, his eyes never left Emily's. "Besides, I'm sure dear Emily will want the information I wish to bare."

"Sebastian." Kyle's voice was hard. "Don't let him play this game. Just take him."

Something in Andre's words must have peaked Sebastian's curiosity though because he stayed put. Ignoring Kyle he spoke to Andre. "What do you want with Emily? She burned you, get over it. You're old it won't take you long to totally heal from that."

Andre gave an exasperated sigh and uncrossed his arms. "I'm growing tired of this." His eyes narrowed as he stared at Kyle and Tyler with great intensity.

Emily felt a wave of throbbing pressure that seemed to be pressing into her mind. It was agony. She pressed her fingers to her temples trying to stop it. She saw that Sebastian was doing the same thing.

Kyle and Tyler dropped to the floor. Whatever Andre was doing, caused them to pass out. At least Emily prayed they had just passed out. Ivy strained fiercely against the ropes that bound her to the chair to no avail. The pulsing power became too much for her and her head lolled until she too was unconscious.

Andre clapped his hands once with finality. "There now, that's better." The pressure in the room receded, but didn't completely dissolve. "Now that the children are asleep, we adults can get down to business." Power surged again seeming to bounce off all of the walls. Two chairs slid across the room behind Sebastian and Emily.

"Have a seat my friends." When they didn't move his eyes narrowed again. "I said sit down."

A strong pulse of power pushed them both into the chairs and pinned them there. Emily tried to move her arms away from her sides and found her efforts were useless. If Andre had this sort of power why did he have to use rope on Ivy? Sebastian looked as though he wanted to speak but couldn't.

"Are you comfortable Emily?" Andre asked drawing her attention back to him. "Can I get you anything?"

He tried to take on the role of a good host but Emily wasn't buying. "You've got us here just get on with it. This doesn't need to be a production. If you're going to kill me just do it." She stared at him defiantly. Of course, she didn't have a death wish, but there was no point in any pretense of survival. This was where she was going to die. Andre was going to drain the life out of her. She didn't see much point in delaying the inevitable.

The head vampire laughed again. "So feisty aren't you? I don't plan to kill you my dear girl. I owe you a life debt after all."

"What are you talking about?" Emily asked.

He ignored her question and continued. "You see, this isn't the first time I've visited this little town. I passed through about five years ago. My clan was heading a few states over to be with friends. We were only supposed to be here for a night but there were… unfortunate complications." He moved to Emily's side and brushed a hand on her cheek.

She tried to turn her head and couldn't. The power still lingered around her body, not allowing her to move. "Don't touch me!" Emily snapped. "What does any of this have to do with me?"

Out of the corner of her eye, she could see Sebastian. He was watching her and Andre's exchange with open fury. His eyes burned with it. The power that shackled Sebastian didn't allow him to free himself, despite his vigorous attempts. Sweat dripped from his forehead, displaying the amount of strain he was exerting.

Andre removed his cold fingers from her cheek. He clasped his hands behind his back and began pacing. He weaved around all of the imprisoned slayers as though they weren't even there. "It appeared that we were being tracked by a slayer. It was tragic what happened. I was going through a violent faze back then you see." He stopped and faced her. "Cruelty isn't usually isn't usually in my nature."

Sebastian snorted and rolled his eyes.

The narrow eyed glare Andre shot him was full of venom and barely contained hostility. When he turned his attention to Emily, the hardness had dissolved. "As I was saying, before I was so rudely interrupted, I am not normally cruel. I just couldn't allow her to go back to her people and tell them we were in the area. I made her suffer that night." He stopped pacing and gazed at her, as though trying to will her to understand.

Emily glared back. "I still don't see-"

He put a hand up silencing her. "Back then I had this theory. I thought it would be marvelous to utilize a slayer's strength and abilities by turning them to my side. Obviously no slayer would willingly cross over so when I captured this particular slayer it was the perfect opportunity to test the theory. I still think it would have worked if it wasn't for that blasted creature she was blood bonded to getting in the way." He waved a hand dismissing the thought. "It is said that a slayer who is given the blood of my kind can't take it." He smiled at Emily considering. "I think if given the proper nurturing care they could tolerate the change." He sighed regretfully. "No matter, he spoiled it."

This was ridiculous. Was he planning to turn her? He said that he owed her a blood debt. Her mind raced as it tried to put it all together. Nothing made sense. He moved closer to her again breaking through her thoughts.

He bent so that he was about three inches from her face. He smiled wistfully at her for a moment before shattering the world as she knew it. "You know? You have her eyes exactly. The same beautiful shade of blue. You have the same bone structure too. The resemblance really is uncanny."

Emily's breath caught in her throat. "What... are... you... saying." She put great emphasis on each word. Annoyance was rolling off Emily. The fear that had taken her over at the first sight of Andre was dissipating to make room for the irritation.

Andre put a finger to his lips considering. "Is it possible you didn't know? That you still don't know? Hmm..." Abruptly he dropped his finger and peered at her. "Emily, do you know of whom

I'm speaking?" He didn't even give her a chance to respond. "Now I know you know her. Her name was Melissa."

Emily's heart fell to the floor. In a single instant, this monster had turned her world even more upside down than it already was. "No," she whispered. Her mother couldn't have been the one he tried to turn. Her mother was not a vampire slayer. She was a mom who liked to garage sale and bake cookies.

Andre wiped the tears from her face that she didn't even know were there. "Did you even know she was a slayer?" He shook his head regretfully. "I'm amazed your father never told you." He sent a look at Sebastian. "Or that the other hunter slayers never did, especially that one. You my dear are an important part of the underworld now. If I were you, I would be demanding answers." He attempted to show compassion. Genuine sensitivity wasn't his actual goal. It was clear he was amused by it all. "You've missed out on years of critical training. That's a shame."

Speaking wasn't an option at that point. Emily swallowed hard, fighting back the heaving sobs that wanted to break through the surface. This could not be happening. She kept her eyes on the floor. Breathing deep she tried to push down the emotional flood that threatened to overtake her.

Andre didn't speak anymore. Pleased with himself he went to a vacant chair and sat with his hands on his knees observing the unraveling of his dirty work in action. Satisfaction crossed his features and he smiled slightly as he watched her. It didn't even seem to matter to him that he had totally shattered someone's world.

The misery that had enveloped her was being quickly replaced by rage. Emily could feel it coursing through her veins making her blood run hot to boiling with every passing second. Her heart still hammered but no longer with fear. She wanted to fly out of the stupid chair and rip that abomination, that murderer to shreds.

Emily envisioned the window near Andre shattering, blowing shards of glass pouring over him. She pictured her invisible bindings crumbling to dust and falling to the floor. Most of all she pictured what it would feel like to kill Andre with her own bare hands. Normally, she couldn't really imagine herself as a slayer. Right now, she wanted nothing more than to claim that heritage and use its power to take out Andre for good. The fact that she had been lied to her entire life wasn't lost on her either, but she didn't have time to think about that now. Revenge took precedence and she could almost taste the beauty of it. She wanted it. She wanted him.

There was an instantaneous shift of power in the room that was palpable. Andre felt it too. His eyebrows rose slightly in response but he showed no other visible reaction. Emily knew the changed was hers. She could feel the pent up power flowing through her. She pushed it out as hard as she could. Still picturing what she wanted harnessing her fury into a tangible weapon. Andre's power that bound her to the chair dissolved. The window at the far side of the room near Andre crashed inward sending a spray of shattered glass raining down at the end of the room. The door to the den made a splintering sound and came off its hinges crashing against the opposite wall of books.

Without any further hesitation Emily reached for her knife and leapt off the chair at Andre. She had the element of surprise on her side. He never had a chance to move against her. Her force knocked the chair backwards to the floor. The two of them grappled both trying to gain the upper hand. Emily found an opening and buried her knife to the hilt into Andre's shoulder. The wound wouldn't kill him but it would hopefully slow him down at least. He clawed at her arm and the marks burned.

She didn't cry out though. She refused to give him the satisfaction. She yanked the knife from his shoulder and struck again. She aimed for his heart, he moved just in time making the blade hit near the shoulder again. Blood poured from the wound profusely.

With a grunt he pushed her off of him and she scrambled to her feet before he could pin her. In the blink of an eye Andre was on his feet preparing to spring. He was losing a lot of blood. At the moment, that wasn't a deterrent from his attack. He lunged for Emily but she dodged and spun around.

This put her at his back. Using this to her advantage, she plunged the knife into his back close to where the heart should be. Andre fell to the floor. Emily breathed hard as she waited for his next move. The breath burned in her lungs, they felt as though they were on fire. It astonished her that she was doing as well as she was. The fatigue was beginning to weaken her, though she refused to quit. He wasn't getting up this time one way or another.

Was he dead? As impressed as she was with her new found fighting skills she doubted she hit the heart. Reaching down, she pulled the knife out and hesitated. This was always the part in a scary movie where the supposed dead guy came back for one last attack. That wasn't happening. Using what little strength she had left she hurled Andre's body over so he was facing her.

His eyes were open and staring. He wasn't dead though not yet. Thoughts of her mother lying helpless in her hospital bed flashed before her eyes and that was the only encouragement she needed.

She pressed the tip of the blade to his chest. She would have to get through the ribs and penetrate the heart. The blow to his back must have been close. Otherwise, he wouldn't have been so debilitated. As she broke the skin Andre spoke.

"This won't bring her back," Andre choked. His whole body shook with the effort to speak but his voice wasn't much above a whisper.

It took everything Emily had not to bludgeon him to death. "Maybe not, but it will make me feel better." She pushed the blade in another inch.

Andre gasped and tried to swipe at the hilt. The effort was pointless. His strength had dwindled enough that Emily didn't even budge her position. "Kill me if you must but my work is already in effect." He coughed and a trickle of blood ran out of the corner of his mouth. "Lina and I have made a faction of soldiers to deal with this miserable little town. You won't-" His words were cut off with another bout of coughing. He retched a fountain of blood that pooled around his head thick and viscous. It didn't *at all* look human.

Emily swallowed back nausea at the sight of the blood. She reached up to tuck hair behind her ear that had escaped the pony tail earlier and left a wet track down her jaw. She hoped absently that it wasn't blood. "Where is this Lina? What about the newborns?"

"They will come to you soon enough," Andre sputtered. He attempted to sneer at her but it was just sickening with all the blood. If it was even possible, his face had gone even more of a fish belly white giving it the pallor of chalk. It looked as though if she blew air at him he would turn to dust and disappear.

"Tell me and I'll make this quick." She put more pressure on the hilt to emphasize her point.

The dying vampire sighed causing blood to gurgle in his throat. "Never." He closed his eyes for a second before regaining focus on her. "Your mother wanted..."

Emily never found out what her mother wanted. Her name on his lips was the final straw for Emily and she drove the knife home strong and true. Andre was still staring at her, but he no longer saw her. Emily Jameson had just killed another vampire, and not just any vampire. She had managed to cut the thread of life from a head vampire. She fell back on the floor, leaning back on her hands with a sigh of relief.

There was only a moment of calm before the room erupted again. The fallen slayers as well as Sebastian were free from Andre's spell now that he was gone. Sebastian jumped up and ran to her while the others came back to life more slowly and disoriented.

"Are you alright," Sebastian asked with concern. He offered her a hand up and she took it.

She wiped her blood stained hands on her pants with disgust. "Yeah just peachy, how about you?" Despite her exhaustion, her voice sounded falsely perky and upbeat. If it wasn't for the carnage at her feet it would have seemed as though everything were normal.

"Honestly? A little bummed that you stole the glory and got Andre... but whatever." An approving smile tugged at his lips and spread into an actual grin.

Emily stared at him incredulous for about five seconds before breaking into a smile herself. "Why Mr. Sebastian? Are you actually smiling? Apparently I should kill head vampires more often."

"Don't let it go to your head Jameson." Just like that, Sebastian's mask was back on. Even through the guarded facade, his gorgeous eyes still shown with pride. "Good work and I'm sorry about your..."

Emily waved off his sympathy. "Don't worry about it. It is what it is." She was really good at hiding her true emotion. Emily wasn't about to let Sebastian or anyone else know how much Andre's confession had really gotten to her. She did plan however, to let Sam know what she thought on the subject. For the moment her emotions were in check. It felt like ice had crystallized around Emily's heart keeping her whole. Any minute reality would set in and shatter the sharp shards of ice that were stabbing into her soul, tearing her already formed wound wide open.

"Bass? What happened?" Kyle was still trying to drag himself to his feet.

With a dramatic flourish of his arm Sebastian gestured at Emily. "Well, it would appear that Emily stole the show and did our job." He bowed to her... actually bowed.

Emily giggled embarrassed. "Stop it."

"Way to go Em," Tyler said proudly. He brushed the hair out of his face as he watched Andre's dead form lying broken on the floor. "That is frickin awesome."

Ivy stared at Emily as though she had never seen her before. The normally rude girl had bruises on her face and some definite swelling. Emily could tell Ivy was amazed. It was kind of satisfying to show the other girl up. Maybe now she wouldn't treat Emily with such hatred, probably not though.

Before they could leave for the compound Sebastian said they had to take care of business at the house. As a team, they collected the bodies of Andre and Charles and hauled them to the back yard. The seasoned slayers explained to Emily and Tyler that the old ones took longer to turn to dust. It would happen eventually, but that wasn't good enough. In matters of the supernatural, time was of the essence. They couldn't afford to take the chance an unsuspecting human stumbled across the bodies before they vanished. That would cause an epic uproar that wouldn't be easily dealt with.

Once they were in a pile Kyle lit a match and set them on fire. Emily had never seen a fire blaze up as quickly as that one had. One second they were looking at a pile of *really dead* vampires and the next into the bright flames of a bon fire.

Within just a few minutes, the bodies were turned to ash that would leave nothing behind but a scorch mark in the grass. Sebastian and Tyler gathered rock from the flower beds to put around the fires circle. If anyone ever came back here, all they would think was that the people that lived in the house had weenie roasts in the summer.

The fire had been bitter sweet. It had symbolized the close of a horrible event. With that closure, came the mark of the beginning of more death to come. It didn't smell bad, weirdly enough. It actually just smelled like any other bon fire. Emily supposed that was for the best. It wouldn't pay to have neighbors come to investigate why the odor of burning flesh was in the air.

When they left, they did so together. No one spoke and that was okay. They were all preoccupied with what had happened and with grief for their fallen brother. It wasn't awkward though. For the first time in a long time Emily felt like she was in the right place with her life. So with her new family, she went home.

EPILOGUE

The day after the raid went by in a blur. That was probably thanks to the fact that Emily had slept twelve hours of the day away. When she woke up she still felt like crap but at least she was rested.

Aside from a little muscle fatigue her body was in pretty good condition. Who would have thought a person could escape multiple vampire attacks with only minimal soreness? She might not be like the average vampire slayer, but at least she healed like one.

Alexander had decided there must have been something wrong with the summoning process. Emily clearly had displayed slayer characteristics during the raid and her extra abilities proved she was not a regular human. He vowed to help her track her history and get to the bottom of things. Little did he know, Emily was a very relentless person when it came to such important things. She planned to hold him to every square inch of his promise.

After a bit of searching she found that everyone was conferring about the prior day's events in the kitchen. Alexander, Sebastian and Ivy were sitting around one of the tables eating sandwiches. Apparently the only food a big tough vampire slayer knew how to make was bread with meat and cheese.

Kyle and Tyler were standing by one of the long counters engaging Beth Thomas in what looked like nothing more than flirty banter. She seemed interested but shy and awkward. The poor girl had been through a lot and was probably very confused. Beth would be returned home in a day or so and therefore, put back into reality. Emily wondered if Alexander would alter her memory so that she would have no recollection of the recent attempt on her life. In her opinion that would be the best thing for her. Then, maybe she would have some chance at a semblance of normalcy. No human needed nightmares about being almost bled to death by an undead creature of the night.

Emily was still confused for crap's sake and she was smack dab in the center of this mess. The big Gothic house where they had taken down Andre would be a prominent fixture in her own dreams for quite some time. She wondered absently what Sam was going to think about her recent revelations and accomplishments. At this point she didn't honestly care all that much. Nevertheless, she didn't want to hurt him. He obviously didn't want her in this life and with good reason, blamed it for her mother's death. Either way though she couldn't help the bitter taste left in her mouth at the thought that she had been deceived all her life.

Calling Lucy was going to have to be a priority in the near future too. Before she had fallen asleep she had seen that she had five missed calls and just as many text messages from her friend. She was freaking out because of Emily's last text. Understandably she didn't comprehend the meaning of it and was in panic mode. Emily wasn't sure what the exact rule was for telling humans about the Underworld but she would have to break that rule when it came to Lucy. She was Emily's best friend and she knew she could trust her with this. After all, hadn't Lucy already confided that she was connected to the paranormal world?

It was intriguing to think that Lucy could be psychic. It was either strongly coincidental that they were friends given they both had supernatural powers or they were brought together for a reason. It scared her to think that Luce might be fated to join her in this world. Lucy was definitely strong enough for it. In all actuality she was probably stronger then Emily. She for sure had more fighting skills. Karate had been a normal part of Lucy's upbringing. George had said it was necessary in case she was ever mugged or attacked because of her disability. Maybe there was more to it than that.

The two different groups were deep in conversation both planning and flirting. The ones planning knew that Lina's counter attack with the Newborns was sure to come soon. Now that Andre was dead the female vampire wouldn't rest until his killer was brought down as well as any others she could manage in the process. Andre had said that their goal was to demolish this town. The reason why was still a bit of a mystery. What was so important about Lakeview?

Alexander explained that Emily and Tyler's training was going to have to get going immediately, so that their powers could be utilized effectively. This part excited Emily. If she was going to be a weapon of mass destruction against the undead she was going to have to bone up on her skills.

The other priority was trying to figure out what was going on with her and Sebastian. Admittedly it was a small problem in comparison to the one that currently plagued their small town but it was a problem none the less. He was so infuriating. Even still, the same parts that enraged her about him were endearing too. They definitely had a connection even if neither one of them knew what that was. It mattered what he thought and she hated that. No one had ever mattered in that way. Sure she cared about Lucy and cared what happened to her but it wasn't the same. This was raw and borderline obsession. She was going to have to get a handle on it. Having any type of crush on anyone right now was the last thing she needed in her life that was growing more and more complicated.

So basically in a nut shell, Emily found out she is apparently a powerful vampire slayer hailing from a family of hunters. Life as she knew it wasn't at all the way things worked, she had a heart gripping crush on someone she didn't even fully know if she wanted. Her best friend was some kind of psychic. Her new secondary best friend was hot but also held mystical powers to aid in the cause of killing the undead. Oh and a newly formed army of vampires were attacking her town with one of their main objectives being to take her life. Yet again, just another day in the life.

What the future had in store was a mystery. Emily was scared, confused and oddly a little excited. It wasn't the thought of killing the vampires that excited her though. It was more the idea that she was a part of something bigger than her. It was up to her and the other slayers to save Lakeview before any other innocent people were either killed or changed into the walking dead. She was going to have to figure out something with school and her job but that was okay somehow. The fight against the evil that lurked in the shadows of her town was more important. She might not have a lot of ties in Lakeview but she would defend it till the bitter end, or die trying.

ABOUT THE AUTHOR

Having lived in the same rainy town within Washington State her entire life, she loves life regardless of what it may bring. Though Nicole was initially born with her eyesight, she is now completely blind. Despite the odds, she has overcome adversity and doesn't allow anything to get in her way. Writing has always been a passion of hers throughout her life and this books stands as a testament to her determination. Look out world, Nicole Rae is here to stay!

Nicole has also been successful, as a blogger. Her blog, Playing the Blind Card, is used to bridge the gap between the blind and those with their eye sight, using humor. You can visit her blog at www.playingtheblindcard.blogspot.com.

For more information, please visit Nicole Rae at
www.authornicolerae.blogspot.com
www.facebook.com/authornicolerae
and on Twitter @NicoleRae83

14605358R00130

Made in the USA
Charleston, SC
21 September 2012